MW00532016

The Royce Buchanan she had known was clearly in the voice now.

All right, Anne-Marie addressed him silently, if it's you, it's you. So be it. She swallowed hard. "How about Friday morning at eleven?" she said into the phone.

"Friday, as in tomorrow?"

"Yes," she replied, glad she'd found the courage to get it over with. "Tomorrow, at eleven."

"Then the first order of business is getting you here, I guess." He gave her directions to his ranch, and Anne-Marie jotted them on a scrap of paper.

As he talked, the image of that young man from years before kept coming to mind. She wondered whether she ought to reveal her identity, confirm his. But she couldn't make herself say the necessary words. "All right, Mr. Buchanan, see you tomorrow," she said when he had finished.

"It's Royce, by the way," he replied.

She felt her stomach drop. But it didn't matter. She'd already known. That brash young army officer, the **first man she had ever loved, had come walking back** into her life again—just as curiously, though far less emotionally, than the way he had left it.

"And I'm Anne-Marie," she whispered.

Dear Reader,

Each and every month, to meet your sophisticated standards, to satisfy your taste for substantial, memorable, emotion-packed stories of life and love, of dreams and possibilities, Silhouette brings you six extremely **Special Edition**s.

Now these exclusive editions are wearing a brand-new wrapper, a more sophisticated look—our way of marking Silhouette **Special Edition**s' continually renewed commitment to bring you the very best, the brightest and the most up-to-date in romance writing.

Reach for all six freshly packaged Silhouette **Special Edition**s each month—the insides are every bit as delicious as the outsides—and savor a bounty of meaty, soul-satisfying romantic novels by authors who are already your favorites and those who are about to become so.

And don't forget the two Silhouette *Classics* at your bookseller's every month—the most beloved Silhouette **Special Edition**s and Silhouette *Intimate Moments* of yesteryear, reissued by popular demand.

Today's bestsellers, tomorrow's *Classics*—that's Silhouette **Special Edition**. And now, we're looking more special than ever!

From all the authors and editors of Silhouette **Special Edition**,

Warmest wishes,

Leslie Kazanjian,
Senior Editor

JANICE KAISER
The Lieutenant's Woman

Silhouette Special Edition

Published by Silhouette Books New York

America's Publisher of Contemporary Romance

For Narda Krum, with love

SILHOUETTE BOOKS
300 East 42nd St., New York, N.Y. 10017

ISBN: 0-373-09489-2

First Silhouette Books printing November 1988

Printed in the U.S.A.

Books by Janice Kaiser

Silhouette Special Edition

Borrowed Time #466
The Lieutenant's Woman #489

JANICE KAISER

Four years ago Janice Kaiser combined two new beginnings in her life: her second marriage and the start of her writing career. A former attorney, Ms. Kaiser is frequently asked if she misses law. "The answer is no," says the author of over ten books. "I prefer the creativity and freedom of writing." An experienced traveler, Ms. Kaiser likes to set her novels in places she's been to and loved. She always tries to ground her romances with realistic touches and says her first concern is the reader's pleasure.

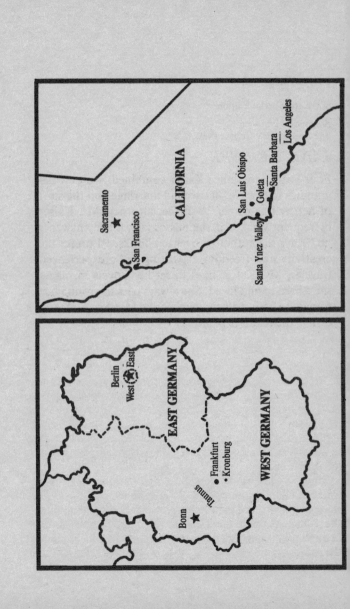

Chapter One

He sat in his shorts on the edge of the examining table looking at the doctor, a corpulent, balding young man with pale blue eyes. Royce Buchanan remembered when doctors had always seemed older and wiser. This one, he thought, had probably been born about the time he was in high school.

The doctor was peering down at the file in his hands, looking very thoughtful. He seemed to be making a diagnosis based on the papers he was examining. Then he glanced up, frowning slightly.

"Why don't you get dressed, Mr. Buchanan, then come back to my office. We can talk there." He gave a cursory smile and left the room.

Royce got off the table with a sigh and went to the hook where he had hung his clothes. As he slipped on his trousers and shirt, he glanced out the window through the venetian blinds at the palm trees lining the street. The fronds were moving gently in the breeze. Perhaps a mile away, he could see the Pacific over the rooftops, a narrow band of blue stretching across the horizon.

California. It seemed so unlikely to be living here after years of slogging it out in the smokestack world of Detroit, building an auto parts manufacturing company from nothing. Yet here he was, not yet fifty, retired from the hurly-burly of the business world, and with enough money in the bank from the sale of his company to buy half the businesses in Santa Barbara.

He smiled, knowing he was no more suited to the life of an idle millionaire than the man in the moon. Yet he was in California, living in a brand-new twelve-room mansion, an enormous palace that signaled his success to the world.

How far he'd come in his forty-nine years. The house he'd grown up in back in Mount Clemens had a quarter the square footage of the swimming pool that spread out behind his new home like a small lake. His hundred acres kept him a discreet distance from his neighbors. In the Santa Ynez Valley it was land, not just fences, that made good neighbors, the real estate man had told him.

It was a perfect life. That's what he had been telling himself for the past three months. Yet there was one inescapable fact that brought the whole proposition into question—he was all alone.

After he zipped his trousers he stepped into his loafers. Then he looked into the mirror over the small basin in the corner of the room. The tanned face looking back at him was relaxed, confident. He ran his fingers through his thick brownish-blond hair, took a deep breath and slowly exhaled. The pressure he'd lived with for years was a thing of the past now.

He didn't have to project rates of return, growth curves, profits. He didn't have to think about what the analysts were forecasting or whether a change in the tax laws would undercut his capital investment plan. He didn't have to worry about dividends, difficult directors, bankers or corporate raiders.

Now that he was a man of leisure, his concerns were different. He occupied himself with decisions about whether he should run six, eight or ten miles in the morning, whether he should go to Tahiti for a month, or to China, whether buying his daughter and her husband a house would be a kindness or a disservice. There wasn't anything else that mattered. And he had discovered that adjusting to his new life-style was the most difficult challenge he'd ever faced.

There was a soft knock at the door, and the nurse who'd shown him to the examining room stuck her head in.

"Oh, excuse me, Mr. Buchanan. I thought you'd left."

"No, I'm afraid I'm just a slow dresser."

The woman, a slender redhead in her late thirties, blushed but seemed in no hurry to withdraw. She had eyed him when they first spoke, subtly signaling her interest. She couldn't have known who he was, so she wasn't flirting with his money. He wore no rings, and neither did she. That was probably what it was all about.

"I guess you're lucky I didn't have to tie my shoes," he said with a wry grin. "I might be here another half hour."

She smiled more broadly than his faint attempt at humor warranted. "Take your time. I didn't mean to rush you."

Glancing into the mirror, Royce straightened the collar of his polo shirt, then slapped his lean, muscular flanks with the palms of his hands. "No, I'm all set. Just have to see Dr. Gilchrist."

"You remember where his office is?"

"I think so. But if you'd care to show me the way, I wouldn't mind." He walked to the door, and she waited long enough for him to move close to her. He caught a faint whiff of her perfume before she turned and headed up the hall.

He followed her, his eyes sliding down to her rump, past the curve of her hips to her calves and ankles then up her body again. Several doors down she stopped abruptly and spun around. Though the movement was graceful, she had executed it quickly enough that he was sure she had been hoping to catch him looking at her rear end. She nearly had.

"Doctor will be back in a few moments, Mr. Buchanan," she said, indicating the empty office. "Please have a seat, and he'll be with you shortly."

He slipped past the nurse, taking another whiff of her perfume before ambling over to a chair. He looked back toward the door as he sat, noticing her smile a final time before she disappeared up the hall.

Royce leaned back, feeling weary all of a sudden. He wondered what the redhead was thinking, what, if anything, she had actually hoped might happen. Was it merely idle flirting? Or was she as lonely as he? Six months earlier he wouldn't have given her two thoughts, but now...

He gazed vacantly at the diplomas and framed certificates on the wall and considered whether that was what fate had in mind for him: marrying a nurse, settling down on his ranch and letting her take care of him for the next thirty years. He shivered, not from distaste but at the thought that he had been reduced to such speculation. Perhaps the problem was that he had let too much time elapse since he'd had a woman.

"Well, Mr. Buchanan," the physician said as he entered the room. "Sorry to keep you waiting."

"That's all right. This is my last appointment today," he replied ironically.

"Wish I could say the same." Dr. Gilchrist sighed as he eased himself into his high-backed chair. He leaned forward, resting his elbows on the desk. His expression grew serious. "I don't know exactly what to tell you about your backache. It's probably muscular—the spine doesn't seem to be involved—but normally this kind of injury, if that's what you'd call it, isn't associated with jogging."

"I run a lot more than most folks."

"I realize that. I'm inclined to recommend the obvious: cut back for a while and see if it improves."

"I don't suppose it's all that big a deal. But it's been bothering me for three weeks or so, and I thought I ought to find out if it was somehow connected with running."

"You say you've never experienced this sort of pain before?"

"Not that I recall. Of course, I never paid much attention to things like this in the past. I guess I'm listening to my body a little more now than I used to."

"That's good. I wish more people did."

Royce shrugged. "I don't want to turn into a hypochondriac."

"Don't worry about it." The doctor leaned back. "I know you came in for answers, but I don't have anything to suggest other than a period of experimentation, adjusting your level of exercise." He smiled lamely. "You're in wonderful physical shape, Mr. Buchanan. I wish I were half as fit myself."

"Well, I'll cut back for a few weeks and see what happens."

"I could send you to the hospital for a battery of tests, of course, but I really don't see the point. Not yet, anyway."

"I'll just ease up."

The physician steepled his fingers. "There is something I might recommend, come to think of it. Something else you might try."

"What's that?"

"Yoga."

"Yoga? You mean you're into holisitc medicine?"

"No, I was thinking of it in terms of exercise...stretching and flexibility. I discovered it through my sister, as a matter of fact. She's a fanatic. I looked into it, and I've referred several patients to a local practitioner. I regard it almost as a kind of physical therapy."

"Can't I just do calisthenics?"

"It's not the same thing, I'm afraid. We're not talking about exercise per se. Developing flexibility and strength in combination is what it's all about. I had a patient who is a computer operator, for example, complaining about terrible headaches. Her ophthalmologist couldn't find anything wrong with her eyes, and we finally concluded it was the way she sat and held her body all day—a posture phenomenon. Yoga adjusted her spinal alignment, and the headaches went away.

"I also had a auto accident victim with a shoulder injury. Yoga helped him regain flexibility and reduced his discomfort."

"Maybe it's worth a try."

"I must warn you, though," he said with a smile, "it seems to be mostly a woman's sport. The classes are made up primarily of housewives. Some men don't feel comfortable in the setting."

"If it fixes my back, I couldn't care less."

The doctor reflected for a moment. "You know, a good way to start might be with a therapeutic massage. It's something like having yoga applied to you. The official terminology is Zen

Shiatsu, but Anne-Marie calls it a sports massage." He reached for his telephone index.

Buchanan felt a little twinge at the mention of the yoga instructor's name. Anne-Marie. He'd known a woman by that name once—a girl, actually. But that was a long time ago—more than twenty-five years earlier—in Frankfurt, Germany.

"Given your predilections," the doctor said as he perused the index, "I imagine the sports angle would appeal. Yes, here she is." He looked up. "Shall I see if she can take you?"

"You're the doctor. If you think it would help, I'm game."

"I think it's worth a try. Besides, Anne-Marie is a delightful lady. If you like her, you can discuss taking one of her classes." He reached for the phone and dialed.

After a lengthy wait, the doctor rolled his eyes. "I hate answering machines," he said to Royce. Then he spoke into the phone. "Mrs. Osborne, this is Dr. Gilchrist. I'm referring a patient with back problems to you. I believe your sports massage might be the ticket. Please expect a call from a Mr. Buchanan."

He put down the receiver, then jotted something on his prescription pad. When he finished, he slid the paper across the desk to Royce, who picked it up. The name Anne-Marie Osborne, along with a telephone number, was written in the doctor's scrawling hand.

"You can call and get particulars from her," he said. "I'm not sure about her fees, but they're reasonable. And she can tell you about her class schedules, et cetera, if you're interested."

Royce stared at the slip. The Anne-Marie he had known was named Keller, and she was a German girl. Nearly eighteen the last time he'd seen her. Anne-Marie. How long it had been since he'd thought of her.

"Do you have any questions, Mr. Buchanan?"

He shook his head. "No, Doctor. Thanks. I'll give your yoga person a call and see if she can help me." He got to his feet.

The doctor rose, as well. "And try cutting back on that running, too. Forty miles a week is a lot, even without a backache."

Royce nodded, then extended his hand. "I'll let you know how the massage works out." Then he headed for the door, realizing he wasn't quite sure himself whether he meant the regimen or the instructor.

There was a fine sheen of perspiration on her brow. Her heart was beating nicely, her blood surging steadily through her veins. Anne-Marie was aware of her body—every inch of it, every muscle, every limb. She felt herself relaxing into *Savasana*, melting into the mat. The tension from the exertion of her exercises had begun transforming into deepening relaxation. Her breathing slowed. She felt good, mellow, vital.

Outside, somewhere in the large trees that spread protective boughs over the roof of the house, she heard a bird singing. Though it probably was near, its song seemed to be receding into the distance, fading with the calming pattern of her thoughts.

As she relaxed, her mind took an unforeseen turn, evoking an image, an unexpected one from the past. Anne-Marie was in the Taunus back home—the home of her childhood—running through the forest, Spatzle, her dog, loping along behind her.

She was fourteen and running as fast as a deer, leaping over branches and ferns, Spatzle barking at the wind and frolicking after her. *"Kommen Sie her!"* she shouted as his bark echoed through the woods.

Then, when she reached the crest of the hill, she fell to the ground, breathless and exhausted. Her great lumbering puppy came to her, panting, lapping at her face before tensing and bounding off after a squirrel.

Anne-Marie saw herself staring up through the deep green boughs overhead at the blue sky, and she heard a bird sing, just as she did now, thirty years later. A tiny smile bent the corners of her mouth as the image lingered in her mind. It was a rare little trip into the past, but a happy one. She felt a deep sense of contentment.

The bird outside her window in Santa Barbara, and the one in the Taunus, were momentarily silenced by the sound of soft knocking. Anne-Marie had been alone in the house, but she realized Christianne must have come home from school.

"Yes," she said, just loud enough for her voice to carry through the door. "Come in. Come in."

She heard the door opening, but her eyes remained closed, her body motionless. She waited through the silence that followed, expecting her daughter's voice. Instead, it was a deeper, masculine voice—Kurt's.

"Sorry, Mom. Didn't know you were doing your exercises."

"It's you, darling!" Anne-Marie said, opening her eyes and turning to look at the tall young man standing in the doorway.

He wore jeans and a T-shirt. He leaned against the door frame, looking a bit sheepish.

"I didn't expect to see you," she said softly, not wanting to jar herself too abruptly from her meditative state.

"I'm interrupting. I'll wait downstairs."

Anne-Marie had closed her eyes again, but the happy little smile was still on her face. "No, give me a minute. I'm almost through. Sit down," she said, lifting a finger from the mat and gesturing.

She heard him walk the few steps to the straight-back chair, his running shoes squeaking on the wooden floor. She relaxed, wanting to center herself for a moment before coming up.

Kurt tapped his foot, causing an impatient thumping sound Anne-Marie knew he wasn't aware of. He was preoccupied with something else—Tracy, undoubtedly.

"Are you staying for dinner?"

"I was planning on it."

She opened one eye a crack and peeked at him. "That's a surprise. What's with Tracy? Is she working or something?"

He grinned. "Yes, but that's not the reason."

"It can't be that my college man actually wants to see his mother."

Silence greeted her comment, and Anne-Marie began wiggling her toes and slowly rotating her feet to bring life back to her limbs. Then she bent a knee and rolled onto her side to face Kurt, her head resting on her arm as she looked at him. She smiled, and he smiled back.

It amazed her that her young son was now a man. The freckle-nosed kid in the Little League uniform just a few years ago was now off on his own, a visitor to his mother's home. She studied the handsome, slightly arrogant face that appeared unusually serene at that moment.

"You almost look sad," she said tenderly. "Everything all right?"

"Yeah. I was just thinking about Dad."

"Do you miss him?"

He let his eyes drift along her pink leotard and tights. "I was wondering what he'd think if he could see you now. He wouldn't believe it."

Anne-Marie grinned. "I was a chunk when Daddy was alive, wasn't I?"

"You've always been my beautiful mom to me. But you were a little heavier then, yes."

"A little? I weighed *eighteen* pounds more eight years ago." She sat up and wrapped her arms around her bent knees, looking at herself in the mirrored wall opposite, trying to see herself through Ted Osborne's eyes. The long-legged, dark-haired woman was indeed slender—svelte, even—and, more important, in prime physical condition.

"With the possible exception of the track or swim team," Kurt said, "there's not a girl on campus in half as good shape as you are. And none of them have the flexibility. It's amazing how many are fat."

The compliment made her smile. "They're probably all bloated from birth control pills. That's one thing I don't have to worry about, thank goodness."

Kurt didn't say anything, but a quirky little smile appeared on his face.

"You haven't said why you came home. Is anything wrong? Is it money? Do you need a loan?" She grinned. "Or were you thinking in terms of a grant?"

He shook his head. "None of the above."

"It can't be for some of my good old-fashioned home cooking, or 'Mom's healthy-icky cuisine,' as your sister calls it."

"Not that, either."

She looked at him for a moment, then straightened her back and crossed her legs into the lotus position. She stared serenely into the mirror. Her ebony hair was gathered at the back of her head, but several tendrils had fallen down onto the white skin of her neck.

A thought struck her, and she turned to Kurt. "Tracy's not pregnant?"

"No, nothing like that." He paused. "I wanted to talk about you."

"Me?"

"Yes. I've been so wrapped up in my own life lately, I haven't stopped to think about you. I figured it was time."

"Well, if it's my impending old age you're concerned about, I'm just fine, thanks. I still hardly have a gray hair in my head, thank God. Your father bet me I'd have gray streaks by the time I was forty-five. I think that's one bet I'll win."

Kurt still didn't say anything. Anne-Marie glanced at him. He was looking awfully wistful.

"Some days I think about your father, too, and wonder what it would be like if he were still here."

"He'd be really proud of you."

"He'd be proud of us all, Kurt. He loved his family."

"Yes, but you've done so much. There's not a woman in the world your age who looks so good, who's taken charge of her life like you have, who's managed to be happy, despite everything."

Anne-Marie laughed. "So, it's my happiness we're talking about?"

His expression turned sheepish. "I guess I'd better come clean. Tracy told me about you and Don."

Anne-Marie stared at him for a moment, then nodded. "I wish Don had listened to me. I told him we ought to keep it quiet until everything was worked out."

"Are you going to do it? Are you going to marry Don?" he asked hopefully.

"I'm considering his offer."

Kurt screwed up his face. "'Considering his offer'? What kind of a way is that to talk about someone who wants to marry you? Don't you love him?"

"I'm thinking it over. All love doesn't come complete with bells and whistles, you know. Marriage is the sort of thing you have to consider very carefully."

"You make it sound like buying an insurance policy."

She chuckled. "Well, they're different, of course, but at my stage in life a person does tend to be more pragmatic about marriage. It's not only a matter of love. There are other people I have to consider—Christianne, for example. I know that may be hard for you to understand, considering the way you feel about Tracy, but time changes the rules of love and marriage, believe me."

"Well, I'm not trying to stick my nose into your business, but I guess it does have an impact on me and Tracy."

Anne-Marie's brow furrowed. "Yes, to be honest, that's one of the things that's concerned me most. When Don first started talking about marriage, I raised the point, but he said we shouldn't let your relationship with Tracy affect us either way."

"I think that's right."

"But do you two want us to marry? Do you like the idea of getting a stepfather who might end up being your father-in-law, too?"

"If you'd be happy, yes."

Anne-Marie didn't say anything for a moment. She looked into her own eyes in the mirror. "In some ways, marrying Don seems like the most logical and natural thing in the world. Since Carole and your father are both dead, we've practically been like a family anyway. But in another way, it seems somehow... wrong."

"Don't you love him?"

She closed her eyes, thinking. Then she looked up at her son. "Maybe I'm just not used to the idea of marrying one of your father's and my oldest friends."

Kurt grinned. "I thought you weren't looking for bells and whistles. I'd have thought friendship was exactly the place you'd want to start... at your stage in life."

She eyed him, suddenly feeling uncomfortable with the conversation. "I'm not ready for the rest home, Kurt."

"Just kidding." He looked a bit wistful. "It could never be like it was with Dad, though, could it?"

"Your father was very much like Don in many ways. I think that's one of the reasons I'm so fond of him."

"I'm fond of him, too." He shifted in the chair. "What I'm trying to say is...Tracy and I have talked about it, and we really like the idea. You've got our blessing."

Anne-Marie smiled at him. "I do appreciate that, honey. But to be honest, I can't make that consideration top priority. Naturally, I'd think long and hard before I'd do anything to hurt the two of you, but I'm certainly not going to marry Don to please you and Tracy.

"Frankly, I haven't worried as much about you as I have about Christianne. She's still at home. Don would become her stepfather, creating a major disruption in her life—"

"You can't let her hang-ups get in the way of your happiness."

Just then the telephone rang, calling faintly through the closed door of the studio. She started to get up, but Kurt stopped her.

"I'll get it. You stay where you are. It's probably for the brat, anyway." He went out the door, then scrambled down the stairs.

Anne-Marie took a deep breath and again looked at herself in the mirror. No, it probably wasn't for Christianne, she thought. It was more likely the Mr. Buchanan whom Dr. Gilchrist had referred to her. A little twinge went through her at the thought.

When she had played the message back on her machine and heard the name Buchanan, emotions had washed over her—emotions rooted in the distant past. But she knew it couldn't be he. Ted had come home from the office once years earlier with a story about a new client named Buchanan. Her heart had missed a beat then, too. But it had been a false alarm. It always would be. There were many Buchanans in the world. And Royce Buchanan was long gone from her life.

She heard Kurt on the stairs again. She turned her head as the door opened.

"It's for you, Mom. Some guy calling about yoga."

"One of my students' husband?"

"I don't know. Said his name was Buchanan."

"Okay. I'll take it on the extension in my bedroom."

The feeling struck her again as she got to her feet. But Anne-Marie knew she was reacting to something in her past. Perhaps the memories that had come to her off and on all morning had unsettled her; they'd certainly made her a little testy about the prospect of her marriage to Don Nelson.

She walked erectly, with measured strides, to the telephone in her room. "Hello?" She waited for the response, expecting a voice that clearly wasn't Royce's.

"Mrs. Osborne?"

She could detect no discernible clue. It could be he, but it could be anybody. "Yes?"

"My name's Buchanan. I was given your name by Dr. Gilchrist. He thought one of your therapeutic sports massages might be the answer to my back problem."

Anne-Marie listened intently to the voice but still wasn't sure. "Yes, I got the doctor's message, Mr. Buchanan. Is this a long-standing problem or something recent?"

"It's fairly recent. I mean, I've had backaches in the past, but none that lasted. The doctor doesn't know the cause for sure. Says it's muscular. Lower back. He thinks it might be a result of my running, though I don't know why. I've run for years."

The voice did seem vaguely familiar, in a distant way, but she still wasn't certain. So many years had intervened. She agonized, feeling more and more tense by the moment. She badly wanted the relief of knowing it wasn't he. "Back problems have a way of sneaking up on you."

He chuckled. "Unless you run fast enough."

The laugh was familiar. Ice water filled her veins. Something told her it was Royce Buchanan, but she was afraid to find out, afraid to ask.

There was a long silence on the line. Her mind was churning. She was wondering if he could know. She doubted it. He'd known her when she was German. Now she was American. Her English was flawless. Only an expert could detect her place of birth.

"Mrs. Osborne?"

"Sorry. You say you run. You mean jog?"

"Well, when you're serious, you run. I run."

Something in the man's tone brought that young American officer of twenty-odd years ago vividly into her consciousness. The confident, vaguely irreverent manner of speech she heard now could easily be that of the man she had known.

"Running could well be the problem...if only indirectly. We all develop muscle imbalances. And certain activities and postures accentuate them. Sitting a great deal, for example, will shorten certain muscles in the leg and add stress in the back when our body tries to compensate. The purpose of Zen Shiatsu and yoga generally is to create flexibility and symmetry, to enable the muscles to work harmoniously."

"The doctor recommended it, so I thought I'd give it a try. How do we handle this? Do you have an office?"

"Well, normally I make house calls, but . . . I don't know if I can take on a new client at the moment."

"You aren't going to give me a big sales pitch, then turn me away, are you?"

Anne-Marie realized that was precisely what she was trying to do. "There are other yoga instructors in the area. I could give you a name."

"For this sports massage?"

"Well, no. The nearest I'm aware of for that is in L.A."

"Look, Mrs. Osborne, what's your usual fee?"

"Thirty-five dollars an hour."

"We'll make it seventy for this first go-around. This therapy may not help—my problem could be totally different from what the doctor thinks—but we might as well find out."

"Yes, we might as well find out," she said with resignation.

He chuckled. "I like your attitude, Mrs. Osborne. You sound like somebody I can do business with."

Anne-Marie knew she was being sucked into a situation she had no desire to be in. Of course, she wasn't absolutely sure the man she was talking to was Royce Buchanan, but he seemed very much like a mature version of the man she had once known.

"I regard my work as an art form as much as a business, Mr. Buchanan."

"*Macht nichts,*" he said. Doesn't matter.

Anne-Marie tensed. "I beg your pardon?"

"What I mean is, I'm only interested in the result. When do we do this?"

The Royce Buchanan she had known was clear in the voice now. All right, she addressed him silently, if it's you, it's you. So be it. She swallowed hard. "How about tomorrow morning at eleven?"

"Tomorrow?"

"Yes," she replied, glad she'd found the courage to get it over with.

"I guess you'll need my address. Do you know the Santa Ynez Valley?"

"I've driven through it. But you're a ways outside Santa Barbara. I hadn't realized."

"I'll pay you for travel time, if that's a problem."

"No, you've been more than generous."

"Then the first order of business is getting you here, I guess." He gave her directions to his ranch, and Anne-Marie jotted them on a scrap of paper.

As he talked the image of that young man from years before kept coming to mind. She wondered whether she ought to ask him a question or two, reveal her identity, confirm his. But inertia gripped her. She couldn't make herself say the necessary words. "All right, Mr. Buchanan, see you tomorrow," she said when he had finished.

"It's Royce, by the way," he replied.

She felt her stomach drop. But it didn't matter. She'd already known. That brash young army officer, the first man she had ever loved, had come walking back into her life again—just as curiously, though far less emotionally, than the way he had left it. "And I'm Anne-Marie," she whispered.

Chapter Two

Royce Buchanan stood at the wall of glass opening onto the Santa Ynez Valley. The lawn sloped down to the sparkling blue water of the pool, and in the distance beyond were pastures speckled with livestock. He stared at the tranquil scene for a few minutes, his arm leaning against the sliding-door frame.

The yoga instructor, he decided, was just another woman named Anne-Marie. She wasn't the German girl, the young art student he'd once known, though something in the voice vaguely reminded him of her. Still, the conversation had set him thinking.

The girl he had known would be—he stopped and calculated—close to forty-five by now. It didn't seem possible. Royce couldn't picture her as anything but the leggy beauty she'd once been—the girl with the raven hair, the girl with the endearing accent, the girl he'd once loved.

Anne-Marie's textbook English had been beautifully pronounced but stilted, and the emphasis sometimes fell on the wrong syllable, making him laugh. How sweet she had been that first time she'd told him she loved him—her face turned up to his, her pale, pale gray eyes glistening with emotion.

A lump formed in his throat at the memory. Anne-Marie Keller had been gone from him for more than half a lifetime, yet the tender recollection of that first love still came to mind occasionally. Sometimes months would pass before he would think of her again, but her sweet disposition and lovely face never faded. She would always be with him. Perhaps it was true what they say—first loves never die completely.

Royce opened the slider and stepped out into the warm air of late afternoon. It was May. The days were getting long; the sun was still well above the western hills. He gazed over the land that spread out from the hillock where the house stood. The greenness was virtually unbroken except for an occasional house or barn and the white board fences that seamed the terrain.

The open sky above was cloudless, but Royce felt strangely confined. The urge to change into his running togs struck him, as it often did when he was in such a mood. He craved the feel of the open road under his feet, the kiss of the dry California air on his face.

He was as free as a man could be, yet he felt like a squirrel in a cage, trapped by an inexplicable longing. Though he was supposed to cut back, the only hope for relief was to run, even if he simply ended up where he had begun—alone.

Anne-Marie sat alone in the kitchen, listening to the clock that had been on her grandmother's wall in Kronberg for decades. Half an hour earlier Christianne had returned, excited to find her brother home. The girl had convinced Kurt to take her to the beach so she could show him off and feel older than her years, though of course she hadn't admitted that to him.

Anne-Marie was glad for the opportunity to be alone, to think. She told them dinner would be ready when they got back, but she hadn't managed to do much more than peel the potatoes. In her confused state of mind she had put the water on to boil but had forgotten to put the potatoes in. The lid rattling under the billowing steam reminded her of the oversight, and she got up to take care of it.

Since the telephone call, Anne-Marie hadn't thought about anyone or anything but Royce Buchanan. Though he was as remote as the country she had left behind, she was surprised to discover how much he remained a part of her.

For a very long time, Royce had been nothing more than a memory, much like Germany and the heavily wooded hills of the Taunus where she had grown up. He was a familiar yet dusty antique, like the language she never spoke anymore and had half forgotten. But suddenly here he was, again in her life.

Years ago Ted Osborne, the young American accountant, had taken her away from all that—away from her native land and a broken heart. Ted, twenty-eight then, had been on an extended assignment in Frankfurt. She had been twenty, finished with her course of studies at the art institute and working as a commercial artist in Frankfurt.

They had met at a café near the Neues Theater on the Schweizerstrass. He had courted her for six months, married her and taken her home to California. Now she was his widow, as American as he had ever been, with two children who knew little more about her native land than well-informed tourists did.

Her husband had died of a heart attack as a relatively young man. Despite her loss, Anne-Marie was well adjusted and happy with her children, her friends and Don Nelson, the man in her life.

Thinking of Don gave her a feeling of reassurance, especially in contrast with the unsettling effect of Royce Buchanan. Don was like Ted—a giving man, a sensible person who had his priorities straight. It was no accident that Ted and Don had been partners—they were cut from the same cloth. In their way, they each gave a profound and lasting meaning to the word *love*, valuing her as she should be valued.

Both were different from the brash American lieutenant she had once known and loved. How much bigger than life Royce had seemed to her then. When she came face-to-face with him again, she expected disappointment. People and things from the past were often smaller than one's memories of them, much as her father's house in the Taunus had been when she and Ted went back for visits.

Still, the prospect of seeing Royce frightened her a bit. Certainly she was mature enough to cope with the unusual experience, but he *was* associated with one of the greater traumas of her life. The fact of the matter was that she wore what he had done to her like a scar on her soul....

"Schwärm, Meine Mädchen," Grandmother said. "It's just a crush. Your father understands these things far better than you."

"But I love Royce. And Papa wants only to ruin my life," Anne-Marie cried, tears glistening in her eyes.

"This young man is a soldier. He will move on. You should understand that, even at your age. What your father does is best."

Her grandmother sat at the heavy wooden table in the kitchen, peeling apples, taking great care that the long, unbroken band of skin fell neatly into the heavy crock on her lap. The old woman looked up through the thick lenses of her eyeglasses, her flat blue eyes magnified so that she looked to Anne-Marie like a wise, plump owl.

"Papa is cruel to tell me I shall never see Royce again. I love him. And he loves me—more than his life. He told me so!"

"Pfft! You're a silly girl, Anne-Marie. These are things all men say to virgins. Did I not tell you this when you were sixteen?"

"Grandmother, you don't understand!"

"I've been on this earth a good time longer than you, my girl. Don't presume to tell me about men and the ways of love."

Anne-Marie turned away from the table and went to the window. She stared out at the lead-gray sky and the somber winter face of the woods that lay beyond the small meadow behind her father's house. The Taunus had always been her home. She loved it as she loved and respected her father and her grandmother, the woman who had raised her after Mother had died. Anne-Marie had never once even dreamed of defying Herbert Keller, but she considered it now.

Before Royce, leaving the Taunus, much less leaving Germany, hadn't been a consideration. But he had told her such beautiful stories about Michigan, the Great Lakes and the woods in the North where he had fished and hunted as a boy. America seemed at once so remote, so modern and so primitive.

Royce had showed her pictures of his family home in Mount Clemens, near Detroit. It was a modest cottage compared to Father's house, but Royce had said it was only a starting point. He would be a rich man one day, he'd told her. A good mind and hard work were all you needed in America, he had said. And he had a good education, too. That made his success doubly certain.

None of that really mattered, though. Anne-Marie would live with him in an Indian tent on the prairie, if that's what it took. She loved him more than she had loved anyone in her whole life.

As she stared at the bleak scene in the falling darkness, she pictured Royce's handsomely irreverent face, his wide, craggy smile and strong white teeth, his deep-set eyes under his blond brow. Royce, it seemed, was always smiling. He was fearless, unafraid of the world and totally sure he was going to conquer it.

He wanted to marry her, he had said, to take her home to America. And he would, too, because she would find a way.

Anne-Marie turned around and looked at Grandmother. The woman sensed her eyes and looked up. She met Anne-Marie's gaze, then reached for another apple.

"Trust your father," she said. "He is a good man. He knows what is best."

"I love Papa. And I love you, Grandmother. But you are both wrong about Royce." She considered her next words before uttering them. "And you are wrong about me, as well."

The woman put the apple and paring knife down in the bowl and looked up crossly, wiping her plump hands on the front of her apron. Anne-Marie knew her grandmother was responding to her tone as much as to her words.

"I'm not a virgin," Anne-Marie said simply. "I have made love with Royce. That is why he will be my husband."

For once Grandmother was speechless. Her eyes opened wide with dismay. She sputtered, then turned bright red. "Anne-Marie," she finally managed, "go to your room at once!"

And she went, though she was no child, and it was wrong to treat her as such, just as Papa was wrong in his plan to keep her from seeing Royce. She knew he would be upset when Grandmother told him the news, as she surely would. But that was all right. The time had come at last for her to be a woman, not a girl.

The hours seemed to drag eternally until Father came home. From her room, she could hear him speaking with his mother. *"Was? Was? Nicht Anne-Marie,"* he said over and over. Finally, after more long minutes of agony, he knocked sternly on her bedroom door.

"Ja?"

Herbert Keller towered in the doorway. His expression was grave, his eyes dark under his heavy brows. He was a man of only average height, but his demeanor as well as his broad chest and shoulders made him seem much larger. He wore a traditional gray wool suit with the jacket unbuttoned. A gold watch chain hung from his vest pocket and over his slightly protruding stomach.

At the sight of him, Anne-Marie suddenly lost the resolve she had been cultivating. His stern expression brought the little girl in her rushing to the surface. She was glad she was sitting down, because she was sure her knees would have buckled.

Her father was staring hard, neutralizing any intention she might have to risk an untruth. "Anne-Marie," he said slowly, enunciating each syllable, "is it true?"

She didn't want to falter. She longed to be brave, but she couldn't withstand his gaze. Her eyes dropped submissively. *"Ja, Vater,"* she whispered. And when she looked up, he had left the room and closed the door.

For a long time Anne-Marie sat on her bed, feeling weak and inadequate. She was miserable. Not long after Father had left her room she heard him leave the house. She assumed he was going outside to cool off in the winter air. As she waited, she decided to talk to him as soon as he returned, to say the things she had planned to say earlier.

But Father didn't come back for a long time. She and Grandmother had a light supper without speaking two words, then Anne-Marie returned to her room, finally going to bed.

She lay awake staring into the darkness, fear growing in her by the minute. She had already decided that her father's absence was purposeful, that he was working against Royce in some way, though she wasn't sure what.

Herbert Keller was not a terribly important man, but he had influential friends, and he was respected. The American soldiers in the Frankfurt area were sometimes a problem, and the politicians frequently became involved in military matters affecting the civilian population.

Anne-Marie wondered if her father could have used his connections to take some action against Royce through his commanding officer. She resolved to ask him in the morning. After all, she had a right to know.

The next day, when Anne-Marie awoke, scattered snowflakes were falling randomly in the crisp winter air. The ground was lightly dusted with them, as was the birdbath and the heavy wooden lawn chairs that sat like headstones in the garden.

She looked out her bedroom window, watching the sparrows scratching and pecking at the frozen ground for several minutes before remembering she wanted to talk to Father before he left the house.

She turned and looked at the alarm clock on the night table. It was past eight-thirty. She had overslept. He might be gone.

Anne-Marie quickly ran a brush through her hair, slipped on her bathrobe and hurried to the kitchen. Grandmother was sitting at the table with a large cup of coffee poised at her lips. She wore one of her flowered dresses, an unbuttoned cardigan and an apron, as always.

"Where is Papa, Grandmother?"

The woman looked at her with mild annoyance. "*Guten Morgen*, Anne-Marie," she said flatly.

"Oh, good morning, Grandmother. Has Father gone already?"

"Yes, he leaves early. You know that." She gestured toward the basket of breads and the plate of cheeses and cold cuts on the table. "Have your breakfast."

"I'm not very hungry, thank you." She looked woefully at her father's empty chair. "I wanted to speak with him."

"You must get up early to speak with your father. He works very hard so that there will be more for you and your children when he is gone." Grandmother didn't say "your *German* children," but Anne-Marie heard it, nonetheless.

"Yes, I know." She stepped to the table and took a piece of black bread, broke off a corner and popped it into her mouth. Her grandmother didn't say anything, but Anne-Marie heard disapproval in her silence. "I shall speak to Papa this evening," she said, and left the kitchen.

She quickly bathed and dressed, then sat at her window. The snow was falling a little more heavily than before, but it was only a shower, not a storm. She imagined Royce out somewhere in the countryside with his tanks in the snow. She had never seen him in his combat uniform, but she pictured how commanding he would be. She visualized him directing his men, perhaps standing in his jeep and shouting orders, vapor from his breath billowing in the chilled air.

It was Saturday, and he had told her he would be back at his base by that night. They would meet as usual the next afternoon at the café on the main square in Kronberg. Father certainly wouldn't approve, but Anne-Marie was determined to be there, no matter what.

She looked at her clock again. Because it was Saturday, Herbert Keller would be home by midafternoon. Anne-Marie knew the conversation would be a pivotal one in her life. And although she was afraid, she was eager to get it over with.

The minutes seemed to drag on interminably. Even the snowflakes seemed to take forever to reach the ground. But she knew there was nothing to do but wait.

When she grew tired of sitting at her window, she got her sketch pad from her drawer and slowly flipped through the pages until she came to a blank sheet. She began drawing a portrait of Royce from memory, capturing perfectly the square jaw, his tapered, slightly pointed nose. Her friend Brigitte from the art institute said Royce looked Irish, but that was only because he resembled United States' President Kennedy, with his thick blondish hair and handsome, toothy grin.

Before long she had finished the sketch, rather proud of the likeness though the artistic merit was nothing exceptional. She propped the pad against the pillow, lay on her stomach on the bed and stared at it. "So, Mr. Buchanan," she said to him in English, "will we be married?"

But her fantasies contented her only for a little while. As time passed she grew more and more anxious that her father had indeed taken major steps against Royce. His quiet, unexplained disappearance the night before became ever more ominous in her mind.

By late morning she couldn't stand the waiting. She wanted to talk to Royce, but that wasn't possible. Still, she decided she had to get word to him, to warn him, though of what she wasn't quite sure. Just before noon she slipped on her coat and told her grandmother she was going into Kronberg to post a letter.

"Must you go?" the old woman asked. "The roads are not good. Can't it wait for your father to take on Monday?"

"No. Besides, I'd like the air." And so Anne-Marie took off on her bicycle, wanting to get to the post office, not to mail a letter, but rather to call the headquarters of Royce's unit to leave a message for him.

As she leaned her bicycle against the front of the building in the village, she felt like a sneak. But the stakes were rapidly rising. Her whole life could be hanging in the balance.

It was too risky to call from her father's house. Though Grandmother's English was not good, the woman would easily guess her purpose in making a call. And Grandmother was blindly loyal to her son. The safest course was to phone from town.

Royce was not yet back from maneuvers, as Anne-Marie expected, but the clerk, a young man from the South of the United States whom she had spoken with once before, took her message.

"Am I supposed to put down what it is your father knows, ma'am?" he asked with hardly disguised curiosity.

"No, Lieutenant Buchanan will know."

"All right, ma'am. I'll put it in his mail slot. He'll get it tonight or tomorrow mornin'."

And Anne-Marie went out into the cold winter air. She didn't want to go home. What she really wanted was to see Royce at that very minute. But she would have to wait. And she had to see her father first. She had to tell him she would be marrying Royce Buchanan no matter what. Nothing on earth would stop her.

Anne-Marie sat in the café on the square the next afternoon watching the door, her hands wrapped around a mug of hot chocolate. Three old men in caps and wool coats were drinking beer at a table near the bar. A woman across the way was sipping tea and reading a book. The café was otherwise empty.

Anne-Marie had arrived half an hour early. After her talk with Father the previous evening he had become furious at her defiant spirit and told her that seventeen was too young to make any decisions about marriage. She was forbidden to see the young American officer ever again. But her father's harshness had only strengthened her resolve.

The first chance she had after breakfast, Anne-Marie had slipped out of the house and ridden her bicycle into Kronberg. The shops were closed, so she went first to the train station, where she bought a newspaper and a copy of *Time* magazine. She regarded it as the first tangible step of the day toward a new life as an American.

When she grew tired of the station, she had walked her bicycle up the hill to the square. On the way a *Polizist* passed by in his patrol car, observing her closely. She felt uncomfortable, wondering for a moment if she might be arrested. But then, she had committed no crimes—not against the law, at any rate.

She knew perfectly well that her father would be enraged at her disappearance, but she was unsure what he could do about it. It worried her that he might come looking for her in the village, though he couldn't be certain that was where she had come.

Over the laughing voices of the old men, she heard the telephone against the wall ring. The barmaid went to answer it. Anne-Marie watched with fear and suspicion.

"Fräulein Keller?" the woman called over the men's voices. She looked at Anne-Marie questioningly.

"Ja?"

"It's for you."

Anne-Marie went to the telephone, her heart thumping, not knowing whether to expect her father's voice or Royce's. *"Hallo?"*

It was Royce, and she let out an audible sigh of relief.

"Sorry, darling," he said anxiously, "but I can't meet you. I'm tied up. The colonel asked to see me. I tried calling your house, but—"

"It's about me? Your colonel wants to see you about me?"

"Why do you say that?"

"Didn't you get my message last night?"

"What message?"

"Oh, Royce," she moaned, "my father knows about us. He knows everything. I told him."

There was a dead silence.

"Why?" he finally asked.

"Because he didn't want me to see you again. It was time for the truth, my darling. I told Grandmother we would marry."

Another pause. "Then they know everything?"

"Yes, I had to say it."

"Hmm. That's why they wouldn't talk to me when I called your house."

"Father is very angry."

Royce didn't say anything.

"Darling, will it be all right? We'll go to America. We'll be married, won't we?"

"Yes, of course—eventually. But we can't now. It's pretty complicated, you see. I need my commanding officer's approval. And you're not yet eighteen."

"But nearly so."

"Yes, but it complicates things, Anne-Marie. I was thinking later... at the end of my tour of duty."

"I know we haven't talked specifically of it, but Father has done this now. He wants to stop us." She felt tears of desperation forming in her eyes.

"I've got to think," he said vacantly.

"Oh, Royce. Will you come? Will I see you today? I can't go home without seeing you."

"Yes, but I have to see the colonel first. I must leave now. Give me an hour or two."

"I can't wait here in the café. Father will come eventually. I've been gone a long time."

"All right. Go to the Schlosshotel. He won't look for you there. Wait for me in the lounge. I'll make reservations for tea. Just give my name if anyone asks. Say you're meeting me and you had to come early."

"Whatever you say."

"I'll be there as soon as I can."

"Royce?"

"Yes?"

"Ich liebe Dich."

Chapter Three

"Mom!" Christianne exclaimed when Anne-Marie led the ace of spades. "That was stupid. The queen hasn't been played."

"Maybe *she's* got it, dummy," Kurt said to his sister.

"No, she doesn't," the girl replied, tossing it from her hand to the middle of the table.

"She's right," Anne-Marie said woefully. "It was a stupid lead. I wasn't thinking."

"What's happened to you, Mom?" he asked with a touch of concern. "You used to whip our butts at hearts. You were always the grand strategist."

She shrugged. "I don't know. I guess my mind's not on the game."

"Well, take your trick," Christianne said, gesturing toward the cards. "It's too late to shoot the moon. Kurt's already taken a heart."

"Two," he said, "thanks to you."

"You might be in college," the girl replied, "but you obviously haven't learned anything useful, like playing cards."

Kurt reached over to ruffle his sister's dark hair, but she leaned back, out of his reach.

"Getting slow in your old age, too," she teased.

"Hey, pip-squeak, watch your mouth."

Anne-Marie was staring at her cards, only half hearing her children's banter. "Oh, dear, I've left myself without a lead."

"Throw your lowest heart. Maybe Kurt kept all his high ones."

"Very funny," he said. "You're getting so you think you know everything. Maybe it's time for me to teach you a real game, like poker."

The girl sat upright. "Would you, Kurt? Would you really?"

"I know I'm being a party pooper," Anne-Marie said, looking at the score sheet in front of Christianne, "but I've just about lost anyway. Would you two mind if we quit?"

"Ah," the girl moaned, "I was about to whip Kurt's butt."

"Christianne, that's hardly the way for a young woman to talk. You're fourteen—you should show more discretion."

"Kurt said the same thing a minute ago."

Anne-Marie glanced at her son. "He ought to use better judgment, too."

He rolled his eyes and looked disgusted as Anne-Marie began gathering the cards.

"I was going to break down and make you two apple strudel, but I didn't have time," she said, "so I'm afraid there's no dessert."

"How about ice cream?" Christianne asked hopefully. "And I don't mean that tofu stuff that's been rotting in the freezer for three months."

"I don't know if there's anything else."

The girl got up. "I'll go look." She bounced out of the room, heading for the kitchen.

Anne-Marie noticed Kurt watching her and gave him a smile. "It's good having you home for dinner, even if it's only because Tracy had a baby shower to attend."

"In a month I'll be home for the summer."

"If it's anything like last year, we won't see much more of you than when you're up in San Luis Obispo. And imagine, I thought we'd be seeing more of you if you went to Cal. Poly.

rather than MIT. The truth is, Tracy's the only one who's benefited."

"Now, Mom . . ."

"Oh, dear. Am I sounding like a mother again?"

"It could be because you are one."

"I don't mean to be so maudlin. This has been kind of an off day for me. I'm not myself."

"Yeah, what's gotten into you, anyway? Did my asking about Don bother you?"

"Oh, no. I don't know what it is. I was thinking about home some . . . when I was a girl."

"I figured as much. Wiener schnitzel, boiled potatoes and cabbage for dinner instead of bean sprouts."

Anne-Marie touched her stomach. "Yes, and I've been feeling guilty ever since we ate."

"You've got to lighten up on this health business. I know because of what happened to Mrs. Nelson and Dad's heart attack you're into prevention, but you kind of overdo it."

"If I didn't look and feel better, I'd agree with you, Kurt. But the older you get, the fewer compromises you can make at the dinner table. For some people it's all or nothing."

"Bad news," Christianne said glumly as she came dragging back into the den. "There's nothing but the tofu."

"If it's really important, I suppose we could go to the store and get something else," Anne-Marie said with a conspiratorial glance at her son.

"Could we, Mom?" the girl asked. "*Two* ice creams in one month?"

Anne-Marie grinned. "Your brother told me I should lighten up on the food program."

Christianne looked at Kurt with a mischievous grin. "Maybe you're learning something in college, after all."

"Don't get the idea we're going to make a habit of this," Anne-Marie warned.

The telephone rang in the kitchen.

"That's probably another class scandal awaiting your ears," Kurt said sarcastically.

The girl scowled at him and bounded toward the telephone. Anne-Marie put the cards in the carton.

"It's for me," Christianne called out. "If you go for the ice cream, I vote for Rocky Road."

Anne-Marie gazed at Kurt. "I guess we've been given our assignment."

"Come on, Mom," he said, getting to his feet. "I've got time before I have to pick up Tracy. I'll drive you."

Anne-Marie went upstairs for her purse, and they left Christianne chatting away with one of her friends. As they descended the front steps of the large old house she and Ted had inherited from his parents, Anne-Marie took a deep breath. The usually cool marine air was rather warm, reminding her of the spring evenings she used to know as a girl on the Taunus. Since Royce Buchanan's call, everything seemed to remind her of those earlier years.

They went to Kurt's old Ford Mustang parked at the curb. He held the door open for her. "Watch the bad spring in the seat if you don't want to get goosed."

She started to comment on his choice of terms, having been reminded of the poor example he'd set for his sister earlier, but she held her tongue. He was nearly twenty-one—for all intents and purposes a man. It was time she stopped being only his mother and became more his friend.

Kurt closed the door for her, then went around to the driver's side and got in. They drove down the dark street, the soft night air blowing in the window, fluttering wisps of her hair against her neck.

"So, what got you thinking about the Old Country?" Kurt asked, as though he were reading her mind.

She considered telling her son about Royce's call but decided not to, thinking it might somehow worry him. Since Ted had died, Kurt had been very protective of her—both consciously and unconsciously—when it came to other men. Don Nelson had been the only one he had ever approved of, and that was because Don had been practically a surrogate father to him for years. Tracy's closeness to her father was another contributing factor.

"I was thinking about my father and grandmother," she finally replied.

"It's been a long time since you've talked about them."

"That was a different world for me, Kurt. Another lifetime."

"Do you ever get the feeling you'd like to go back?"

"To visit, sure. But you and Christianne are my only real family, except for my cousins." She looked out at the houses of Santa Barbara. "I'm sorry in a way that you never had a chance to get to know Germany and my family."

"We all went a couple of times. And Christianne's going back this summer to stay with your cousin Kirsten."

"Yes, but that hardly counts. I would have liked for you to get to know Grandfather Keller before he died. If you had, you might understand why I say you're so much like him."

They were nearing the shopping center where Anne-Marie usually bought groceries. Kurt geared down and turned into the parking lot.

"I thought you said I was like Dad."

"You're like him in ways, too. Your father was very loyal, concerned about his family. We always came first in his life."

"What about Grandpa Keller?"

"He was, too, in his own way, though more bullheaded about it than your father."

Kurt pulled into a parking space in front of the store and turned off the ignition. "What are you saying, Mom? That I'm bullheaded, too?"

"You can be a little stubborn, my dear. And that's not necessarily bad, unless it's taken to the extreme and you abuse it."

"Did Grandpa abuse it?"

"Sometimes, yes."

"Like when? When you wanted to marry Dad and leave Germany?"

"No. By that time your grandfather was pretty well resigned to the fact that I was going to lead my own life. But earlier, when I was younger, he wasn't so open-minded."

"What happened?"

"Oh, it's been so long ago that it doesn't matter anymore. Besides, Grandpa is gone." She reached for the door handle.

Kurt stopped her. "You cooked dinner. You're tired. I'll go in." He opened his door, got out and closed it. Then he leaned in the open window. "What flavor will it be?"

"I guess we'd better make it Rocky Road."

"To please the princess?"

Anne-Marie gave him a disapproving look. Then she took a five-dollar bill from her purse and handed it to him. Kurt smiled, took the money and went into the store.

For a while she sat in the dark, staring at the bright lights of the supermarket. A gentle breeze blew through the open windows of Kurt's Mustang. It wasn't a cold breeze, but Anne-Marie shivered. Her mind was somewhere else. She was already back in Kronberg. It was winter, twenty-seven years ago, and she was at the Schlosshotel waiting for Royce Buchanan....

The waiter, a gaunt young man from the village with wispy hair and a self-important manner, came for the third time in three hours to where Anne-Marie sat in the lounge, waiting. She looked up at him uneasily, aware that his face was vaguely familiar, though he himself showed no outward sign of recognition.

"Would you like something now, *Fräulein*?"

Anne-Marie had said no to the question the previous times he had asked, explaining that she would wait for Lieutenant Buchanan. But she was beginning to feel a little foolish. Teatime had passed, and she knew her story was beginning to look suspicious.

"*Vielleicht.*" Perhaps.

"And what would the lady like?"

"Mineral water," she said casually. "And ice."

The tiniest hint of a smile touched his lips as he bowed and moved back a step before turning and walking toward the bar.

Anne-Marie shifted uneasily in the deep leather chair, where she had been waiting impatiently for hours. There seemed to be relatively few guests in the hotel, an old Victorian castle originally built for the widow of Kaiser Frederick III by her mother, the Queen of England. Its park, golf links, gabled roof and chimneys seemed more English than German, hence a little alien to the surroundings and to Anne-Marie.

She had been to the hotel only a few times before, though she had grown up just kilometers away. Once, when she was eleven, she'd come with her father and grandmother to a wedding party. It had been a nice spring day, and champagne had been served in the garden overlooking the park. Anne-Marie remembered that occasion best because Father's friend had given her half a glass of wine and she'd gotten dizzy on the few sips.

More recently, soon after she had met Royce, he had brought her to the *Schloss* for lunch. It was a favorite place of the Americans, perhaps because General Eisenhower had made the old castle his headquarters at the end of the war, and they, along with the British, could claim a piece of it.

After they had eaten that day, Royce had arranged for them to see Eisenhower's staff room up on the top floor of the hotel, under the gabled roof. The young officer had walked back and forth in the room in his green uniform with the silver first-lieutenant's bars gleaming on the shoulder, his chest puffed, savoring the feel of the floor under his feet—where the Commander in Chief himself had once walked.

"I imagine the butlers and the chambermaids did more in here over the years than Eisenhower," he said with a mischievous grin. "But it feels good to pace around a little."

"I'm sure they've changed the carpet, Lieutenant," she had said with a laugh.

Royce had put his arm around her waist then and kissed her on the temple. It was the first time he had kissed her.

Anne-Marie remembered that summer day happily, smiling at the recollection when the waiter returned, carrying a silver tray over his shoulder. He placed a liter bottle of mineral water on the table beside her, along with a small ice bucket, a glass and a bowl of lime wedges.

"Would you like for me to pour, miss?"

"*Bitte.*"

As Anne-Marie watched, the young man picked up a pair of silver tongs and put several cubes of ice into the glass, then poured from the open bottle and withdrew. She took the glass immediately and sipped from it.

From the entrance to the lounge the maître d', a distinguished-looking silver-haired man wearing a tuxedo, looked in at her with suspicion. In pants and a heavy sweater, she was more suitably dressed for a walk in the park than for the evening hours. And, though she was trying to conduct herself with dignity, she knew her youth was apparent. Young ladies of seventeen did not spend three hours alone in the lounge of the Schlosshotel.

The first guests, dressed for dinner, had begun descending for cocktails. Through the lead-paned windows Anne-Marie could see that twilight had fallen and that it would soon be dark. What if Royce didn't come? What if she had to return to her father's house without seeing her young officer?

She looked at the mineral water, the ice bucket and the limes. If Royce didn't come, she'd have to pay for it. She'd had only a ten-mark note and some change in her purse when she left the house that morning, but that was before the hot chocolate in the café. The mineral water was only two marks fifty in the store, but they would easily charge three of four times more here. On top of everything else, she now had to worry that she would be unable to pay her bill.

She took another sip as a sinking feeling came over her. What was happening? Was Royce's meeting about her? Had Father done something to undermine their relationship?

All sorts of dark thoughts were swirling through her mind when Royce suddenly appeared at the door. He was in his uniform, his unbuttoned trench coat over it, his hat in his hand, his thick hair a little mussed. He looked haggard and grim as he walked directly to her. She rose to her feet.

"Sorry," he said, not smiling. "I was afraid you'd given up on me." He kissed her cheek.

His skin was cool, and he smelled of the outdoors, with barely a hint of the American cologne he usually wore.

He took her by the hand and pulled her to an adjacent couch, where they sat side by side. Anne-Marie looked at him questioningly. He still hadn't smiled. He was looking into her gray eyes. She saw pain, and maybe fear. It was the first time she'd seen fear in his eyes.

"What's happened?" she murmured.

"Colonel Johnson did want to talk to me about you. You were right about that."

"Father?"

Royce nodded, looking at her from under his fair brows, his blue eyes dark and glistening.

"What has he done? What did he say?"

"I don't know, exactly. I guess the channels are very convoluted."

"Very what?"

"It's complicated—German relations with the military."

"What have they said to you?"

Royce looked around. "It's a long story. I'll tell you everything, but aren't you hungry? We missed tea. Shall we have dinner?"

"Royce! What did my father do? I must know!"

He took her hand in both of his. "He doesn't want me to see you again. He thinks you're too young."

"I know this. Wasn't there more?"

"Yes, but let's talk about it over dinner. I'm starved. Aren't you?"

"I'm not hungry. I can't eat anything, I'm too upset. Besides, I'm not dressed for dinner. They've been looking at me strangely here already."

"The hell with them. You're with me now."

"I'd rather not eat here, Royce."

"All right," he said, getting up. "We'll go someplace else then."

Anne-Marie took her coat, then saw the waiter approaching as Royce started to lead her toward the door. "Wait," she said, stopping him. "The mineral water." She gestured toward the table. "I haven't paid for it."

He was reaching for his wallet as the waiter came up to them.

"Wieviel kostet?" How much is it? Royce asked in rather awkwardly pronounced German.

Anne-Marie and the young man both suppressed smiles.

"Eight marks, *Mein Herr.*"

Royce handed him a ten-mark note, and they headed for the door.

Outside it was nearly dark. The sky was still pink through the trees to the west. Anne-Marie had slipped on her coat and held the lapels closed over her neck with one hand as she took

Royce's arm with the other. Vapors issued from their mouths in the chilled air.

"May we walk in the park before we go?" she asked.

"If you like."

They followed the walk around the building and were soon on a path leading out into the open field. Royce didn't look at her. He maintained a somber visage under the peak of his hat. His mind seemed to be off somewhere—perhaps with their problem. Anne-Marie sensed something ominous.

"What will happen to us?" she asked after a while. "What did your colonel tell you?"

Royce didn't answer immediately, but he stopped walking. Then he turned to her and took her arms, gripping them tightly through her coat. For a long time he stared at her. His face was in shadow, but she saw the fear again, and moistness in his eyes.

"They want me to leave," he finally said.

"Leave? Where to?"

"Colonel Johnson wants me to take an assignment in Korea. They want me to go tomorrow."

"Tomorrow! Korea? That's on the other side of the world!"

He bit his lip. His thumbs dug deeply into her arms.

"I'll go with you."

Royce slowly shook his head.

"You aren't going. You won't leave me. Tell me they can't make you go."

"I could refuse. But Colonel Johnson said it wouldn't help my career, or his, for that matter. I wouldn't necessarily have legal problems because of your age, but I'd definitely have political problems. Apparently your father has friends in high places, and they've put pressure on to have me transferred. He's determined to stop us."

"You won't let him, Royce."

"If I were a civilian, it would be easy. But he's got me between a rock and a hard place with the army. I'm an officer, and he knew enough to offer the carrot along with the stick."

"What does that mean?"

He touched her lower lip with his finger, smiling for the first time. "It means if they ship me out of Germany, if I go, the matter is closed. No more legal *or* political repercussions."

"And you'll let Father scare you away?" She felt emotion start to boil up within her as the implications became clearer and clearer.

"That's what I want to talk to you about."

"Your Colonel Johnson said to come and tell me goodbye. That's what this is, Lieutenant Buchanan, isn't it?" Anger surged through her blood. Anne-Marie turned on her heel and started back up the walk toward the *Schloss*. But Royce grabbed her arm and stopped her.

"Anne-Marie, I'm not finished. You've got to hear what I have to say."

"What is there to say? You're going to Korea. I'm staying in my father's house, and that is that. *Nein?*"

"No, that's not all."

"What, then?"

"I'll only be in Korea for eighteen months. Six months after that my military obligation will be complete. They think they're going to turn me into a regular army career officer. Johnson has taken me under his wing. That's why he wants to save me, pull what strings he can to get me out of this. I've decided to let them believe that. It's in my interest. Then—"

"What about *my* interest, Royce? You're forgetting about me."

"No, I'm not. But you're only seventeen, Anne-Marie. That's half the problem. Eighteen months from now you'll be going on twenty. Then they can't stop us from doing what we want. The army won't have me by the collar, and your father won't have you. In two years I'll be a free man."

"Two years is forever." She heard her voice crack. "Two more springs, two more summers, two more autumns. Two years of watching the trees change their colors. Why can't we marry now?"

He pulled her against him and kissed the top of her head. "We can't, my darling. For the moment they're bigger than we are. You can't fight city hall."

"What?"

He laughed and lifted her chin. The tears were streaming down her cheeks, and he brushed them away with the backs of his fingers. He smiled for the second time. "I love you, Anne-Marie." Then he kissed her softly on the lips.

She pressed her cheek against his chest and felt the warmth of his body. And as she held him tight, she saw a hare appear suddenly on the path a dozen meters from where they stood. The small creature seemed to look at them for several moments, then turned and scampered away into the darkness.

Anne-Marie couldn't help wondering if the hare was an omen. It had vanished as quickly as it had appeared—just as her lieutenant would, now that Father had interfered. The question was, would she ever see Royce again?

Chapter Four

A sliver of the California sun peeked over the string of low hills to the east, its first rays striking Royce Buchanan on the side of his sweaty brow. He breathed deeply and easily as he ran, the only sound the thumping of his feet on the dirt road. He had already gone six miles by his calculation, the first few in the hazy light of predawn, the remainder in daylight.

Fifty yards ahead a jackrabbit hopped onto the road and sat transfixed for a moment, watching him approach. Then it turned and loped along ahead of him, stopping occasionally to see if he was still following. The game continued for a while until the rabbit rounded a bend and disappeared. It seemed to Royce a fitting sequel to his dreams of the night before.

The moon had been about to set in the west when he awakened from a fitful sleep. He couldn't doze off again, so he got up and went to the sliding glass door of his bedroom. There he stared at the moon and the valley, a canvas of silver gray.

The vaguely uncomfortable feeling that possessed him had emanated from his dreams. He had been in a faraway place, perhaps Germany, searching for Anne-Marie Keller.

The conversation with the yoga instructor had brought Anne-Marie to his mind, and he had spent the previous evening sitting in the darkness, listening to music, drinking wine and thinking about that brief but tortured period of his life. It struck him as strange that a little incident like that telephone conversation could release a whole chain of memories—memories that had been locked away unexamined for years, like an old photo album.

But his dreams the night before had been even more immediate and full of the sharp, distressing emotions that had gripped him as a young man. Only once since Anne-Marie had slipped through his fingers and into the arms of another man had his failure tormented him so.

That had been five years earlier, several months after his divorce had become final. The guilt and misgivings, and especially his feelings of inadequacy, had turned his mind back to Anne-Marie.

In his isolation and loneliness, memories of his first love came to haunt him. He thought about her for days during that difficult period. For a while he seriously considered going back to Germany to try to pick up her trail, to find out where she had gone, whether she was still married, if she was happy.

But he never had. The impulse had faded as he gradually recovered from the trauma of his divorce. And once he had gone back to work—back to the living, consuming present—Anne-Marie retreated again to that small compartment of his subconscious where she lived.

But the previous night she had found her way into his dreams. She had been an elusive, tantalizing figure, staying just beyond his reach, barely within sight. He had begun running after her, but no matter how fast he ran, he couldn't catch her.

Then he awoke to the sight of the moon dropping in the western sky, surrounded by a silver halo. It looked so peaceful, yet his heart was beating heavily from the endless chase. He wasn't exhausted, though. He craved the fatigue, the pursuit of the dream. After putting on his running clothes, he had headed off in the fragile air, Anne-Marie Keller still on his mind.

As he ran, he realized he was chasing something still. If it wasn't Anne-Marie, it was something or someone else. But in the growing daylight, on an isolated road in the Santa Ynez Valley, at the rim of the North American continent, he saw the face of that German girl with the ebony hair and gosling-gray eyes.

And he yearned for her as he had yearned for her that other day, two years after they had parted. In his mind he saw her father's house again, enveloped by the deep, silent forest she so dearly loved....

The taxi sped along the winding road from Kronberg, deeper into the Taunus, moving faster even than Royce Buchanan's eagerness to see Anne-Marie warranted. He adjusted his tie again, leaning back into the seat, looking out at the dirty snow left behind by the storm that had hit Europe the week before.

When the driver turned into the lane where the Keller house was located, Royce leaned forward in anticipation. For a month he had been mentally rehearsing this moment, composing speeches for every conceivable objection she might raise to his sudden appearance.

She hadn't answered his last letter—the ten-page epistle he had written from Fort Hood in Texas, just before his discharge. But in a way, he'd half expected that she wouldn't.

Anne-Marie was a proud girl. He had disappointed her two years before when he left Germany without her. It was clear that she had doubted his love. And though she was wrong about that, he *had* had misgivings. He had been twenty-three, and she would still have been in high school if she'd been an American. When Colonel Johnson pointed that out, her youth had really struck him for the first time.

And Royce had begun doubting his own maturity. "Give her a chance to grow up without you for a while," the colonel had advised. "Then see how you feel about each other."

It had been an opportunity for him to do a little growing, to test the love he felt. And once he had emotionally accepted the notion of a separation, he had embraced it. Though he wrote to Anne-Marie to express his love, he tried to limit those outpourings. If they were really to be separated, he decided the relationship should truly go on the back burner, giving them both an opportunity to grow up.

And when she didn't answer his letters, it became easier to detach himself from her. Anne-Marie became for him a delicate blossom in a terrarium he had placed on a shelf, waiting for the day he would take her down and enjoy her to the fullest.

Now that day had arrived. He knew he had risked coming to her when she was unready. She might also have stopped loving him. But as Colonel Johnson had said, "If your love isn't strong enough to last, you shouldn't be together."

They were nearing the house, and Buchanan leaned forward to tap the driver on the shoulder. *"Können Sie hier halten?"*

The man nodded and stopped at the side of the road. The Keller house was less than a hundred meters ahead. Buchanan wanted to walk the last small stretch and give himself time to calm his mind. It was a Sunday morning. And unless things had changed radically, Anne-Marie would be home with her father and grandmother, observing the family time to be together. He spoke to the driver again.

"Bitte, warten Sie auf mich." Please wait for me.

He got out of the taxi and walked up the road. Although he really had nothing but the little money he had saved while in the service, after his discharge he had gone out and bought a fine suit and topcoat, gold cuff links, an expensive Italian silk tie and a pair of hundred-dollar shoes. His hair was grown out to civilian length. He looked and felt affluent, mature, responsible.

When the Keller house came into view, Buchanan felt his pulse pick up. He was eager to see the expression on Anne-Marie's face when she saw him. He expected her to be shy initially, perhaps even cold. But he was certain of his love for her, and equally certain of her love for him.

As he neared the house he noticed a finger of smoke curling from the chimney, indicating an inviting fire. He pictured himself sitting beside it with Anne-Marie while they drank tea, rediscovering each other.

Herbert Keller remained an unknown, though. He couldn't expect the man to embrace him, but his protective attitude toward his daughter would have to have softened by now, considering she was already twenty. But if it hadn't, Royce knew he could deal with it. This time, nothing could get in the way of their love.

He had reached the house, stopping for a moment to gaze at it, surprised by its tranquil facade and unpretentious demeanor, considering all it represented. How many nights in Korea had he pictured this house in the Taunus? How many times had he seen Anne-Marie at the door when he finally returned?

He went to the foot of the stairs, scraped his shoes, then slowly went up the wide porch. He walked directly to the door and knocked. A long, silent minute passed before the door opened and an old woman appeared, the grandmother he had seen only a time or two before.

"Guten Morgen. I am Herr Buchanan. I have come to see Anne-Marie," he said in careful German.

The woman looked at him through her thick glasses with suspicious eyes. She shook her head, then finally said, *"Warten Sie einen Augenblick."* Wait a moment.

The door closed, and Buchanan waited, shifting his weight from foot to foot impatiently. After a minute it opened again. Herbert Keller, heavier, ruddier, stood like a bull in the doorway. He wore slippers, a white dress shirt open at the neck, and trousers supported by heavy suspenders. *"Ja?"*

Buchanan repeated his request.

"I'm afraid Anne-Marie is not here, Mr. Buchanan," Keller said in heavy English. "She is married and gone from home."

Buchanan stared at the man, hearing the words but not believing them. "Married?"

"Last summer."

He shook his head, unafraid of showing his disbelief. "She can't be."

The man stared at him blankly, showing neither bitterness nor compassion. Royce was certain it was a trick, though. And he felt so frustrated that he considered pushing past the man and searching the house. But before he could act on the impulse, Keller turned and called something unintelligible back into the house.

As he waited, Buchanan wondered if the father had decided on this marriage ploy by himself or if Anne-Marie was in complicity. Whatever the case, he knew it wasn't true. It couldn't be.

The grandmother, carrying something, came up behind her son. Herbert Keller took the object from her, turned and held up a large framed picture for Buchanan to see. It was Anne-Marie in a wedding dress, standing in the garden, a bridal bouquet in her hands.

Keller passed the photograph back to the old woman. Then he took a small gilt-trimmed album from her and extended it to Buchanan, who took it with quivering fingers. Inside was a picture of Anne-Marie in her wedding dress, once again in the garden. But beside her this time was a tall blondish man with a round, good-natured face. They were both smiling, holding hands, looking very happy.

Buchanan flipped through a few more pages, his gut churning. There were pictures of Anne-Marie and her husband with her father and grandmother. There were pictures with another older couple, undoubtedly the parents of the groom, and pictures with children Buchanan didn't know. It was all alien, unbelievable.

The only truth he recognized was the smile on Anne-Marie's face. It was a truth he had seen countless times before in his mind's eye, a truth he had experienced on innumerable lonely nights in Korea. The only things different were the context . . . and the man beside her.

He slowly closed the album and handed it back to Keller, believing for the first time what the man had told him. A deep sense of emptiness descended as he stared at the man filling the doorway. Perhaps she was married, but she couldn't be happy. Not without him. It was a false happiness in the pictures. He was the man she loved.

"Anne-Marie has a baby in the summer, Mr. Buchanan," Keller said, as though reading the younger man's thoughts. *Don't think anymore of her,* he seemed to say. *She is lost to you forever.*

Royce felt his shoulders sag under the weight of the news. He had never felt more defeated in his life. *"Es tut mir leid, Sie zu belästigen,"* he finally mumbled. I'm sorry to trouble you.

He turned then and walked away, hearing the door click shut behind him. If the taxi hadn't been waiting, he'd probably have walked off into the woods until he dropped. But the driver was ready to take him on to the station, the airport, the States and the rest of his life. At that instant Royce Buchanan knew that whatever happiness or success he managed to find in life, it would be qualified.

In his despair, and amid the tears that filled his eyes, an awful truth struck him: in abandoning Anne-Marie, in leaving Germany without her, he had made a terrible, terrible mistake.

At seven-thirty Anne-Marie stepped into her studio wearing gray tights and soft blue leotard. She had awakened early and begun thinking instantly about Royce Buchanan. The courage she had felt the previous afternoon and evening had abandoned her, and she wasn't at all sure she wanted to see him.

Almost certainly he didn't know it was she who'd be coming to his house, and her foreknowledge almost seemed unfair now. Still, she was glad she wasn't the one to be surprised. Or would it have been better that way, encountering him without an opportunity to prepare herself?

She went to the middle of the room and faced herself in the mirror, assuming the *Tadasana* position, her toes touching, her legs straight, her spine tucked in slightly in a catlike tilt, her breastbone elevated, her arms and shoulders relaxed. She was as graceful as a ballerina, though her strength and flexibility were more harmonious, more balanced than even the most accomplished dancer's.

After holding the pose for a minute, she bent forward at the waist into the *Uttanasana*, until her face touched her shins. She wrapped her arms around her ankles and breathed easily, folded in two like a rag doll. She let her body relax into the stretch at the back of her thighs, aware of every inch of her body.

She proceeded through her routine, moving easily from one pose to the next, testing her limits with a natural effort that left her body feeling vibrant and alive. Though the objective was in part to clear her mind, Anne-Marie couldn't help thinking about Royce Buchanan—and worrying.

There was no reason to expect any unpleasantness. Indeed, he might not even remember her very well. Some people had a way of letting go of the past entirely. Seeing her might be no different to him than running into an old friend from high school or college. *What a small world! How've you been? I didn't know you'd left Germany. Wow, you've really lost the old accent, haven't you? So, when did you get into yoga?*

Anne-Marie hoped it would go that way; it would be so much easier. She could ask him about his wife and family—surely he had them. Men his age did. They could show pictures of their children and trade stories about them. People did that.

Maybe, if it wasn't too uncomfortable for them, they could even laugh about that brief time years ago. How strange to think that they, now strangers, had once been so close to marriage.

Incredible as it seemed, they had been lovers once. Anne-Marie shivered at the thought. The unfamiliar man she would be seeing only hours from now had been the first man she'd been with, the man to whom she had given her virginity, the man who had preceded even Ted into her heart and into her life.

Despite the pep talk she had been giving herself, she realized she really didn't want to see Royce. His place in her memory was a comfortable one at last, and seeing him again might upset that, might reawaken her to long-ago pain. When she thought of him now, the recollections were pleasant. They were memories of young love, first love. A happy marriage, children and a contented home life had erased the pain, but they hadn't obliterated youthful pleasures.

The girl of seventeen who lived on inside her could still love Royce Buchanan as he had been then, could still dream, could still pretend. Probably every woman was like that, she decided, harboring in her heart the girl she'd once been.

But the man she was to meet later that morning was a different proposition altogether. He wouldn't be the same man she had known, any more than she was the same woman. In the interim she had been the wife of Ted Osborne, and the man in her life now was Don Nelson. Those were the men who had helped form her identity, who had helped define the person she had become.

And her children. She was the mother of a fourteen-year-old girl and a young man, himself not many years from marriage. Before very long she would likely become a grandmother.

She had a well-formed personality, tastes, values and a life-style that were the product of years of living. She was comfortable, content with the love of a gentle man with whom she shared so much. Why, then, did the prospect of seeing Royce spark such emotion in her?

Anne-Marie finished her routine with a headstand and a shoulder stand, the king and queen of yoga poses. She had worked harder and longer that morning than she had intended. Noting the time, she lay on her mat and relaxed only briefly, deciding she'd take another shower before heading off for Royce Buchanan's ranch in the Santa Ynez Valley.

Royce moved through the rambling house like a restless cat, a glass of cranberry nectar in one hand, a rubber ball that he squeezed to strengthen his grip in the other. His back didn't hurt so badly, and he wondered if it hadn't been simply an ordinary strain, something that would heal itself given enough time. Perhaps the doctor and the massage therapist were unnecessary, a waste of time.

But this Anne-Marie Osborne would be arriving soon, and, his backache aside, the treatment might turn out to be pleasurable. Besides, he was curious about her. An encounter with an unknown woman always sparked curiosity in a man.

He remembered Jessica Sarver, the management consultant from Chicago he'd hired to do a study of the organizational structure of his company about seven years earlier. Their contact the first half dozen times had been over the phone. She was all business, cool as a cucumber. And by the time she was due to arrive at his office, his curiosity about her was considerable.

As it turned out she was younger than he expected, with ice-blue eyes and a matching demeanor. She was attractive in a handsome sort of way, married and dead serious. Though at the time his marriage was on the rocks and Jessica offered the kind of challenge tailor-made for a man in his position, he let the subterranean tension between them pass without acting on it.

Neither of them had given the other an overt indication of interest, but he knew it was there, and that it was mutual. They both had held back, and he still wasn't sure why. Perhaps there was more satisfaction in being wise than in acting on the desire they felt.

He wondered if Jessica Sarver was still married and if she would remember him favorably if they were to run into each other. With so many women in the world it seemed pointless even to conjecture about it. Within an hour's drive were plenty of nurses, businesswomen, divorced socialites and, for that matter, a yoga instructor or two. He decided it was wisest to wait and see what opportunities fate dealt him.

He was headed back toward the kitchen for more juice when he heard a vehicle out front. Putting his empty glass and the ball on the counter just inside the kitchen, he went to the entry hall and opened the front door.

In the parking area down the slope, a hundred feet or so away, was a white Honda Accord under the canopy of giant oaks. In the mottled sunlight a woman was at the trunk of the car, apparently unloading some gear.

She wore a baby-blue jogging suit, and as she withdrew her head from the rear of the vehicle, he could see her shoulder-length ebony hair. It was swept back on the sides and curved under in the back. She was slender, and she moved with the grace of a gazelle to the driver's door, where she took something from the seat before returning for her gear.

There was a youthfulness about the woman, yet a maturity, as well. Buchanan couldn't guess her age, but as he watched, something about her struck him—an odd, elusive familiarity.

She picked up her case and looked toward the house for the first time. She was too far away for Royce to see her features clearly, but she definitely touched off a spark of recollection. As she moved up the walk through the trees, his eyes were riveted to her face, slipping down only occasionally to take in her body.

With each step she took, the woman became more familiar, more evocative of someone else, some other experience, some other lifetime. The walk twisted behind a large oak in front of the house, and as she came around the tree, a surprisingly pretty, smiling face came into focus.

In the milliseconds that followed, he was aware first of her beauty, then of the lilt of an eyebrow—a mannerism deeply reminiscent of someone from the past—and finally of the face itself. Her face. Anne-Marie Keller's. It was older now, he could see, but it was still beautiful. She stopped at the edge of the porch and put down her case.

"My...God," he stammered. "Anne-Marie...it's you!"

She laughed, tilting her head to the side as she had years before when she was shy or embarrassed. "You didn't know, did you, Royce?"

"Lord, no," he said, extending his hands to her, the shock still filling his head with short-circuited thoughts. "Did you?"

She put her hands in his, nodding apologetically. "I wasn't positive until you said your whole name at the end of our conversation. And then I was too stunned to say anything."

"I can't believe this," he said, shaking his head. "It's really you." He squeezed her hands, rubbing the backs of them with his thumbs.

She looked so good to him. There were smile lines at the corners of her eyes that hadn't been there before, and the skin at the top of her chest showed some age, but she seemed remarkably youthful. "You look fantastic," he said, glancing up and down her trim, vibrant body.

She nodded gratefully, the little smile he had always remembered touching the corners of her mouth.

"And so do you."

"I can't believe this," he said again, laughing with delight. Then, because he had to, he pulled her to him and gave her a big hug. Her fragrance was not at all familiar, but he liked it. He held her a little longer than he should have, testing the feel and scent of her, like a man trying to separate fantasy from reality.

Anne-Marie laughed with amusement, her gray eyes dancing as she pulled back a little to look at him. "I hate to think how many years it's been," she said.

"Good God," he said, shaking his head and grinning. "When Dr. Gilchrist first mentioned your name—Anne-

Marie—I thought of you, that little girl I fell in love with in Frankfurt. But I didn't dream that…" The words stopped. He stared at her, disbelieving.

"I guess I should have said something, but I didn't. I don't know why."

"It's a hell of a shock," he admitted with a laugh. "But I'm glad. I couldn't be more pleased."

She looked very shy just then, reminiscent of the young girl she'd once been. He stepped back, breaking the awkward moment that followed, gesturing toward the open door. "Well, come in for heaven's sake."

She reached for her case.

"Let me get that for you."

"No, I've got it." She picked it up, giving him a smile as she walked past him into the house. She stood in the entry, looking into the large, nicely appointed rooms that carefully maintained a balance between elegance and comfort.

"Well, it's not much like that little place in Michigan you showed me the picture of once. Remember?" She turned around and watched him close the door, then walk to where she stood in the middle of the entry.

"Yes, that was my launching pad, my childhood home. As I recall, I told you I'd climb a little."

"I remember."

He touched her arm. "Put your gear down. Let's go into the front room and talk." Without waiting for a reply, he took her case from her hand and set it down against the wall.

"I don't have a lot of time, Royce. I've got a yoga class at the Goleta Racquet Club at two."

"We'll have to cut the therapy short, then." He looked deeply into her pale eyes, remembering. "I was just having a glass of juice when I heard your car. Can I offer you one? Or something else?"

"Juice or water—anything's fine."

"Go on in and make yourself at home. I'll be back in a jiffy."

Anne-Marie turned from him and wandered into the exposed-beamed living room filled with overstuffed couches piled high with decorator pillows. He watched her for a moment, noting the pleasant curve of her hips, her remarkably trim figure. Then he headed toward the kitchen.

"What happened to the old accent?" he called to her over his shoulder. "The last time I saw you, you were definitely a German girl."

"I'm an American now, Royce, and quite a bit older," he heard her call back.

He pushed his way through the swinging door and went to the refrigerator. Indeed, she was an American now. And a woman. A very lovely woman.

He took a bottle of juice from the refrigerator, then turned toward the door he had come through, staring at it for a moment. For some reason the image of the jackrabbit he had seen on the road that morning came to mind. Maybe what he'd been running after all these months was Anne-Marie—the woman who'd just walked in his front door.

Chapter Five

Anne-Marie ran her fingers lightly over a pillow. She glanced around the room, seeing money everywhere. When Royce had said he lived in the Santa Ynez Valley, she figured he was pretty successful, but she hadn't pictured such affluence. What had he done to attain these heights? And what about his wife? Where was she?

The room, the entire place, was silent about the lady of the house. Though the home was large for one person and tastefully decorated, it had a masculine feel to it. The soft touches of a woman were missing. Perhaps his wife didn't spend much time there. Or perhaps there wasn't a Mrs. Buchanan.

Anne-Marie reflected on their brief interaction since her arrival and during their phone conversation. She could recall no clue about his marital status. And yet there was a distinctly independent character to Royce's demeanor. He had the feel of a man alone. Why would he be alone? she wondered.

"Do you like cranberry juice?" came his now familiar voice from the kitchen.

"Yes, fine," she called out.

"I've got guava, pineapple-coconut, apple-banana—you name it."

"I like cranberry if it's not too tart."

Anne-Marie thought of the irony of being in Royce Buchanan's house after all these years. What was even more remarkable, he seemed so very much the same. He looked good, though there was a ruggedly handsome maturity about his face in lieu of the freshness of the young officer she had known. But that shouldn't be surprising. So many years had passed.

Lord, she thought, he had been only a couple of years older than Kurt was now when they were lovers. How incredible that seemed.

"Thought I'd bring you a sample of my cranberry juice," he said, entering the room, "before I pour a whole glass." He walked toward her with a tiny glass of rose-colored liquid in his hand. "I have my juices specially shipped, and cranberry can be tricky. This is actually a nectar diluted with concord grape."

"It wasn't necessary to bring a sample, Royce," she said, taking it from him. "I'm not so particular." She looked up into his deep-set blue eyes, which seemed always to squint and smile.

The lines at either side of his strong chin were evident when he grinned at her. "All part of the service."

"It's very nice," she said after a sip.

Royce rested his hands on his hips, shaking his head as he looked down at her. "God, you look good, Anne-Marie. Like one of those sweet dreams you wake from and wish had never ended."

"Heavens!" she replied with a laugh.

"I know, I'm sounding . . . sentimental."

They looked at each other for a long time, then Anne-Marie finished the bit of juice and handed the glass back to him. He took it, smiling broadly.

There was an energy in him that she found disconcerting. She folded her hands around her knees and rocked back, gazing up. "Where's your wife?"

"In Michigan."

"Do you keep a home there, too?"

"She does. I don't make her feel very welcome here." He paused dramatically, then a mischievous grin crept across his face. "We've been divorced for years."

"Oh," Anne-Marie said with an audible sigh, "I see."

"How about you?"

"I'm widowed. My husband died several years ago."

"I'm sorry."

They stared at each other again, their mental calculations obvious. Anne-Marie was uncomfortable and felt the need to comment.

"Ted and I were very happy."

"That makes it worse, I guess. He must have been the tall blond fellow your dad had a photo of. The one with you in the wedding picture."

She looked at him with surprise. "How...what are you talking about?"

"After I was discharged, I went to your father's house to collect you, but you'd married the summer before. He showed me your wedding picture."

"I didn't know. Papa never told me you'd come back."

"It doesn't surprise me." Royce smiled, remembering. "He had some advice for me, as I recall. 'Forget Anne-Marie.' Or words to that effect."

"That sounds like Father."

"He told me you were pregnant, I think to make sure I wouldn't interfere."

"I did get pregnant right away, but I lost the child." She looked up at Royce wistfully. "Papa didn't care for you, did he?"

"No."

"He died a number of years ago. I imagine you weren't aware."

"I'm sorry to hear that."

Her smile was sad, and a bit reflective. "Well, that's all over now, isn't it?"

"So, your husband was an American. I had no idea. I'd assumed you'd married a German and lived in Europe all these years."

"No, Ted was as American as they come. His family was from Wisconsin, originally. But he grew up in California. Right here in Santa Barbara."

Royce shook his head. "Funny. I always pictured you living across the Atlantic, raising a brood of German kids. And you were out here on the West Coast the whole time, and I didn't know."

"Yep, practically a native."

"Jeez...." He shook his head again. "You had other children?"

"Two. A son, twenty, a daughter, fourteen."

"Unbelievable, Anne-Marie. You could pass for thirty."

She scoffed. "I stay in shape, but I couldn't pass for thirty. I feel better than I did then, though." She laughed. "Come to think of it, I was pregnant at thirty."

He looked at her for a long time, the corners of his mouth threatening to break into a smile, the tip of his sharp nose almost twitching with amusement. "Come on," he said, extending his hand, "you can help me get the juice."

Anne-Marie took his hand, and he lifted her from the couch with surprising strength. He turned and led the way toward the kitchen, still gripping her hand firmly.

She followed him, aware of the tanned, well-developed triceps extending from the sleeves of his polo shirt, his muscular shoulders and trim waist. She didn't tend to notice men physically—not as a matter of course—but Royce Buchanan seemed to leap out at her. He came at her from both the present and the past, making her feel a bit the seventeen-year-old girl in his presence.

Royce didn't let go of her hand until they were in the kitchen, a large room full of gleaming imported tile and fine wood cabinetry. It looked untouched and virginal, like that of a model home.

"Do you have a housekeeper?" she asked, settling against a counter while he poured the juice.

"I have a woman who comes in to do the housework." He turned and looked at her. "You were noticing how clean the place was and figured I couldn't be the responsible party."

"I'd forgotten about that."

"What?"

"The way you comment on a person's train of thought."

"Did I do that back then, too?"

"Uh-huh. I remember it now."

"Must be ingrained in the genes or something. My ex used to complain about it. Drove her batty sometimes."

"It never bothered me." Anne-Marie realized she sounded a little too compliant. "I just noticed it, I guess."

Royce had filled two tall crystal glasses with juice, and he brought one to Anne-Marie. He stood very close to her, as he might if they were in intimate conversation at a cocktail party.

"Well, this calls for some kind of toast." He paused to think. "Dr. Gilchrist is the obvious choice, for making this delightful surprise possible, though I suppose eventually we'd have met in the frozen-food section of some supermarket." He paused to think. "How about to our children? My daughter, Sybil, is twenty-one. The love of my life. She just got married at Christmas. I've been in a depression ever since." He smiled wryly as if to say it wasn't *entirely* true.

"I like that," she replied. "To our children."

They touched glasses, and she tasted the juice and Royce's cologne at the same time. It wasn't the way she remembered him smelling.

"You don't wear the same cologne as you used to," she said before she realized the words were out.

"No, I imagine I don't. What's it been...twenty-five, twenty-six years?"

"Twenty-seven."

"I don't recall what I wore then." He sipped his juice. "I noticed you smell different, too."

Anne-Marie was embarrassed by the drift of the conversation and eased past him to escape, walking casually to the window, where she looked out at the hilltop covered with oaks. "Your place is lovely, Royce. And it's a beautiful setting."

"Come on, then. If you don't mind drinking and walking, I'll show you around."

He took her outside first, to the top of the sloping lawn overlooking the pool, around the side of the house where they could see the barn partway around the hill, through the small formal garden outside a glassed-in sun room filled with flowering plants. Then they went back through the public rooms and eventually into the master suite, which, though elegant and attractive, immediately struck Anne-Marie as a monument to masculine self-indulgence.

There was a waterfall and spa in a glass-enclosed tropical garden off the master bath, an exercise room, a sitting room with every conceivable audio-visual gadget made and a large bedroom with a king-size bed. An antique carved elephant tusk hung over the Oriental headboard. There were paintings on the walls, all of which Anne-Marie knew by her training to be expensive and of exceptional quality.

"It's a bit ostentatious, I know," he said, "but it took me almost a quarter century to afford it, so I feel justified in flaunting it."

"It's a lovely home."

She was standing a bit uncomfortably in the middle of the large bedroom, her tennis shoes sinking into the extra thick carpet. Royce ambled over to the bed and dropped down on the corner of it, looking at her with a rather longing, nostalgic expression, his hands clasped between his knees.

A mat of blond hair speckled with gray showed at the V of his shirt. The slightly mussed hair on his head was still thick, though somewhat longer than the way he had worn it as a young army officer. The only gray was in the sideburns—just a tinge at the edges. He looked very thoughtful.

"Mind if I ask you a brutally frank question?" he said.

"No," she replied, only a little uneasy.

"Have you ever regretted that we never got together, that we never married?"

"That *is* a brutally frank question."

"You don't have to answer it."

"I was happily married for sixteen years, Royce. And I would be happily married still if my husband hadn't died."

"That's not exactly an answer to my question."

"At first I thought of you, of course. But when I fell in love with Ted . . . well, he was the man in my life. It must have been that way with you and your wife...at least when you were first married."

"I'd given up on you, yes. I married someone else. But I never forgot you."

"One doesn't forget."

"That's not what I meant."

She was perplexed. "What are you getting at? Why the questions?"

He got up from the bed, then crossed to where she stood. He took the nearly empty glass from her hand and put it on a table. Then he returned, placing his large hands on her shoulders.

She wasn't prepared for the intimacy in his touch, though something in his mood seemed to have been pointing toward it almost from the moment she walked in the door. Anne-Marie felt her heart thumping in her chest. She felt his thumbs sliding over the curve of her shoulders and sinking into her flesh. There was an ominous intensity in his eyes—an intensity that mesmerized her as it had mesmerized the young woman she had once been.

"I have only two real regrets in my life," he said in a voice gravelly with emotion. "One was leaving you behind twenty-whatever years ago. The other was just now, hearing that I hadn't meant more to you than I did."

"I didn't intend to demean our relationship. We were both young, Royce. And it was a long time ago."

"I haven't thought of you incessantly, Anne-Marie, it's true. Sometimes you wouldn't come to mind for weeks or months at a time. But you were always there. And I've lived with the fact that I made a mistake in not marrying you when I could."

"I honestly can't say the same."

"I know. And if my marriage had been happier, I might feel the way you do." He paused a moment, then smiled. "But that's all in the past. This is now, California, you and me. Again."

"I hardly think—"

He stopped her by touching a finger gently to her lips. "What I'm getting at, if you'll forgive me, is that there'll be three things in my life I'll regret . . . if I let it happen."

She searched his eyes, fearful. Yet she felt herself slipping into his mood. And she remembered so vividly the desperate love she had once felt for him. Royce had set her heart—the same heart that had beat so fervently for him in the Taunus—rocking again.

"What's the third?" she murmured.

He ran the tips of his fingers along her cheek and chin. "The third is if I let this day, this minute, pass without kissing you."

And it was Germany again. She did want him to kiss her. She wanted him as surely as the girl in her continued to live. His need, and the emotion it stirred in her, were as compelling as the strong fingers that dug into her shoulders.

Royce lifted her chin. Then he lowered his mouth to hers, covering her lips tenderly, sensuously with his own. It was the same sweet kiss she had known long ago, the same man, an awakening sensation of the same love.

As his kiss became more eager, as he pulled her more firmly into his embrace, Anne-Marie felt something come alive inside, something, for all her self-awareness, she hadn't experienced for a long, long time.

She was lost in his arms, lost in an unlikely dream that couldn't be happening. For many minutes she let her body melt into him, tempting the danger. The kiss became more eager, their lips and tongues hungrier, greedier.

His body was pressed hard against her, the firmness of his loins wedged against the softness of hers. The contact excited her, and as he crushed her in his arms, her eyes closed and she grew weak.

When the kiss ended her head rolled back, exposing her throat. He kissed her neck, dragging his tongue along the side of it until she moaned with pleasure.

Then she felt him lift her into his arms and carry her to the bed. She lay there for moment on the cool Thai silk bedspread, watching his eyes, which seemed almost grim with desire. His energy made her feel fragile.

He sat on the edge of the bed, beside her, stroking first her cheek and hair, then her shoulder. His fingers trailed lightly over the skin at the opening of her top. Then he grasped the zipper and pulled it down slowly, without taking his eyes off hers.

Anne-Marie looked at his strangely familiar face, now weathered by the drama of life. He was so much more experienced than the young officer who had once seemed so mature and wise. She could tell instantly that this man, who could have been the father of the other, knew much more about love. He knew it was not the act that excited but the quality of the lovemaking. He was gentle because gentleness allowed time to savor. She could tell all that just by the way he touched her.

When he pulled back her top and unfastened her bra, Royce took a few moments to admire her breasts. And he seemed to know his admiration excited her further.

By the time he leaned over to kiss her nipples, they were erect and pulsing in expectation. Then he tenderly and slowly kissed her from her navel to her neck, bringing her flesh vibrantly to life.

She stroked the head that moved over her half-naked body, giving herself up to the sensation as he undressed her completely. Her eyes were half-closed as he removed his clothes, pulled back the spread and moved her onto the sky-blue sheets.

When he moved against her, naked, she touched his face, running her finger from the corner of his mouth to his broad chin. Then he leaned closer, brushing his cheek against hers, deeply inhaling her scent, nuzzling and kissing her neck.

"And there's another thing I don't want to regret my whole life, Anne-Marie," he whispered into her ear. "Loving you as you should be loved, as I should have loved you before."

He kissed her deeply then, probing the depths of her mouth with his tongue, running it along the edges of her teeth and lips.

"Oh, Royce," she moaned, digging her fingers into the thick hair at the back of his head, grasping him with her strong hands.

A deep, bearish sound emanated from his throat as he shifted his pelvis over hers. His hand ran up the flat plane of her belly to her breasts, caressing them until they were as hard as his loins.

Then he wedged her knees apart and slipped his between them. He was nearly upright, above her, his broad, matted chest powerful, dominating. Her instinct was to submit, though part of her was frightened, uncertain.

When he drew his hands down her torso, over her ribs and abdomen, she tried to relax. When he lifted her knees and slipped his hands under her buttocks, she tried to let her body go. When he leaned over and kissed her belly, she moaned. And when he lowered his face to her soft mound, washing her with his breath, she gasped and closed her eyes.

Anne-Marie had never been kissed so intimately, had never known such pleasure. The ecstasy of the sensation was a shock, and her breath wedged in her throat. Each flick of his tongue heightened her excitement, sent a river of fire through the center of her.

The feeling was exquisite. She tried to give herself to him completely, to surrender her body totally. Her legs opened wider, her hands reached instinctively to grasp the headboard for support. Within moments she was throbbing with desire, with intense yearning for him.

Each delicate stroke of his tongue brought her closer to the fever point. Her nails dug into the headboard. Her hips began to gyrate. His caress quickened. Then, when she was about to explode, she stopped him.

"Please, Royce. Please take me," she pleaded.

He moved onto her then, his body blanketing her. She felt him large and hard against her inner thighs. As his arousal found her, her urgent hunger rose to near desperation.

Anne-Marie felt an anxious, virginal desire but without the fear. She wanted him badly, as badly as he could have wanted her. Her loins ached for him, convulsing instantly as he gradually penetrated her.

The heavy musk of his body surrounded her, the scent familiar, though the familiarity was borne from the distant past. He surrounded her physically, enveloping her. Royce Buchanan was on her, around her, in her, consuming her, filling her. She clawed at his back, fighting for more of him, opening herself to him, surrendering, resisting, demanding.

She moaned as he thrust into her again and again, filling her, rocking her. "Oh, oh, *Mein Gott!*" Her cry of pleasure seemed to release Royce to his fulfillment, and sent her after him into a frenzied, shuddering climax.

Then they lay still for a long time, her legs wrapped around his hips, their moist skin welded together, her small but still firm breasts flattened under the weight of his chest. He kissed her temple and the damp hair pressed against the side of her face and neck.

She felt the beat of her heart in her throat, felt his on her chest. They were locked in the ultimate embrace, and yet, he was a stranger.

When Royce had regained himself, he arched off of her a little. He lovingly looked down into her gray eyes. "Oh, Anne-Marie," he murmured. "In my rashest fantasy, I didn't dream this would happen. It couldn't be better than this."

She looked into his eyes, her breathing still heavy. She slowly rolled her head back and forth. "No," she whispered. "It's never been like this before." There was awe in her voice—she heard it herself. And it frightened her.

He kissed her lightly. She gazed at him with wonder but also with growing dismay. What had happened *was* rash fantasy— a wild, irrational act. She had walked into his house, and twenty minutes later they were making love. The realization horrified her.

How could she have let it happen? Were the memories of her first love that strong?

Her sex life had begun with this man; now it had come full circle. And she had permitted it. She had let that first time happen all over again, submitting as helplessly as she had the first. On both occasions she had acted out of desire and instinct. And somehow it didn't matter that she was a mature woman who should have known better. She had simply let it happen.

Her thoughts must have been playing openly on her face, because his brow furrowed. "What are you thinking?" he asked, his voice husky. "Is something wrong?"

"I'm wondering how this happened."

"There's obviously still something between us. I acted on my feelings, and I assumed you did, too. Time doesn't always kill love."

She looked into his eyes, horrified. He couldn't really believe that. Yet his eyes *were* full of love. But love was about people, not sensation. What they had shared was a festival of the body, not the mind and heart. Didn't he understand that? Was he blind?

"Maybe I've always loved you," he murmured.

"No," she mumbled, pushing gently at his chest to indicate she wanted him to move away.

Royce withdrew himself, rolling off of her, letting the cool air of the room envelop her moist, still throbbing body. Anne-Marie took the sheet and pulled it modestly over her, leaving him naked beside her.

"What's wrong?"

"I can't believe I let this happen," she replied, her voice cold and a touch indignant. She glanced at him, embarrassed that the incongruity of who she was and what had happened seemed so obvious.

Royce looked a trifle distraught. "I don't understand. Did I say something to offend you?"

"No, it's what you did . . . I mean, what *I* did."

"We. We simply acted on our feelings."

"We made love, that's true." She looked away, unable to meet his eyes.

"I'm sorry if this sounds corny, but what I feel now is not that different from what I felt for you over twenty-five years ago. This wasn't only lust, for God's sake."

She shot him a hard look. "I'm not questioning your motives. I'm not challenging you at all. It's my own weakness that's upset me."

"Please don't chastise yourself, Anne-Marie. Was it really so terrible that we made love? After all, once we loved each other a great deal."

"That's my point. I'm not a foolish girl of seventeen any longer. And I'm not hopelessly in love with you. But I'm lying naked in your bed as though my whole life up to now has been irrelevant."

"What are you trying to say? That *this* was irrelevant? That *I'm* irrelevant? Why doesn't the love we shared qualify as part of your life?"

"Because this isn't me! I'm my children, my home, my job. I'm a mother, a member of my community." Her eyes teared with frustration as she looked at him. "And I'm engaged to be married to another man!"

Royce was rocked by her words. He stared incredulously. A tear overflowed her eye and rolled down her cheek. Anne-Marie wiped it away impatiently with the back of her hand.

"Engaged?"

"Yes," she replied. "And this was as unfair to you as it was foolish. I don't know how I let it happen."

"You're going to marry somebody else?"

"That's what 'engaged' means, isn't it?"

He was stunned. And hurt. Her words were cold water poured on his sweetest dream. He looked at their clothes, discarded in hasty clumps on his bedroom floor, the fossils of an earlier passion. It had lived only minutes ago, but it could have been twenty-seven years.

After reflecting for a moment, he gave a half laugh. What absurdity! He had behaved as naively as an adolescent boy.

She touched his arm. "I'm sorry, Royce. I didn't mean to be sharp. I'm upset with myself, not you. I'm so sorry I let this happen. Please forgive me."

He looked at her, wanting equally to take her into his arms and push her from his bed. "Well, you treated me to a novel experience, I'll say that much."

"I wasn't being frivolous. I was weak. Perhaps you meant more to me once than I was willing to admit. Perhaps I was acting on those memories. I don't know how to explain it."

"Well, if you had a good time, maybe the morning wasn't a total waste," he said snidely.

"Don't demean it."

"Demean it? You're the one calling it a mistake. I found it damned nice."

"It was nice. It was lovely. But that's not important."

"I'm glad you're able to rise above mere pleasure."

"Please don't be angry. You've got a right, but please don't."

"All right. Let's forget about it."

"That's not what I meant, either."

He felt his anger begin to boil. "What the hell did you mean?"

She lowered her eyes contritely. "I've got a class to teach. I'd better go. May I use your bath to clean up?"

"Certainly. Help yourself."

Anne-Marie slipped out from under the sheet, picked up her clothing and headed with long, graceful strides toward the bathroom door. He watched, observing her trim body, devoid of even an ounce of extra fat. Her thighs and hips were lean, the muscles beautifully toned, her posture impeccable. What a lovely, damnable sight, he thought.

As the door closed he clenched his fist and drove it angrily into the bed. The same feeling went through him as the day Herbert Keller had closed the door of the house in Kronberg and he had retreated into the bleak European winter without her.

He stared at the closed bathroom door, resolving that it wouldn't happen again. He knew, absolutely and without any doubt, that they had the potential to love each other as much as they had twenty-seven years ago.

Chapter Six

She took a quick shower, dried herself with one of the thick, fluffy bath sheets piled on the counter, then dressed. She was still numb, half doubting the reality of what had happened but convinced she had made a terrible mistake. When she returned to the bedroom, Royce was gone. She called out to him, thinking he might be in the exercise room, but she received no response.

He had made the bed. His clothes were gone from the floor, all evidence of what had happened erased. On the corner of the bed she saw an envelope with her name on it. She picked it up and opened it. Inside was a note and a check.

I was a businessman for many years. You have to work for a living, and I know time is money. Thanks for a nostalgic trip to the past. I hope it hasn't caused you any problem.

Royce

The check was for seventy dollars. Anne-Marie sensed he didn't mean any disrespect by it—some people really did equate time with money. He couldn't be expected to know her feelings. She took the note but left the check on the bed.

As she walked through the house, she saw no sign of him. She decided the note was his goodbye. Perhaps avoiding another confrontation was intended as a kindness. She wasn't sure. Glancing into the living room, she noticed the sliding door to the outside slightly ajar. She went to it to look out.

Royce was standing on the lawn, halfway down the slope to the pool. He was staring across the valley, the warm afternoon breeze ruffling his hair. His hands were in his pockets; he was motionless. His face wasn't visible, but Anne-Marie imagined him to be looking into the past.

The image was a sad one. She had the urge to go to him, to put her arms around him, to tell him it wasn't a dream or a trick. The passion, the love, was real. But she knew that was true only because of their memories, not the reality of their lives. And life was an ever-changing road. The Pacific Coast of America was not the Taunus of Germany.

She turned and walked across the living room to the entry hall. She stopped and looked back, taking a deep breath to savor the smell of his house, the sight and feel of it. It had been an unusual morning. One she would remember for a long time.

When he heard her car start, Royce went back inside. He headed for the bedroom first, to make sure she was gone. He stared at the bed, trying to convince himself that what had happened was real. But he had erased all the evidence himself; he had picked up the clothes and made the bed. As before, he had only his memories—fresher, more immediate than the old ones—but still only memories.

With her announcement that she was engaged, Anne-Marie had tried once again to remove herself from his life. But how could she claim to be engaged to someone else and still make love with such passion?

Royce didn't believe her. At least, he didn't believe she loved anyone else. Even though they had gone to bed within a half hour of seeing each other, he hadn't sensed the slightest hesitancy on her part. There hadn't been another man, another relationship in her mind at war with what she was doing.

And yet, afterward, she had spurned him unequivocally. She had rejected him as certainly as she had when she had married another man.

He saw the check on the corner of the bed. The envelope and note were gone. He wondered if she had been offended. Maybe it had been stupid. He looked at his own bold and hasty hand, recalling the anger and hurt he'd felt while writing it.

But then he remembered their love, the feel of her naked body, her lips. Crushing the check in his fist, he threw it angrily against the headboard and stalked out of the room.

For a while he walked around the house, feeling the frustration of a caged animal. Then he noticed her equipment case. She'd left without it. He smiled. What was it they said—people left things in places they didn't want to leave, if only subconsciously? He wondered if she'd be back for it.

Then it occurred to him that returning it would give him the excuse to see her again, to take the initiative. It was a long way to Santa Barbara. It would be a kindness to drive it in.

At the thought of being with her again, he felt better. Once the shock of her announcement wore off, he'd be in a better position to analyze her true feelings, to determine how she could possibly be engaged to someone else and not even think about the guy while she was making love to him.

The more he thought about it, the more sure he was that Anne-Marie had thought solely of him. She had behaved as though he were the only man on earth.

She didn't notice her sport bag was missing until she went to get it out of the trunk of her car at the club. Fortunately it wasn't essential for her class. But she would need it, and that meant driving back out to Royce Buchanan's place, unless she could get him to drop it off somewhere the next time he came into town. What a stupid thing to do.

Anne-Marie managed to get through the class, though she clearly wasn't concentrating on what she was doing. Luckily all the students were regulars and were able to follow her absent-minded instructions.

A couple of times she had to be reminded to repeat a pose from the other side when she had blithely gone on to the next one. And once, when she went into a difficult pose, her thoughts were so preoccupied with Royce Buchanan that she forgot to talk her students through the exercise. Coming out of her reverie, she saw eight women parroting her actions without a word of instruction coming from her lips.

After the session one of the students wanted to pay for another series of classes, but Anne-Marie had to tell her to wait because her record and receipt books were in her sport bag. Leaving it at Royce's had proved very inconvenient. When she went out to her car to go home, she flirted with the idea of heading back to his place to get it, but she didn't have the courage. She would call him, instead.

On the drive home, Anne-Marie tried to figure out what it was that had permitted her to fall so easily into Royce's arms. She wasn't a frivolous or superficial person. In fact, she had never had a casual sexual relationship in her entire life. There had only been three men ever—her husband, Don Nelson, and of course Royce.

Obviously she had been able to make love with Royce today because she had loved him once. It had represented an impulsive visit to the past, a brief return to the days of her youth.

That didn't justify it, of course. It had been stupid. And she still didn't understand it. Why couldn't her need, her fantasy, have been satisfied by talking to the man? Why had she let him make love with her? Had it been need, plain raw sexual need?

No, that didn't explain it. True, she hadn't had much of a sex life since Ted had died. What she had with Don Nelson was more symbolic than anything.

But the cause of her slip wasn't mere frustration. It was more emotional than physical. Probably it wasn't much more than impetuosity, she decided, the craving for romance that lived on despite the fact that she was a mature woman.

That sort of thing took a long time to die, if it ever did completely. And there was really nothing wrong with having romance in your heart, as long as you kept it in perspective and under control. Teenagers had to learn to temper their impulses with judgment, and adults were not immune to forgetting.

Perhaps there was a universal law that explained it. After years of being levelheaded, after years of doing the right and responsible thing, surely you were entitled to an occasional trivial regression. Afterward you felt guilty and foolish, but it was out of your system and you could return to the sane life you'd chosen for yourself.

After all, it was no accident that she had forsaken Royce for Ted Osborne. When it came to marriage, home, children, she had chosen the man she truly belonged with. Love had many faces, and she had had the good sense to pick the right one with Ted.

And now Don represented so many of the same things. In her wisdom, Anne-Marie knew she would choose the right course; she would choose Don.

In fact, her encounter with Royce might well have been a blessing, though on the surface it seemed shortsighted, even selfish. It was like a wake-up call, a reminder of how unimportant some things were in comparison with others.

She had lived long enough to know what really mattered in life. Had she still been a girl, what had happened today might have seemed monumental. But from the perspective of maturity and experience, she was able to see it for what it was.

In the long run, an afternoon in bed with Royce Buchanan couldn't be worth a fraction of an evening by the fire with Don Nelson. What she felt for Royce would quickly fade—that sort of emotion never lasted. But the quiet happiness that she'd known in her marriage, and that she was learning to find with Don, could last forever.

Yes, perhaps Royce had done Don a favor, as well. He had jolted her from her lethargy, made her grateful for what she had. It was time now to give Don her answer. After all, she'd told Royce about her engagement. There was no reason in the world she shouldn't make it true.

Anne-Marie pulled into the driveway of Ted's family home, feeling a sense of security that she still shared it with their children and with her memories of him. It was like a refuge, an emotional haven from the adversities of life. That had been her husband's enduring legacy.

She climbed the front steps wearily, hearing Christianne's laughter inside. Anne-Marie loved the indomitable spirit of her child, who reminded her so much of herself when she was young.

As she reached for the doorknob, she smiled. Maybe a little of that zest for life was still alive in her, too. Maybe she wasn't as old as her son thought she was. If her day had proved anything, maybe it had proved that.

She pushed the door open, and what she found made her mouth drop. Royce Buchanan was sitting in Ted's favorite chair, laughing and chatting with Christianne. When he saw Anne-Marie at the door, he slowly got to his feet. Her daughter turned to her.

"Mom," she said, jumping up, "we've got company!"

"So I see." She was staring at Royce, trying to understand his presence.

"You forgot your bag," he said, pointing to the case he had left by the door. "I thought you might need it."

Anne-Marie glanced down at it. "Oh, yes. I did forget it, didn't I? I was going to call." Then she looked at Christianne, wondering what he'd said to her, how he'd explained the situation.

"All the benefit of that therapeutic massage was undone by the drive into town," he said, a hint of whimsy on his face. "My back's really starting to bother me again. I guess I'll need another session."

She closed the door and looked at him severely. "I'm afraid that won't be possible. My schedule is quite full." She glanced at Christianne.

"You see," he said to the girl, "even old acquaintances can't overcome the imperatives of business." He smiled at Anne-Marie. "I told her we'd known each other in Germany...when we were young."

"Weren't you surprised, Mom?" Christianne asked excitedly. "That's like ages ago!"

"Yes, almost ancient history." Anne-Marie gave Royce a look, silently asking him just what he'd said to her daughter.

"I explained that we'd met while I was in the service, before you knew Ted," he offered, apparently reading her thoughts.

Christianne seemed to be watching them both with avid curiosity.

"Well, Mr. Buchanan," Anne-Marie said with deliberate formality, "it was very kind of you to bring my bag back. I appreciate it."

"No problem."

She made it as obvious as she could that she expected him to leave, without actually indicating the door.

"I know you're busy," he said, getting her message, "so I'll get out of your hair. But I was wondering if we might talk a little about your recommendation for treatment. You had to hurry to your class, and we didn't have much of a chance to discuss it."

"I think it'd be best if you took that up with Dr. Gilchrist."

"But he put such emphasis on your brand of treatment. I got the impression he was deferring to you."

She could see he wasn't going to give up easily. Perhaps she should have made her feelings clear before she'd left his place. "All right. I'll walk you to your car, and we can discuss it." She looked at her watch. "I'm afraid I don't have much time, though."

"I understand." He turned to Christianne. "Well, I certainly enjoyed meeting you. You've got your mother's spirit, I could see that immediately. She wasn't all that much older than you when I knew her, you know."

Anne-Marie shifted uneasily.

"Nice meeting you, too, Mr. Buchanan." Christianne smiled broadly, glancing at her mother.

"And remember what I said about the horses," Royce said. "It's an open invitation."

"Oh, yeah! Guess what, Mom? Mr. Buchanan said you could take me and some of my friends to his ranch to go swimming and horseback riding. Wouldn't that be rad?"

Anne-Marie gave him a look.

"I thought she and her friends might enjoy it," he said innocently. "I suppose I should have mentioned it to you first, but in the heat of conversation I got carried away."

"Yes, you are prone to getting carried away, aren't you?"

He had the grace to look embarrassed.

"Well, we'll see about the horseback riding. I can't promise anything, Christianne. We've already planned a big summer for you."

"I know, Mom, but couldn't we . . . just once?"

"We'll talk about it." Her look at Royce was full of displeasure. "Perhaps we can discuss your back now, Mr. Buchanan." She pulled the door open.

Royce turned to Christianne and extended his hand. "It was nice meeting you. I enjoyed our talk."

The girl smiled. "Next time you'll have to tell me all about Mom. I'd like to know what she was really like. Not just what she tells me and Kurt."

"She was a lovely young lady—I'll tell you that much right now. A charming, delightful person."

"Come, Mr. Buchanan," Anne-Marie said, "before you lose all your credibility."

He made his way toward the door, and she let him pass through. "There are some chicken breasts in the freezer, Christianne," she said to the girl. "Would you thaw them out in the microwave for me?" She went out onto the porch, where Royce was waiting, then looked him in the eye. "Dirty pool."

"The horseback riding? I found her very charming. Seeing her reminded me of my own daughter. The invitation was sincere."

"You knew I'd have to bring her."

"Can I help it if there'd be fringe benefits?"

They started down the steps.

"You knew I didn't want to see you again, Royce."

"The feeling wasn't entirely mutual."

"I told you, I'm engaged."

"Yes, I've been thinking about that. Is this some guy you've known very long?"

"What difference does that make?"

"None. Unless he's nothing more than a figment of your imagination."

She glanced at him with annoyance. "Don's not a figment of my imagination."

They headed up the sidewalk.

"Has Christianne met this fellow . . . Don?"

"Of course. Our families have been close for years."

"Why didn't she know you were engaged, then?"

Anne-Marie turned to him with surprise. "What did you say to her?"

"Don't worry, I didn't give away your secret. I was very discreet. But I did find out she didn't know that her mother is engaged."

"It's a recent decision."

"Yes. Very recent, it seems."

"We decided to marry a while ago, but we haven't told our children yet. As a matter of fact, we were planning on a family dinner sometime soon, when we could get them all together for the announcement. I was thinking of doing it this Sunday."

They stopped at his car. Royce sat on the fender and looked up at her. "So... I'm too late."

She gave him a level look. "Yes."

"You really love this guy?"

"Certainly. I wouldn't marry him otherwise."

"Hmm." He rubbed his chin.

"You don't believe me. Your ego won't let you believe me."

"It's not my ego."

"Then what is it?"

"Maybe it was the way you made love."

She spun away. "Please. I've already explained that. It was a mistake, an impetuous act. Nothing more."

"I have trouble believing that, too."

She turned back to him. "Well, it's true. I cared for you once, a long time ago. And I'll admit there's still a physical attraction. I wouldn't have done it lightly."

"That's my point."

She shook her head. "You really don't understand, do you? You think you do, but you don't."

"I'm glad one of us is so sure about what happened this morning."

She straightened, lifting her chin. "Thank you for returning my bag. And if I hurt you in any way, I'm sorry."

"So. That's it, then?"

"I don't know what else there can be."

"This whole thing started with my backache, and that hasn't changed."

"There's no way I could treat you after what happened today."

"What about your yoga class? Aren't the exercises supposed to be good for me? That's what Dr. Gilchrist seemed to think."

"There are other yoga teachers."

"He thinks you're the best."

She looked at him with exasperation. "Royce, why won't you take no for an answer?"

"Let's look at the facts." He held up his fingers to tick off the points as he made them. "You're so much in love with this guy, Don, that you're going to marry him. So an old flame from the past like me can hardly be a threat. You've got what happened today in perspective, and you realize it's meaningless. You're the best yoga person around. And I've got a bad back. I don't see why I can't spend a few weeks in your course and get my injury treated."

"All right. If we can keep it professional, and if you accept the fact that I'm committed to someone else, I'll agree to take you on as a student. But there's no need for it to last more than a few weeks. Once you've learned the poses required for your problem, you won't have to continue."

"Fair enough." He stood up and extended his hand in a gesture of friendship.

Anne-Marie took it reluctantly. Royce held her fingers firmly.

"You may not have been impressed by what happened today," he said, looking at her evenly, "but I was."

Images of their desperate lovemaking flashed through her mind as she looked into his eyes. Feeling a sudden surge of panic, she pulled her hand free, then hurried back to the house.

"Don?" she said, clutching the phone to her ear. She had only been in the house a minute, but her blood was still racing through her veins.

"Anne-Marie. How are you, darling? I'm so glad you called. Tracy and I were talking. We decided it's too long since we've had both families together. We wanted you and the kids to come over for dinner, maybe this weekend. I understand Kurt's going to be back in town...."

"Yes, that would be terrific. We'd like that. How about Sunday?"

"Okay."

"But let's do it here."

"Tracy and I came over last time."

"That's all right. Tell her to make dessert. She does a wonderful job with that nut cake Carole used to make. I'm sure that'd please her. Just have her bring the cake."

"Are you sure?"

"Yes. Funny, but I was calling you for the same reason. I wanted us all to get together."

"You see how we're on the same channel, Anne-Marie? The only thing wrong is that we're running two households when it should really be one."

"That's the other reason I called. I think we ought to talk about that some more."

"You've decided, then?" His voice was hopeful.

"I want to talk a little more. Could we have lunch or something?"

"Sure. Let me get out my calendar. Hold on."

Anne-Marie waited, her heart still beating heavily.

"Here we are," Don said, his voice patient, more familiar to her now even than Ted's.

While he thumbed through his book on the other end of the line, she thought again of her impassioned lovemaking with Royce, and her cheeks turned fiery.

"Okay, tomorrow is...no, that won't work. I've got a Lions Club meeting. I'd skip it, but I'm treasurer, and tomorrow I give my monthly report. It's important because they want to set the budget for scholarships, and the committee has to know where we stand. We can make it for dinner, though. No, wait. Carole's sister, Molly, is driving up from L.A. on business and asked Tracy and me to go out to dinner with her. But there's no reason you can't come along. Why don't you have dinner with us?"

"No, Don. I want to talk to you alone. How about the next day, for lunch?"

"Great. I'm wide open. Not a thing until four o'clock. We can make it a long, leisurely lunch if you like."

"I'd like that."

"Wonderful, darling. Lunch, day after tomorrow, then."

"Fine."

"You okay, Anne-Marie? Everything all right?"

"Yes. Everything is just fine."

"Good. I've been thinking we've got to find more time to be together. Between your classes and my practice, there never seems to be enough time. We've simply got to live under the same roof. That's the only solution."

"Yes, Don. I'm beginning to think that's true."

Anne-Marie parked around the corner from Bradbury's on State Street, where she was supposed to meet Don for lunch. She was about fifteen minutes late, having forgotten that her monthly meeting of the Santa Barbara Fitness Advisory Board was that day. She decided to attend part of the meeting, then hurry over to Bradbury's. After all, first things first.

When she entered the restaurant, she saw Don sitting alone at a booth near the back, his brown hair neatly parted and combed, his large frame bent slightly over the table. He probably had no idea that she intended to accept his proposal. But she couldn't just blurt it out on the phone. It required a more personal touch than that. They were talking about a lifetime of commitment, not a golf date.

Though she knew that Don would be pleased and that the uncertainty wouldn't be hanging over her head anymore, Anne-Marie had been nervous the past two days, thinking about the lunch. Royce Buchanan had been in her mind so much it almost seemed as though it was he she had decided to marry.

At first she'd attributed it to guilt, but then she realized it wasn't that. She had decided she had been trying to purge him from her memory, expelling everything he stood for—sensuality, lust and self-indulgence. It was as though the two men were at war inside of her, almost like good and evil.

When she arrived at the table she noticed two martinis sitting there, the one in front of Don half-empty. "I'm sorry I'm late."

He brightened immediately. "No problem. Hope you don't mind, I ordered you a drink."

"Not at all." She scooted into the booth next to him, kissing him on the cheek. "I'm glad you did." She picked up the martini and took a long sip, feeling the need for something to settle her nerves. She put it down, returning his smile.

"You look beautiful, as always," he said affably.

Anne-Marie didn't doubt his sincerity, but the words rang a little hollow. Or had she merely been hoping for more? "How were the Lions and Carole's sister?" Her eyes moved over his even features. He was pleasant looking, the sort of man who'd play the father of a dozen freckle-faced kids on a television program.

Don chuckled. "In that order?"

"In any order."

She searched his face, looking for a sign. She didn't know what his expression was supposed to tell her, but she'd hoped for a guide to help her find the words that she knew in her heart were meant to be said with passion.

"The Lions are fine, and Carole's sister is not so fine. Her husband is slipping. She finally had to put him in a nursing home."

Anne-Marie had forgotten about that. A wave of guilt went through her, and she murmured, "I'm sorry to hear that." Then, remembering the purpose of their lunch, she took Don's hand. "I've missed you," she said, hoping the words didn't sound as thin as they felt.

"I've missed you, too, Anne-Marie." He squeezed her hand. "In fact, I meant to pick you up a bouquet or something, but Alvin Edwards, the guy with the drug stores, came in just before I left, so I didn't have time."

"It was sweet of you to think of it, though."

He picked up his drink and drained half of what remained. "Next time."

The waitress came to the table. "Would you like another drink, or do you care to order?"

Don looked at Anne-Marie. "Shall we have another round?"

Normally she didn't drink much hard liquor, but this time she felt the need. "If you're having one, I'll join you."

"Two more martinis," Don said, and the woman left.

Anne-Marie took a long swallow of her drink.

"Nice to have a leisurely lunch, isn't it?" he said, fingering his glass.

"Uh-huh."

He waited while she took another sip. "So, you were thinking of a family dinner with the kids, too."

"Yes, Kurt will be back. I thought it would be a good opportunity."

"For what?"

"I told you. I've been thinking about us."

"And . . . ?"

"Well . . . do you still want to marry me?"

"Of course. You know how long it's been. It's seemed inevitable for years."

"Yes, there has been a certain inevitability about it."

Don looked at her, but Anne-Marie didn't bother to try to explain the remark. She felt frustration, almost annoyance, though she tried to tell herself it was only her mood, that she had to press on. For an instant she had an impulse to tell him about her encounter with Royce, but in the end, she decided not to.

Although Don was very understanding, it would take a lot of explaining to put Royce Buchanan in perspective. Even Ted, who knew the entire story, had recognized Royce's impact on her and felt a certain discomfort about him.

"You said on the phone you'd been thinking about us. What have you been thinking, Anne-Marie?"

"That I've been unfair to you. That you deserve an answer. That the logic of marrying is . . . irrefutable."

She remembered Royce's face as he sat on the fender of his car, saying, "You really love this guy?" And she did love Don Nelson, as she had loved Ted Osborne. Royce didn't understand that kind of love, that's all.

Don took her hand again. The waitress came with their martinis, and he waited to speak until she had placed them on the table and left.

"Are you trying to tell me that you'll marry me?"

For some reason her eyes filled, and she looked at him, feeling the tears brimming. She nodded, biting her lip. Don smiled and scooted closer, putting his arm around her shoulders.

"I thought this was what you'd say, but... I'm... really happy. I've wanted to marry you for a long time." He kissed her temple, and she looked up at him, her tears overflowing and running down her cheeks. She took her napkin and blotted her eyes, trying not to smear her mascara.

"I don't know why I'm so emotional."

"I do. This doesn't happen every day." He picked up his drink. "I'd like to propose a toast to my lovely fiancée."

Anne-Marie took her glass, and they clinked them together. "To you."

They drank. She briefly closed her eyes as the alcohol slid down her throat. In her mind's eye she saw Royce Buchanan handing her the glass of fruit juice in his living room. And she remembered the hunger he had so quickly evoked in her. She had to repress a sob of emotion.

"The kids will be thrilled," Don enthused. "When shall we do it? Do you have a date in mind?"

"No. I thought we ought to wait a few months anyway. Perhaps sometime this autumn."

"Yes, the fall would be good. Well after tax season. It would be murder trying to get a wedding ready and two hundred clients' tax returns wrapped up at the same time. Of course, the worst of it is over now, but there are still loose ends."

"Okay, tentatively this fall." Anne-Marie drained the rest of her martini.

"And we have to get you a ring. I assume you'd like to pick it out. Most women do."

"I think we should select it together."

"Yes, certainly. We'll go out this weekend. How about Saturday? I'm playing golf with Walter Kranich first thing in the morning, but I'll be done by noon."

"Saturday would be fine."

The waitress returned, smiling, as though she knew what had transpired. Somehow, though, Anne-Marie didn't feel the joy she should have. It was as if she was participating in a terrible fraud. And the culprit was Royce Buchanan.

Chapter Seven

Anne-Marie was in the kitchen, putting away the last of the dinner dishes. Don, Tracy, Kurt and Christianne were playing penny-ante poker at the breakfast table. Right after the cake and ice cream had been served, Don had told the children about their plans to marry.

Then, to make a little ceremony out of it, he'd taken the ring they'd selected the day before out of his pocket. It was just over two carats, marquise cut, set in platinum. Tracy and Kurt had received the news with glee, though for a while Christianne had fallen into a stunned silence.

Kurt had suggested poker, and Anne-Marie was happy to get everyone occupied. She looked at the group that would, in not too many months, officially become her family. It gave her a warm feeling to see them together. Kurt and Tracy's happiness also added to her joy.

Don had done so much to fill the vacuum left by Ted's death, she reflected. And seeing him that way, particularly in light of Carole and the way they all had felt about one another, had never seemed a slight to him.

Since their lunch at Bradbury's, Anne-Marie had thought about their plans a lot. The logic of it made a great deal of sense to her, and she even speculated that the tentativeness between them physically would abate once they were living together.

Don was conservative, traditional. He was aware of appearances and uncomfortable with illicit weekends away. As a result, they hadn't managed much intimacy, since both Tracy and Christianne were still living at home.

Anne-Marie heard the spirited bidding and stopped what she was doing to watch the poker players.

"So what does that mean?" Christianne asked.

"It means Don raised you five cents and you have to put in a nickel if you want to see his hand," Kurt replied.

He was leaning back, his arm behind Tracy, as he grinned across the table at his sister. Christianne perused the list of poker hands Don had written out for her on a slip of paper.

"Can I put in more?"

"Sure, you can raise him again," Kurt said with a chuckle, "if you're willing to lose a week's allowance."

"How do you know she's going to lose?" Tracy said, pushing back her long blond hair.

"Because I can see your hand."

Tracy poked him with her elbow before putting her cards down on the table. "You aren't supposed to look."

"It's all right. I folded."

"Can I bet a dime?" Christianne asked.

"You only have eight cents left," Kurt pointed out.

"Then lend me a dime."

"Are you good for it?"

"You can borrow ten cents from me," Don said, pushing some coins toward the girl.

"No, Don," Kurt said, "you can't finance a raise against yourself. I'll lend it to her." He tossed a dime over to his sister. "But if you have another 'flush' with hearts *and* diamonds," he said, shaking his finger at her, "I'll skin you alive."

"Oh, lay off," Christianne said. "They were all red, weren't they?" She pushed the dime he had given her into the pot. "I bet you ten cents."

"See your five and raise you five," her brother corrected.

"Let's see, that's ten to me," Tracy said, pushing in two nickels.

Don put in five pennies. "Okay, young lady, what do you have?"

Christianne put down two aces and a two and a three.

"A pair?" Kurt said with dismay. "You bet like that on a pair?"

"It's not a pair. It's four aces. Remember, Tracy said twos and threes were wild."

Tracy nodded. "That's right, I did." She groaned. "And I had a flush."

Don tossed his cards down. "Look at this, first decent hand I've had all evening. Full house. A natural one, too. Not a wild card in the bunch."

Christianne whooped with excitement. "I won! I won! Yippy!" She began raking in the coins.

Kurt laughed. "I guess that's what we get, playing with women and all their wild cards, Don."

"What's wrong with wild cards?" Tracy asked.

"Nothing, except it's sissy. Men don't play with half the deck wild."

"Sore loser," she retorted, lifting her nose.

Don got up. "Well, you broke me, Christianne. I'm out. You girls will have to fight it out with Kurt."

"My deal," Kurt said with a laugh. "Everything but twos and threes wild!"

"Okay!" Christianne said.

They all laughed.

Don walked around the counter to where Anne-Marie was standing. "Your daughter is fearless."

"I don't know where she got it."

"Neither do I. You and Ted were both so mild mannered and even tempered. Solid people."

Anne-Marie suddenly realized it bothered her when he referred to Ted or Carole, which he seemed to do a lot. Not that they shouldn't be remembered. But it just didn't seem consistent with their own plans for a life together. She glanced down at her ring, trying to decide how much she liked the feeling of being committed again.

Don slipped his arm around her shoulders and leaned close. "Or do you have a secret life I'm not aware of?" he whispered playfully.

The question struck deep into her. Her guilt had been building, even as her commitment to Don had deepened during the past few days. "There's always something people don't know about one another, isn't there?" She picked up a sponge, ran some water over it from the faucet and started scrubbing the drain board.

Don watched her mutely. Then the doorbell rang.

She turned at the sound. "Who could that be?" She began rinsing the soap off her hands.

"I'll get it," Don said. He headed off toward the front door.

Anne-Marie finished rinsing her hands and dried them on a tea towel. Over the children's chatter she heard a man's voice along with Don's in the front of the house. She left the kitchen and went through the dining room to find Royce Buchanan standing in the doorway, talking to Don. Her heart nearly stopped at the sight.

Noticing her, Royce smiled. A magnum of champagne was cradled in his arm. "Just brought a little gift for your celebration." He looked at Don and extended his hand. "I guess congratulations are in order."

"Thank you," Don said, beaming. "My goodness, news travels fast."

Anne-Marie was transfixed, partly with horror, partly with curiosity, as she listened.

"Anne-Marie mentioned she was getting engaged when I ran into her the other day," Royce explained. "She also mentioned a Sunday celebration."

"Well, come in," Don said, stepping back. He patted Royce on the shoulder. "Friends are always welcome."

As she watched with disbelief, Royce walked into the room. He stared at her for a moment, his smile fading when her glare didn't soften.

"So, you knew Anne-Marie in Germany," Don said. He turned to her. "Darling, why didn't you tell me an old friend was in town? We could have invited him for dinner."

"I've been so preoccupied with our engagement, it never occurred to me," she replied. Her level look was intended to tell Royce his visit wasn't welcome. "Besides, I thought of this as a *family* occasion."

"I don't mean to interrupt," Royce said. "I only wanted to drop this off." He handed the bottle to Don, who examined it with delight.

"Mmm. Chilled, even. This is awfully thoughtful of you, Royce." He seemed oblivious to the glances passing between his fiancée and their guest. "Well, why don't we open it? And stay and have a glass with us, by all means."

"He may not wish to, dear," Anne-Marie said with forced sweetness.

Don looked at each of them with surprise. "You have time for a glass or two, don't you? Come on, sit down." He gestured toward a chair. "I'll go open this in the kitchen. Don't want to spill on the carpet."

As Don walked out of the room, Royce shrugged.

"Make this short and sweet," Anne-Marie said through her teeth as she walked toward him.

"The guy's hospitable. What can I say? I don't want to offend him."

"You've offended *me* by coming. This is not the sort of day a woman wants to see a former lover!"

"I wanted to add to your joy. My intent, as I said, was to drop off the champagne."

"I don't need your champagne to be happy."

Royce gave her a disgruntled look. "You certain know how to put a damper on one's spirit of generosity, don't you?"

"Who's putting on a damper? You knew I wouldn't want you here."

"I thought you had that 'little slip' in perspective. After all, I don't mean anything to you. I'm nothing more than an object of your momentary weakness."

She anxiously glanced back through the dining room at the kitchen door. "Would you please go!"

"All right. After I've toasted your fiancé. I don't want to be rude. He seems like a hell of a nice guy, by the way. I like him."

Her eyes flashed. "He *is* a nice guy."

"Well, we agree on that much."

"Royce Buchanan, I could kill you!"

The kitchen door swung open, and Christianne came racing through. "Mr. Buchanan, it's you!"

"Well, hi there, princess!"

The girl came to a stop in front of him, beaming. Royce held out his hand, and she took it. "We've been playing poker. Want to play?"

Anne-Marie decided to nip any possible excuse for him to linger in the bud. "Mr. Buchanan isn't staying long, honey. He's going to have a glass of champagne with Don and me, then he's leaving."

"Oh, crap."

"Christianne!"

The girl blanched at her mother's tone and looked embarrassed. "Kurt says that. He did just a minute ago."

"Well, that's no excuse...."

The kitchen door opened again, and Don came out, holding the open magnum. A towel was wrapped around the neck of the bottle. Kurt was behind him, and Tracy followed, carrying champagne flutes on a tray.

Anne-Marie made the introductions, a tight expression on her face. Royce's easy demeanor irritated her.

He greeted the young couple, then Don got everyone seated and poured the champagne. He let Christianne pass the glasses. Everyone got one but her.

"What about the princess?" Royce said, looking at the girl. "She can have a swallow, can't she, Mom?"

Anne-Marie didn't appreciate his interference, especially knowing that he was trying to cull favor with her daughter. The man simply had no scruples. "Well, maybe a taste. Get yourself a glass, Christianne."

She ran from the room and returned an instant later with a juice glass. Don poured in a splash.

Anne-Marie was staring at Royce, trying to decide how much of the emotion roiling inside her was contempt. It seemed too strong a word. But *resentment* was certainly apropos.

"Well," Royce said, lifting his glass, "to the happy couple. Many happy returns."

Anne-Marie wondered just what "returns" he was referring to. His own?

"Thank you, thank you," Don said.

Christianne scrunched up her mouth as though she'd bitten into a lemon.

"What a face!" Tracy said, laughing.

"It's great on cereal, Christianne," Kurt added. "You ought to try it sometime."

"It's not the taste," the teenager said, regaining her composure. "It tickles my nose, like 7-Up does."

Don smiled. "Good champagne, Royce. French, isn't it?"

"Yes," Royce replied. "I've been partial to things European for years."

His eyes met Anne-Marie's. She looked away.

"How is it you two met, anyway?" Don asked.

"I was stationed in Germany while I was in the service."

"Lucky dog. I spent a year in Korea myself. You'd never believe how cold it can get in a Quonset hut there in January."

"I put in some time in Korea myself, Don."

"Oh, then you got the bad with the good."

"You might say so. If I had it to do over again, I never would have left Germany, though."

Anne-Marie felt her neck turn red.

"You had a choice?"

"Believe it or not, I volunteered to go to Korea . . . in a manner of speaking."

"Why on earth would you do that?"

"At that stage in his life, Royce was blessed with the good sense to know when to leave," Anne-Marie interjected.

Don gave her a quizzical look. He turned to their visitor. "Are you in town for long?"

"Actually, I'm here permanently. Moved out from Michigan a few months ago. I bought a place in the Santa Ynez Valley."

"Nice up that way."

"I like it."

Everybody sipped their wine but Anne-Marie and Christianne.

"What do you do, anyway?" Don asked.

"I'm an investor, I suppose you could say. I owned a man-ufacturing company back East, smokestack operation. I sold it, and I'm looking for something out here to put my money into."

"We should talk. I've got clients who are always looking for investment capital."

"I'm sure Royce has plenty of financial advisers already, dear," Anne-Marie said, not liking the drift of the conversation.

"No, as a matter of fact, I'm looking for professional help out here. Are you a broker, Don?"

"Accountant. I'm a partner in a regional firm. Osborne, Nelson and Gobley." He reached into his pocket and took out a business card, handing it to Royce. "Anne-Marie's husband and I were partners."

"I see. Thanks for the card. I'll give you a call sometime."

"I'd be pleased to give you a rundown on the investment climate out here. Maybe we could do lunch." He glanced over at Anne-Marie and saw her dark expression. "Oh, here we are talking business. Sorry, darling."

She saw Kurt looking at her strangely.

"When did you know Mr. Buchanan, Mom? Before you met Dad?"

She glanced at Royce. "Yes. We met at a dance. One of the rare occasions your grandfather let me out of the house. He didn't approve of soldiers—not just American soldiers, any kind. He soon made sure we...wouldn't become too good friends."

Kurt looked at Royce.

"Your mother was almost as pretty then as she is now, Kurt. There were so many guys in love with her. I was lucky to take her out for a cup of coffee."

"Then you dated?"

"Of course they did," Christianne said. "You don't think Mom's stupid, do you?"

"That was all before I met your father," Anne-Marie said.

Kurt's curiosity was aroused. "Did you know our father, Mr. Buchanan?"

"No, I was already in Korea by then. I didn't even know your mom had gotten married. We'd lost contact."

Anne-Marie was glad that Royce had treated the matter discreetly. Not that it mattered a great deal—it was all so long ago. But she did wish he'd leave. Someone might eventually start wondering, though Don didn't seem upset by his sudden appearance.

Her fiancé got up and poured everybody more champagne. They chatted amiably for several minutes, Christianne pumping Royce about his horses. Anne-Marie let herself begin to relax a little when she saw that he wasn't going to say anything to embarrass her.

"You have a family, Mr. Buchanan?" Kurt asked.

"I'm divorced. My daughter, Sybil, is married and living in Florida."

Kurt had a vaguely suspicious look on his face that made Anne-Marie uncomfortable. He was so protective of her. But Royce didn't seem to be bothered. He caught her eye every once in a while, letting a hint of self-satisfaction show. She couldn't help wondering if he was taking pleasure in having so recently seduced her. Strangely, the awareness aroused her.

She looked at Don. He was not exactly oblivious, but she guessed from his expression that he was mostly trying to estimate how many millions Royce might have to invest.

"Well, I've intruded long enough," Royce said after a while. "I'd better be on my way."

"Don't you want to play poker?" Christianne said with disappointment.

"Maybe another time. But thanks for asking." He got up, and so did Don and Kurt.

They shook hands all around, and Anne-Marie and Don went with him to the door. "Be sure and give me a call," Don said. "I'd like to be of any service that I can."

"I'll do that, Don."

Then Royce held his hand out to Anne-Marie. "I'm glad to find you happy again after all these years."

The little smile at the corners of his mouth told her what he was really thinking. Don hadn't impressed him much as a rival. The arrogance of it infuriated her. Then, when he leaned over and kissed her cheek, she was so angry she could have clubbed him.

"All the best," he said.

But Anne-Marie heard, *You really want this guy over me?*

Yes, Royce Buchanan, she thought as she turned and descended the steps. There's more than one kind of love, and you're probably just too blind to see it. You didn't understand that when I married someone else the first time, and you don't understand it now. You might be appealing and seductive, but you don't appreciate the kind of love that makes my home and family more important than anything else in my life.

She watched him wave and get into his car.

"Heck of a nice guy," Don mumbled as he waved back. "Why don't we have him over for dinner sometime?"

The week was a curiously quiet one for Anne-Marie. She talked to Don on the phone a couple of times, and they met for lunch on Tuesday. But there was no word from Royce—not a call, not a note, nothing. She was relieved, a little surprised, but in a way, skeptical. The silence was somehow ominous. What was he up to?

By the end of the week she was beginning to think that he might have seen the light. Perhaps he realized that she was committed to Don, that the incident at his house meant nothing.

But why had he dropped by with the champagne? Out of curiosity? Had he merely wanted to have a look at Don and maybe confirm her story about being engaged? If so, what he had seen must have satisfied him.

Just when she was beginning to doubt that she would ever see Royce Buchanan again, he showed up Friday afternoon for her class at the Goleta Racquet Club. Though his appearance wasn't a total surprise, it gave her a bit of a start. She felt her blood begin to rush through her veins.

He was wearing a jogging suit, and his sandy hair was rumpled from the wind. There was an easy smile on his face as he approached her.

"Hi," he said. "I wasn't quite sure how to dress or what to bring. I neglected to ask."

"What you have on is fine, although baggy clothing makes it more difficult for me to see things like your spinal alignment, muscle tension and so on." She glanced at the women by a bench along the wall who were getting ready for the class. "As you can see, my students wear tights and leotards ... that sort of thing."

"I've got my jogging shorts and a tank top on underneath."

"That would be fine. Take off your shoes and socks, though. We do yoga in bare feet."

His eyes rested on her easily; his look was surprisingly benign. He seemed almost like any new student who had walked into her class. Anne-Marie wondered if she should be suspicious.

"When do I pay you?"

"Oh, it doesn't matter. The fee is thirty-six dollars for six weekly lessons, or you can pay the drop-in fee of seven dollars a class."

"Would you object if I stuck out the whole course—assuming I like it?"

There was an air of contrition in his voice, which made it difficult for her to be stern. And except for his lingering gaze, he was behaving perfectly. "I suppose it's all right."

A few more students arrived, and the women were chatting amiably among themselves as they shed their cover-ups and got ready for class.

"We have a few minutes before it's time to begin," Anne-Marie said. "Tell me about your back problem."

He went over the history of the case, telling her of his discussion with Dr. Gilchrist and showing her the place in his lower back where he had the pain. She had him take off his sweats and try to touch his toes—which he couldn't do—to check his flexibility. Then she ran her fingers along the corded muscles at the small of his back as he bent over.

"I think the problem is with your hamstrings," she said. "They're very tight, and you aren't getting the support in your back that you need."

"My hamstrings?"

"Yes. Most people don't realize how interconnected all the muscle groups are, and how conditions in one place affect you somewhere else. If there's tightness in the ankle, say, it will affect the way we use the muscles in our leg, which can affect the hip region, back and shoulders." She smiled. "The foot bone is connected to the head bone in more ways than one."

"Amazing."

Their eyes held for several moments, and her nerves tautened a fraction. She rushed on. "In your case, Royce, you don't have the proper flexibility at the back of your thighs, and this puts additional stress on your spine. We'll focus on stretching your hamstrings and working your abdominals. That should reduce the stress on your back."

The other students started drifting over.

"Let's get started," Anne-Marie said to the group. "As you can see, we have a new student. Mr. Buchanan is a runner with back problems, and we're going to fix him up with yoga."

Royce nodded and smiled at the women.

"In class, Mr. Buchanan," Anne-Marie went on, "we do a generalized workout, designed to build strength and flexibility throughout the body. Some poses will be easy for you, others more difficult. I'll point out the ones that are especially important for your back problem as we go along. And you should work on those at home. But remember that all the poses are significant because we want symmetry throughout the body. Balance and harmony are the objectives. When our bodies are flexible and strong, we have greater health and much more energy. Any questions?"

"All that for thirty-six bucks?" Royce said.

"All that for thirty-six bucks, plus lots of hard work and dedication."

He was at one end of the line of students as he watched Anne-Marie demonstrate a pose, then talk the class through it. She wore white tights and a teal leotard, her lithe body exquisite as she stretched into the required positions, as graceful as a ballerina, yet as resilient and wiry as a martial arts expert.

He marveled at the trim lines of her figure, her carriage, her grace and strength. She enchanted him. There was poetry in her presence, her movement. And he wanted her.

But except to watch her, he gave no indication of his feelings. He took quiet pleasure with his eyes but betrayed little. He had decided that if he was to have Anne-Marie, it would have to be with guile.

For some reason—probably because of the past—she had set her heart against him. She had convinced herself that her future should be with this fellow Don Nelson, not him. And though the error in that was obvious to him, to her it wasn't. But, deep down, she had to doubt. It was on that he had pinned his hopes.

After the class Royce put his sweats back on and got his checkbook out of his bag. Anne-Marie was talking to a couple of the other students when he handed her his check for thirty-six dollars. She turned and smiled at him, her dove-gray eyes full of life, energy.

"How do you feel? Get a workout?"

He nodded. "It's deceptively challenging. The first impression is that there's not much to it, but after an hour and a half your body feels like it was pulled apart and stuck back together."

"But it's a good sensation. Don't you feel the energy flowing?"

"Yes." She was damned pretty, but he tried not to let his awareness show. Be matter-of-fact, he told himself. Move slowly, very slowly.

"How's the back?"

"Looser. It doesn't hurt at the moment, but it does feel looser."

"Good." She looked genuinely pleased. "Do those hamstring stretches at home. A couple of times a day, if you can."

He nodded. "I will. And thanks, Anne-Marie, I enjoyed the class. See you next week," he said, turning toward the door.

He walked away, feeling her eyes on him, knowing she was wondering why he hadn't made some sort of overture. He was keeping it polite and businesslike. Eventually, if she cared as much as he thought she did, it would get to her, and she'd let him know. He was counting on that, because he was determined not to lose his German girl a second time.

Chapter Eight

The next week it was the same. Royce came to the class, quietly followed her directions, worked hard and showed improvement in his flexibility. Midway through the session the students were leaning with their hands against the wall, bent at the waist, in a modified *Adho Mukha Svanasana*, their legs straight, knees locked, thighs tight, spines fully elongated. Anne-Marie walked down the line, making adjustments. When she came to Royce she ran her fingers down the lower part of his back, feeling for his vertebrae.

He was lean and firm from all the running, though he needed more flexibility. Seeing him in his jogging shorts made her think of the day they'd been together. When she touched his skin or rotated a limb to adjust his position, she couldn't help but remember his embrace, his touch.

"Raise your hands about three inches," she said, bringing her mind back to the business at hand.

He made the adjustment.

"Ah, there!" she said, running her fingers along the cavity of his back. "You see, the bumps from the vertebrae are gone.

That means you're in alignment. That's much more important than bending deeply. That will come as your flexibility increases. But you're doing better. You must be practicing."

His head was between his arms, and he could only see her feet as she stood beside him. "Yes, twice a day."

"Good. Dedication."

"I want to please the teacher."

A little smile passed over her lips as she moved back toward the center of the room. "All right," she said to the class, "on the next exhalation slowly come out of the pose."

The students straightened and turned around to face her. Anne-Marie glanced at Royce but didn't let her eyes linger, though she wanted to. His reticence intrigued her nearly as much as his physical presence. Was that what he intended, or was he simply resigned to the fact that she wasn't available?

After the class she half expected him to say something, perhaps wait for the others to leave so he could walk with her to her car. But he didn't. He just saluted her pleasantly, said goodbye and left.

She realized immediately that she was disappointed, and that worried her. Perhaps it was no more than her pride, but the feeling was quite strong. What was worse, it would be a whole week before she saw him again. And her unhappiness over that was cause for even greater concern.

On her way home, Anne-Marie had a good talk with herself. She was engaged to Don, a man she had a great deal of affection and respect for. That ought to be enough, particularly for a woman of her maturity. She wasn't a young girl who went crazy over men. And yet, if permitting Royce to seduce her proved anything, it proved that certain desires in her were not dead.

True, she was a lot more mellow than she had been as a girl, and she could easily distinguish physical attraction from love— even romantic love. But Royce Buchanan's allure was strong.

Why wasn't what she felt for Don enough? Her father would have said that the human spirit was weak, and the only way to avoid corruption was to avoid temptation. By that logic, it had been a mistake to let Royce attend her class.

But that seemed a very old-fashioned notion. What kind of feelings did she have for Don if she had to guard against her desire for another man? Was there some deficiency in her love for her fiancé?

She knew Don wasn't perfect. Nobody was. But he had many good qualities—things she could truly say she loved. He didn't incite passion, he didn't bring her desires bubbling to the surface, but how important was that in the long run? Those kinds of things had a way of dissipating over time. When the physical attraction had run its course, what was left?

Royce was tempting, but what did he really offer in the perspective of years? With Don she knew. She had the benefit of experience. As a mature woman, she knew what young girls couldn't possibly know.

So why was putting Royce Buchanan from her mind such a struggle?

After dinner that evening, one of Christianne's friends came over so they could do homework together. Anne-Marie went to her studio to meditate. She put some sitar music on her tape deck, lit some candles and tried to find a quiet place in her mind. Before she had much of a chance to fully relax, there was a soft knock at the door and Christianne came in.

"Can I talk to you, Mom?"

"Sure, honey. How's the homework coming?"

"I'm finished. Laura just went home."

"What did you want to talk about?"

"Laura asked me about horseback riding at Mr. Buchanan's—I told her about it last week and said maybe she could go with me. But then I realized he hasn't called. Aren't we going to go out there?"

"I think that invitation may have been a spur-of-the-moment gesture on his part, Christianne. You probably shouldn't count on it."

"You mean, he didn't mean it?"

"I'm sure he did at the time."

"When did he change his mind?"

"I don't know that he has."

"Then why hasn't he called?"

Anne-Marie sighed. She didn't want to get into a lengthy discussion, but she felt it was somehow important to be honest and let her daughter know the gist of the problem. "I think it's because he knows I'm not eager to see him again."

"How come?"

"It's a long story. Let's just say that since I've gotten engaged, Mr. Buchanan's interest in me isn't the same."

"You mean he was hot for you?"

"Christianne, where do you get these expressions?"

"That's a usual one. Lots of kids say it."

"Well, somehow it doesn't sound quite right in regard to your mother."

"So, did he want to marry you, too?"

Anne-Marie hesitated. "I think 'marry' is too strong a term."

"How come you don't want to... whatever with him?"

"Because I'm already engaged."

"I don't see why you want to marry Don. I think Mr. Buchanan's pretty nice. He's handsome, too."

"Don's nice. And he's nice looking. Besides, looks aren't everything."

"You just want to marry Don because of Kurt and Tracy."

"That's not true. I love him."

"Why?"

"I just do." She looked at Christianne, feeling suddenly uncomfortable. "He's very much like your father. You ought to appreciate that."

"I don't think so at all. Of course, I don't remember Daddy real well."

"I assure you, your father and Don were alike in many respects."

"That doesn't seem like a very good reason, even if it's true. Who wants to marry someone just because they're like somebody else? If I were Don and you told me that, I'd throw up."

"Is it really necessary to be so graphic?"

"What do you mean?"

"Never mind. Anyway, Don's aware of my feelings, and he's not uncomfortable with them."

"Does he say you're like his wife?"

"No. Carole and I were friends, but we weren't too much alike."

Christianne shook her head. "I don't think adults are as smart as they think they are."

Anne-Marie laughed. "You may be right about that."

"Then can Laura and I go horseback riding at Mr. Buchanan's?"

She gave the girl a look. "I'd really like to accommodate you, but I'm in a difficult position. Besides, I'm not at all sure he's still interested in having us out there. I can't very well remind him."

"Couldn't you call him up and kind of hint around?"

"No."

"So does that mean we can't go?"

Anne-Marie thought. "I'll tell you what. I see Mr. Buchanan once a week at my yoga class. If he brings the subject up again, I'll take you. Otherwise, we'll just have to forget about it. That way it's in his hands. Is that fair?"

Christianne groaned. "I guess."

"I think that's a very generous offer, considering."

"Yeah, but now I have to wait around for him to get horny."

Anne-Marie started to admonish Christianne but held her tongue. Though her daughter's vocabulary could use some improvement, she had captured the essence of the situation. In the matter of relations between the sexes, so many questions and answers turned on that very point.

That night, as Anne-Marie was readying herself for bed, the telephone rang. Considering the hour, she half expected it to be Royce, though more because he'd been on her mind than for any other reason. But it was Don.

"We haven't talked for a while," he said wistfully, "so I thought I'd give you a buzz."

"That's sweet."

He chuckled. "Seems like no matter how busy I've been or how much is on my mind, I always think of you around bedtime."

"I guess that's good."

"Oh, it is! I didn't mean to imply anything else. It's when a person feels their loneliness most, don't you think?"

"I suppose so."

"Were you thinking about me, Anne-Marie?"

"Uh . . . yes."

"Maybe we shouldn't wait till this fall to marry, tax season or not."

"We have a good relationship, Don. It won't matter a lot if we wait, will it?"

"No, you're probably right."

An empty feeling came over her, and she hated it. "So, how's your week going? Anything interesting at the office?"

"As a matter of fact, I did get a call yesterday from your friend Royce Buchanan."

At the mention of his name, she felt her muscles clench. "Oh? What did he want?"

"'Jt was a follow-up to our conversation at your house. He was interested in hearing about investment opportunities." Don chuckled. "Your running into him might have turned out to be a pretty lucky break."

"If something comes of it for you, I suppose it proves there is justice in the world."

"Huh?"

"Nothing. An idle comment. Any other news?"

"Nope. What have you been up to?"

"Just stretching things." She gave a little laugh but didn't blame Don for not seeing the humor. It wasn't very funny.

There was silence on the line.

Why didn't he do something impetuous, she wondered, like invite her over for a bottle of champagne or suggest a moon-light walk on the beach?

"Well, I've got an early morning meeting, so I'd better get to bed," he finally said.

"Yeah, I've got a class first thing."

"Sweet dreams."

"You, too, Don."

Anne-Marie didn't realize how much she had been looking forward to her Friday class at Goleta until she was on her way to the club. What if Royce wasn't there? What if he'd decided he'd had all the instruction he'd needed? His back was getting better. She hadn't given him any encouragement. Maybe she wouldn't see him again.

She was about ten minutes early, and only one of the students was in the room when she entered. Gradually the others arrived, and at a few minutes past the hour she began the class. Royce hadn't come. Her premonition had been accurate. Anne-Marie was deeply disappointed.

But about ten minutes into the class, he bounded in, apologizing for being late. She felt a surge of excitement at his arrival and let herself watch as he slipped out of his jogging suit. She had the strangest urge to give him a big hug. He smiled shyly as he took his customary place at the end of the line. Anne-Marie felt notably happy.

The class continued, and she had to resist the temptation to gravitate toward Royce. The women were tolerant of his presence—there had been other men in her classes from time to time—but she had to guard against showing any favoritism. They all knew she was a widow, and none of them had to be told how attractive Royce Buchanan was. He'd garnered many admiring glances the few times he'd been there.

Still, she couldn't help looking his way, and, since he was comparatively new, his poses did require a lot of adjustment. When she approached him to change the angle of a bend or point out a tense muscle that was supposed to be slack, she immediately became aware of his cologne and the speckles of color in his blue eyes. As she stood near him, she noticed his lips and remembered the way they'd kissed that day.

It was a foolish game, the sort of errant behavior that had gotten her into trouble in the first place. Why was this man so seductive?

After class Royce seemed to linger. Anne-Marie wondered if he was waiting for an opportunity to speak with her. When the other students had gone, he came over to where she was packing her sport bag.

"Forgive me for interjecting a personal note," he began, "but I've been feeling a little guilty about your daughter."

"Christianne? Why?"

"The past few weeks I've been trying to be considerate of your feelings . . . you know, keeping in line, et cetera. But it occurred to me that I did promise Christianne a day of horseback riding, and I've sort of reneged. I was wondering if it would be too much to ask for you to bring her and a friend or two out, say, Sunday afternoon."

Anne-Marie started to decline, but she recalled her promise to her daughter. What irony. At the time it had seemed safe enough to leave the matter up to Royce, who appeared to have forgotten it.

"I guess it would be selfish to decline an invitation that's really intended for her."

"I hate to put you on the spot. And I hesitated for a long time before bringing it up. But I do feel bad getting her hopes up."

"Which only goes to show how dirty your little trick was."

"Yes, I guess that's another sin I have to pay for."

She studied him. What was it that told her there was more afoot than met the eye? His contrition was almost too contrite—that's what it was. "Two days is kind of short notice."

"Do you have other plans?"

"No, but I'll have to talk to Christianne. I believe she wanted to ask her friend, Laura, along."

"Then you've discussed it?"

"Let's just say that when you cast your net, in Christianne you found a willing fish."

"In all honesty, at the time I was thinking of the big fish, not the small-fry."

Anne-Marie had to chuckle. "I must say, Royce, you're getting more forthright the longer I know you."

He bowed deferentially. "Your positive influence."

She had to laugh. "As my son would say, it's getting a little deep in here."

"Aptly put."

"I'll talk to Christianne and call you this evening. How's that?"

"Fine. Do you still have my number?"

"Yes, I believe I still have your number."

* * *

Christianne was on the porch when Anne-Marie arrived home.

"Hi, Mom. How was yoga today?" she asked, jumping up to greet her.

"Fine."

Anne-Marie was a bit surprised at her interest. And the expectant look on the girl's face gave her pause. Could she have anticipated Royce's invitation? Christianne knew the Friday afternoon class was the one he was in, and that this was the first session since their conversation. Maybe she'd been even more eager for the outing than Anne-Marie had realized.

"Well, good fortune was smiling on you today, young lady."

"Did he ask?"

Anne-Marie was taken aback. "You mean Royce? How did you know?"

"Well, I...I knew he was...in your class," she stammered. "I was hoping he invited us." She looked up at her mother excitedly. "Did he?"

Anne-Marie smelled a rat. "Christianne, did you know Royce was going to talk to me about horseback riding today?"

The girl hung her head.

"Christianne?"

"Well, I sort of guessed." She didn't look at her mother.

"You sort of guessed?"

"I...sort of knew."

"How?"

There was no reply, no eye contact.

"Christianne?"

"Well, aren't you glad? You'd like to go, too, wouldn't you?"

"That's not the point. I want to know what's going on, young lady."

Christianne frowned. "Can't we just drop it? If you don't want to go Sunday, then we won't."

"How did you know it was Sunday?"

The girl turned red.

Anne-Marie took her by the arm and led them both to the porch chairs. "All right, let's hear it from the beginning. I want to know exactly what happened."

"It was no big deal. Honest."

"Big deal or not, let's hear it."

Christianne groaned. "Well, Laura wanted to know what kind of horses they were. She's done a lot of riding, you know."

"And?"

"And so I called up Mr. Buchanan and asked him."

"You called up to see what kind of horses he had so you could tell Laura?"

"Something like that."

"And in the course of the conversation he renewed his invitation, and you said he would have to ask me because if *he* asked, I'd promised you we'd go. Then he said he would talk to me. Is that how it went?"

"Something like that."

"That's what I thought." Anne-Marie shook her head with chagrin. Thinking of Royce's innocent expression made her blood start to boil.

"Why are you so mad, Mom?" she asked. "It's just horseback riding."

"No, it's not just horseback riding, it's ..."

"It's what?"

"It's the principle of the thing. I don't like him sneaking around, conspiring with you. That's what I'm angry about."

"Well, it's not his fault. I mean, it wasn't his idea or anything like that."

Anne-Marie stopped to think about the point, wondering if it had merit, wondering if her emotions had clouded her judgment. "Maybe. But I still don't like it."

"What are you so afraid of, anyway? It's not like you were a virgin or anything."

"Christianne! What kind of a thing is that to say to your mother? I happen to be engaged to Don. I have no interest whatsoever in Mr. Buchanan. Is that clear?"

The girl didn't reply, and they sat in silence for a while.

"Mom, what does the saying, 'The lady doth protest too much,' mean?"

Anne-Marie looked at her. "If you think I'm upset because I care for Royce, you're completely off base. *Completely.*"

"That's what I thought it meant."

Anne-Marie groaned.

"Okay," Christianne said, "if it's such a big deal, I'll call and tell him to forget it."

"You'll do no such thing. You've caused enough trouble already. I'll call him. You go upstairs and do your homework."

"But, Mom, it's Friday."

"Well, do some homework anyway."

Christianne looked at her strangely. "I just realized what you meant when you used to say that when boys pick on you it's because they like you. You must have a real case on Mr. Buchanan."

"Oh, shut up," Anne-Marie said, giving her daughter a gentle shove toward the door.

She went directly to her room to call Royce. There was no answer, and she realized she probably hadn't given him time to get home. It was quite a drive up to the Santa Ynez Valley.

Perhaps it was just as well. She wasn't completely sure what she was going to say. Of course, he was totally in the wrong, having used Christianne that way—or having let her use him. Whichever way it was, he was wrong. He should have leveled with her, told her Christianne had called. Yes, that was his sin.

Anne-Marie knew what he was up to. Royce was taking advantage of the situation. The rat.

She tried his number again, but there was still no answer. What was he after, anyway? He was perfectly aware of her feelings for Don. He couldn't possible be innocent. Or could he?

Perhaps he hadn't really wanted to have her and her daughter out and had been roped into it by Christianne. If that was the case, she owed him an apology. How embarrassing.

She played their conversation over in her mind. No, there was neither regret nor discomfort on his face when he extended the invitation. He was glad for the excuse. She remembered his coy smile, *and* the remark about the big fish and the small-fry. No, Christianne had played right into his hands. Big fish, indeed.

Anne-Marie angrily dialed his number. Still no answer. If she had him there in her grasp, she'd wring his neck. She got up and paced the floor. But what was she going to do about his invitation? By all rights she should point out the error of his ways and decline.

Of course, that would disappoint Christianne and Laura. Was she making too big of a deal out of it? After all, what had he really done that was so horrible? Maybe his intentions were good, even if his judgment was lacking. Nobody was perfect. Perhaps she was overreacting.

Anne-Marie tried Royce's number several more times. Finally, after dinner, she got through. She'd tried so often without success that she was surprised to hear his voice.

"Oh, you're home. Hi, it's Anne-Marie."

"Well, hello." He seemed pleased to hear her voice. "Have you been trying to reach me? I went out for a super long run. Twelve miles. I wanted to test my back."

"How do you feel?"

"Not bad at all. I did some yoga poses afterward, stretched my hamstrings. I think it's working."

"Good. I'm happy."

"So, have you worked things out for Sunday?"

"Frankly, Royce, I have mixed feelings. I found out Christianne had called you, and that didn't please me."

"Maybe I should have said something. I was in a difficult position, and I didn't know what to do. On the one hand, I didn't want to interfere and get between you and Christianne. On the other hand, I didn't like being less than honest with you."

"I suppose it's our fault for putting you in that position."

"Let's not get into fault and blame. The important thing is that you're coming."

"I haven't said that. I haven't made up my mind yet."

"What must I say to convince you?"

"I suppose it's important for you to understand the reason for my reluctance, and to respect it."

"You mean Don?"

"Yes."

"What the hell, bring him along, too, if that'll make you feel better."

She laughed. "I don't need Don to protect me. I'm not afraid of you, Royce."

"Then what are you afraid of?"

"Nothing."

He didn't say anything.

"I'd just like there to be an understanding between us."

"I thought there was."

"Well, I guess we can come, then."

"Good. Would around two be all right?"

"Yes."

"Tell the kids to bring their suits if they want to swim after the ride."

"Okay, I will."

"I'm looking forward to it, Anne-Marie."

She couldn't tell him so, but she was looking forward to it, as well.

Chapter Nine

Sunday was a balmy, breezy day along the coast. But the sun was bright and warm, and by the time they had driven inland to the Santa Ynez Valley, it was quite hot. Christianne and Laura Fine sat in the back seat chattering away, obviously excited. Laura, who was dark like Christianne, though shorter and heavier, tried to sound blasé because of her riding experience, but the spirit of adventure had clearly taken both girls.

When they stopped in the driveway below Royce's house, he came out to greet them. He was wearing jeans, boots and a worn blue shirt open at the neck, which revealed a mat of tawny chest hair. Christianne excitedly introduced her friend.

Royce was charming, and Anne-Marie, who had gotten her bag and wide-brimmed straw hat out of the Honda, stood back watching. She saw instantly that he could enchant a woman of any age. After all, she had been a girl of seventeen the first time she had fallen under his spell.

He told the girls there were cool drinks waiting on the patio behind the house. As they ran ahead, he turned to Anne-Marie.

"So, how's the big fish today?"

"Remembering what a charmer you are," she said wryly.

"Ah," he said, taking her arm, "starting with a compliment. That's a good sign."

"I hadn't exactly intended it that way."

He laughed and squeezed her arm. "Maybe I won't pursue that one."

When they arrived in back the girls had already opened a soft drink and were standing out on the lawn, looking down at the pool and the paddock beyond.

"Care for something to drink?" he asked, pointing at the cooler on the table.

"No, thank you. Not now. Maybe later."

"Do you ride much?"

"Not really. I wasn't planning on going along. If you don't mind, I'll just sit down by your pool, read and get a little sun."

Royce was looking at her much as he had the day she'd come to give him the massage. But he was holding his tongue, not speaking as freely as he had the first time. He was really trying. And she appreciated it.

Still, there was admiration in his eyes. And, in spite of herself, she liked the feeling. She could handle his unspoken desires as long as they went unstated.

"You're welcome to come or stay, as you please," he said amiably. "But those two won't be restrained for long. I'd better have the horses brought up. If you'll excuse me, I'll go in and buzz the stable."

Royce went into the house, and Anne-Marie watched Christianne and Laura. They were testing the water temperature of the pool with their hands. Royce came back out a moment later.

Anne-Marie had put on her hat. She looked up at him, shading her eyes from the sun. "You have somebody care for your horses?"

"Yes." He sat in the chair next to her. "The people I bought this place from were big on horses, but they were moving to New York City and obviously couldn't take them along. Four good riding horses came as sort of a package deal with the house. I considered selling them, but I thought they might be nice for guests. So I hired a young fellow from Los Olivos to look after them."

"Don't you ride?"

"Two or three times a week, mainly to exercise the horses. Frankly, I'd rather run."

"What is this love affair you have with running?"

He looked at her, smiling broadly so that his white teeth showed. "You really want to know?"

"Sure."

"I took it up years ago, after I had a big disappointment. I felt the need to get up and go, to make the ground move under my feet. I've been running ever since."

"What sort of disappointment would make you want to run?"

"Well, you see, there was this girl, a beautiful German girl I'd met while I was in the service. She had shiny black hair and the most wonderful gray eyes you've ever seen. After I was discharged, I went back to Germany to find her, and—"

"That's all right, Royce. You don't have to finish your story."

"The ending's not exactly sad. More bittersweet, I'd say."

"Bittersweet?"

"She's alive and well and as beautiful as ever. It's just that—"

"Please don't."

"I wouldn't have brought it up . . . but you asked."

"I'm not blaming you. Let's change the subject."

"Okay. How's Don?"

"Let's not talk about him, either."

"The weather?"

She gave a woeful laugh. "You see why I didn't want to come."

"Well, I'm not going to ruin your day. The girls are already chomping at the bit." He got up. "Lonnie, my wrangler, should be here any minute. I'm going to get them organized." He gave her a friendly smile. "Feel free to use the house if you want to change." He sauntered on down toward the pool.

Anne-Marie watched him go, sighing deeply. Bittersweet. That was a good way to describe the way she'd been feeling herself. It was nice seeing Royce, but at the same time it was a big problem.

Down at the pool he was playing with the girls, pretending he was going to throw them in. They both shrieked and ran to the opposite side of the pool, enjoying the game.

"I hope you know how to swim," he called to them. "I know a couple of girls who are going to get dunked after this ride."

"You have to catch us first!" Christianne shouted gleefully.

Seeing the joy on her daughter's face made Anne-Marie glad she'd brought her. Christianne had Kurt, but a brother wasn't the same as a father, the influence of a grown man. She'd been deprived in that respect. It was too bad the girl hadn't responded as positively to Don as she had to Royce. Maybe it was because Tracy was still at home and Christianne didn't feel as though she could embrace him in the same way. But she had certainly taken to Royce, making a case for him in their conversation the other day.

Down below, the wrangler came around the hillock from the stable leading three horses—two sorrels and a bay. The girls and Royce immediately abandoned their game. They were beyond hearing, but Anne-Marie could tell they were discussing who would ride which mount.

The younger man helped each girl into the saddle and adjusted the stirrups for them. When they were ready, Royce swung himself up onto his horse, and they headed off toward the road, all three of them waving up at Anne-Marie. She smiled and watched them go, feeling the impact of Royce's presence, even though he was leaving.

When they'd finally disappeared from sight, Anne-Marie looked down at the lounge chairs by the pool and decided to change and get some sun. When she was younger, like most Germans, she'd worshiped the sun. But after she'd discovered its harmful effects on her skin, she'd been much more careful. Now she always wore a hat and virtually bathed herself in sunscreen lotion.

Taking her bag, she went in through the sliding doors to the living room. She looked at the couch where she had sat with Royce that day, feeling a sentimental twinge. But when she came to his bedroom, the feeling grew stronger, more intense.

The bed was made, its surface as smooth as a tabletop. But Anne-Marie saw herself on it, naked, with Royce beside her, loving her, kissing her, arousing her as she'd never been aroused. A tremor went through her at the recollection.

Not wanting to pursue those memories, she turned from the bed and looked around the room, seeing it really for the first time. Before, she had been under Royce's seductive spell and hadn't fully taken in her surroundings. A picture in a silver frame on the writing desk caught her eye. She went to it and picked it up.

It was the photograph of an attractive young woman of perhaps twenty. She was dark, but her eyes and jaw were a feminine version of Royce's. Doubtless, this was his daughter.

Staring at the picture, she wondered about Royce's wife. The woman was obviously dark—Sybil was—and probably attractive. There were hints of Royce in his daughter's features, but her dark good looks must have come from her mother's side.

She wondered what had gone wrong in their marriage. Had they been mismatched from the start, or was it one of those things where two people grew apart over time? Had they ever been happy? Royce hadn't talked about his marriage much.

He was certainly fond of Sybil, though. That was apparent by the way he had spoken of her—the light of his life, he'd called her.

In a way, his budding relationship with Christianne might be nostalgic for him, a reminder of a time when his own daughter was younger and he was everything to her. Did Royce miss that? she wondered. Did his life sometimes feel rather empty and sad?

After another furtive glance at the bed, Anne-Marie went into the bath, where she stripped and put on her bikini. As she changed, she glanced at the glass-enclosed room off the bath with its waterfall and bubbling spa.

Why was the spa on? she wondered. Was he trying to entice her? As she looked at the roiling water, sensuous feelings bubbled up inside of her, and she appreciated how clever he was.

Anne-Marie made herself turn away, wanting to clear her mind of him. She looked into the mirror and adjusted the straps of her suit. It gave her pleasure to see her body, because she did have a lovely figure. For her age it was almost phenomenal.

But it hadn't come easily. By one's late thirties fitness required commitment and dedication. The young could get away with certain things, but an old broad like her, as Kurt kiddingly called her, had to work at it.

Taking her sunscreen, Anne-Marie began coating her body with it. She remembered how Ted used to like to apply lotion to her back and legs when they took the kids to the beach. Her husband hadn't always been terribly romantic, but he had loved her deeply, and he had cared about her happiness, and the happiness of the children, above all else.

When she had finished Anne-Marie put her hat back on, took her bag and returned to the patio. She paused at the table and looked at the soft drinks. She rarely drank them, even the diet varieties, and though she was vaguely thirsty, she decided against one now. Instead she popped an ice cube into her mouth and walked down the lawn toward the pool.

As she went, liking the cool feel of the grass between her toes and the ice on her tongue, she looked out across the valley, wondering if she might spot the riders. They were nowhere in sight.

She took her book out of her bag and stretched out on a lounge chair. Her hat shaded her face, but the sun's warm rays enveloped her, bringing instant, soothing pleasure. A feeling of deep contentment washed over her, and she felt happy. It wasn't just the sun, though; it was more than that. She liked being at Royce's place, even though he himself unsettled her.

Her mind turned to fancy, and she began imagining herself with him, perhaps living with him in this house. She wondered what it would be like to share his home, to share his life.

What would it have been like if Ted hadn't come along, if she had been waiting for Royce when he'd returned to Germany? If they'd married, would they be together still? Or would their marriage have gone the way his had with Sybil's mother?

She wondered what determined those things. Was it the quality of a couple's love? The people themselves? Chemistry? She didn't know the answer.

But as she lay in the sun, her mind drifting, two different Royce Buchanans invaded her thoughts. There was the adult out riding with her daughter, the playful man at the pool, the captivating lover who'd seduced her and shaken the foundations of her life. And there was the other one, the young one. The lieutenant who had broken her heart....

Anne-Marie loved her new party dress, the first really grown-up one her father had allowed her to buy. It was spring, and he'd reluctantly agreed to let her go to the dance, even though it was in Frankfurt and he knew there'd be all sorts of young men attending. But Anne-Marie was studying at the art institute in Frankfurt. She would be on her own before long and would have to look after herself.

"Ja," Father had said, "but young men like to take advantage of a fine young girl like you. Especially the soldiers."

The dance, in celebration of the June youth festival, was held in the Festhalle near the Hauptbahnhof, in the heart of Frankfurt. Anne-Marie went with Brigitte and two other friends from the institute, Siegrid and Emma.

The four had moved around the hall like a covey of quail, each having gotten a lecture from her parents on some variation of Herbert Keller's theme. Among them, Siegrid was the most experienced, having been to the dance the year before. She led the others, explaining the rules and the pitfalls they must watch for.

The dances Anne-Marie had been to in Kronberg were much more sedate affairs, and tiny by comparison. The swirling crowds and live blaring music in the Festhalle were as frightening, in a sense, as they were electrifying.

Anne-Marie was already looking forward to leaving when two young men approached her and Siegrid as they stood near the refreshment table, sipping punch. They were dressed in jeans and sweaters and had shorter hair than most of the other boys. Siegrid had said the American soldiers were usually the ones with short hair, so Anne-Marie wasn't surprised at the strong accent.

"Darf ich um diesen Tanz bitten?" May I have this dance? the handsome young man said cavalierly.

The piercing blue eyes were confident, his smile immediately disarming. Siegrid danced with the other American, and Anne-Marie let hers lead her out onto the floor.

The band was playing a slow piece, and they danced for a while in silence. Anne-Marie noticed his distinctive yet unfamiliar cologne. She'd never been so close to an American before. He was holding her firmly but not with undue familiarity.

"You're an American," she said in English, judging her ability with the language likely to be better than his German.

"One of the good ones."

"Are there good and bad ones?"

"I've heard a lot about the bad ones. But being good myself, I assumed there must be two kinds."

Anne-Marie laughed, and he smiled broadly at her.

"You're a soldier."

"An officer, if that makes a difference."

"Should it?"

"You're frightened, so I was hoping to put your mind at ease."

"Frightened?"

"You're trembling."

"You must be one of the bad Americans, and I fear you."

"I was hoping it was my charm, unnerving you," he said with a grin.

"You're definitely one of the bad ones, Mister..."

"Buchanan. Lieutenant Buchanan. But to lovely girls like you, I'm Royce."

"Something tells me half the girls in Frankfurt know you as Royce."

"There's only one who matters, though. The one with the most lovely gray eyes I've ever seen."

She laughed, and Royce spun her around and around.

They danced twice more, but, though he was persistent, she wouldn't tell him more than that her name was Anne-Marie and that she was attending classes at the art institute.

She wouldn't explain why she didn't want to see him again. Anne-Marie knew with certainty that a visit from him was something her father would never tolerate, so there was no point in encouraging the young officer. Later, when she told him goodbye and left the dance with her friends, he acted like the saddest man on earth.

Meeting him had been an entertaining experience, and she had thought Royce Buchanan attractive and perfectly "delicious"—the word Brigitte had first used to describe him. But she put him from her mind, never expecting to see him again.

Four days later she was summoned to the administration office at the institute, where the secretary told her she had a visitor. Royce was waiting for her in the reception room.

"Lieutenant Buchanan, what are you doing here?"

"I couldn't die without seeing you again."

"Do you expect to die soon?"

"No, but wouldn't wondering about you be a terrible way to spend the next fifty years?"

"Pfft. I thought you would have found two or three more girls by now."

"I told you . . . I'm one of the good ones."

"And what am I to think of that?" she asked, eyeing his handsome face.

"I thought we could start with lunch and figure out together what you should think."

"I will be honest with you, Lieutenant Buchanan. My father wouldn't approve of my seeing you. That is why I said no at the dance."

"Hmm," he said, rubbing his chin. "You assume that because I am a soldier, and perhaps because I'm American, that your father will not approve of me. But you haven't considered that I might convince him that I am one of the good Americans."

"How do you propose to accomplish that?"

"We must figure that out while we have our lunch."

Anne-Marie laughed. "You are a shrewd one, aren't you?"

"Good and shrewd."

"All right, Lieutenant. We will have lunch. But I warn you, it won't be easy to outfox my father."

Anne-Marie turned over onto her stomach and let the hot California sun caress her back. The warmth felt so good, so sensual, and it, combined with thoughts of Royce, aroused her. The rays seemed to penetrate her, stirring her desire.

Perhaps she would always associate the sun with Royce. Their "first time" had been on a warm sunny day at the end of August. She had been seeing him for nearly three months by then, never ceasing to marvel at the fact that her father had permitted it. But her young American officer had indeed been both good and shrewd. Nothing less would have swayed Herbert Keller.

Royce had written a formal letter of introduction, apologizing that his family was not available to meet the Kellers. But he asked if he would be permitted to call, considering his very great respect for Anne-Marie.

The ploy had worked. Royce was accepted, and he was careful not to abuse the privileges Herbert Keller afforded. For several weeks he had come to call, bringing chocolates or some other little gift for the family.

After a time, he was permitted to take Anne-Marie into the village for coffee or an ice cream. But he always brought her home promptly and was unfailingly proper in her father's presence.

And while the father was being seduced in one fashion, the daughter was being seduced in another. Royce began his romance with Anne-Marie in a cautious, respectful manner, but his self-confidence and determination to win her were unfailing.

She was soon completely in his hands and wanting more of him than he would give. The seduction was a slow dance, Royce being careful to avoid any false step that might ruin everything.

She had told him almost from the beginning that she was a virgin, and he seemed to respect that. Perhaps it explained the slow pace at which he had progressed, though Anne-Marie always assumed his consideration was a product of his love. When they were alone he kissed her passionately, carefully nurturing her instinctive, womanly desires.

But by the end of the summer they both knew that their love had come to the point where it must be consummated. They loved each other insatiably. All that was lacking was the opportunity.

It was Anne-Marie who suggested that they sneak off for a picnic in the woods of the Taunus. At the end of August each year her grandmother went to Bad Schwalbach to visit her sister, leaving Anne-Marie at home. Between sessions at the institute, she would be alone at the house while her father was at work. She would never consider having Royce come to the house, but she told him she would go with him into the woods if he could manage to get leave.

With some effort the rendezvous was arranged, and they met at the park in Kronberg. It was midweek, a time when the woods would be relatively free of people. On the weekends the Taunus was teaming with hikers, nature-lovers, bicyclists, thousands of visitors from the cities and towns. But during the week it was practically deserted.

Still, they took a relatively unused trail and went deep into the woods, Royce carrying the lunch basket Anne-Marie had prepared. When they had walked a very long way from his car, they struck off through the trees, leaving the trail and a chance encounter with a hiker behind.

They finally came to a small glen carpeted with rich grass and wildflowers. There they spread out their blanket, which became their private little island. It was the first time they had been together with any real privacy, and Royce kissed her hungrily, sensing her unexpressed desire for him. But Anne-Marie was frightened, and he knew it would have to come slowly.

They had worn their swimsuits under their clothes so that they could get some sun, and as they removed their outerwear, Anne-Marie felt shy at being so close to naked in his presence. But she stretched out on the blanket with the summer sun beating down on her. Once she was on her stomach, she reached back to unfasten the top of her suit to avoid a tan line.

Royce sat silently beside her. She felt his eyes, knowing that he wanted her, knowing that they were alone and it could be done. After a while he leaned over and kissed her bare shoulder. She didn't open her eyes, but she enjoyed the fantasy.

Soon his fingers found her skin, and he lightly caressed her with sensual feathery strokes. His touch aroused her instantly, and she felt the place between her legs pulse eagerly. Still, she held her pose and let him continue to arouse her with his patient, loving touch.

It wasn't very long before her body ached for him, ached for that first penetration. But for the moment, with her eyes closed, it was just a fantasy—the dream of a girl turning into a woman. Only the delicate stroke of his fingers made this any different from the touch of the young officer she had so often fantasized about in her bed.

When the pulsing had become very strong and she felt herself moistening with desire, Anne-Marie moaned softly. In response Royce kissed the corner of her mouth, letting the tip of his tongue touch her lips. Then he took her by the shoulders and gently rolled her over so that she was on her back, looking into his smiling, irreverent face. Her breasts were naked, and he savored them for a long time, the prize finally won, finally within his grasp.

She reached up then and took his face into her hands. *"Ich liebe Dich,"* she whispered.

"And I love you." He dropped down to her waiting mouth, kissing her deeply, taking the firm ripeness of her breast into his hand.

Their lovemaking progressed rapidly. Desire swept over them. They kissed hungrily, their fingers sinking into flesh, their tongues foraging into each other's mouths. Anne-Marie's brain was burning with a blind, desperate yearning. She couldn't get enough of him. She wanted more. She wanted fulfillment.

Royce helped her remove the bottom of her suit, and she lay naked before him. Nothing could stop them. She had to know his love, know his body, submit completely.

And when he stripped away his suit, she looked at him, not frightened by his sex, because in Germany bodies were commonly seen, even by youthful eyes. But never had she seen a man aroused.

He lay down beside her, kissing her tenderly and caressing her body with care, not wanting to frighten her in the final stages. She felt her heart hammering in her chest, knowing the last moments of her innocence were upon her.

"I love you so much, Anne-Marie. I want us to be together always," he whispered. "Remember that. Above all, I love you."

And when he had raised her fever of desire higher than her fear, he lifted himself over her. Slowly, every so slowly, she opened her legs to him, knowing what she must do but still ignorant of the way it would feel. It could be painful, she knew, and, looking into his eyes, she bit her lip, moaning with dread when the tip of him first touched her.

But he lightly kissed her as he eased himself into her moist hollows. And when he came against her, he paused before pressing firmly into her, tearing her maidenhead. A little cry of pain came from her throat, but it was more from the expectation than from the actual sensation. The pang only lasted a few moments, then the wonder of it dominated all other awareness. She let herself open to him, and he took her deeply.

Chapter Ten

Anne-Marie was lingering in half sleep, dreams of Royce Buchanan blending quiescently with her memories of him. The gentle breeze had picked up, and the parched air, smelling of dry grass, oak and eucalyptus, flowed over her, lulling her, keeping her from wakefulness.

She was aware of voices off somewhere and vaguely cognizant of a presence before she felt someone sit down on the edge of her lounge chair. But it wasn't until a hand lightly touched her bare shoulder that she snapped into wakefulness.

"You're going to burn if you sleep in the sun for long."

It was Royce, the other one, the man with the big house, the pool and horses. She blinked up at him in the sunlight as she turned over, straightening the top to her suit. "Are you back already? I guess I dozed off."

"I hated to wake you. You looked so peaceful—blissful, even."

She smiled at him with embarrassment. "I guess I was dreaming."

He grinned mischievously. "It looked like a dream I'd like to be in."

She almost told him he was, but she didn't. Encouragement was the last thing he needed. Anne-Marie looked around. "Where are the girls?" Then she saw them coming from the direction of the stable. She waved, and they waved back. "Did you have a good ride?" she asked, looking up into the maturely handsome face above her.

"I think they enjoyed it."

She tilted her head in her distinctive manner. "But did you?"

"Sure. There's nothing like the exuberance of kids to make you feel good."

She searched his eyes for the melancholy she'd heard in his voice. "Do you miss your daughter?"

"You always miss them when they're not around."

"I know. I discovered that when Kurt went off to college."

They exchanged the smiles of common experience.

"Hey, Mom," Christianne called from the foot of the garden, "are you going swimming?"

"I hadn't planned on it."

"Oh, come on. Royce said he'd have a water fight with us. You can be on his team. Unless he starts winning. Then you have to be on ours."

Anne-Marie chuckled. "I'm not one for water fights. But I might get in to cool off."

The girls came around the pool.

"Did you have a good time?"

"Yeah, it was super," Christianne enthused.

Laura nodded her agreement. "Mr. Buchanan has really nice horses."

"We ran them and everything," Christianne said.

"Galloped," Laura corrected.

"Whatever."

"I think your suits are still in the car," Anne-Marie said. "Run around and get them if you want to swim."

"You can change in the guest room," Royce added as the girls took off.

Anne-Marie swung her legs off the lounge chair, and Royce got up, taking her hand and pulling her to her feet. They stood looking at each other for a moment before she turned and started up toward the house. He walked along beside her.

"I imagine Christianne and Laura will want something to drink after the long ride," he said. "How about you?"

"I'm a bit thirsty."

"I got soft drinks for the kids, but there's plenty else to choose from in the refrigerator. Lots of juices, and beer. I'm in the mood for a cool one, myself. Care to join me?"

"All right. I will."

They went into the house and to the kitchen. Anne-Marie leaned against the counter as Royce got their beers and opened them. He brought hers to her, glancing at her bikini-clad body.

"You know, you look terrific in a bathing suit. Better than ever."

"You still notice things like that?" she teased.

He laughed. "Hell, I'd have to be half-blind and senile not to notice. I'm not dead yet, Anne-Marie."

There was an intimacy in his tone. Much like that first day. She didn't respond, taking the beer he handed her.

"You know, when I came back from the stable and found you sleeping by the pool, it reminded me of another day."

She felt herself blush. "Please, Royce. Let's not talk about things like that."

He studied her. "I'm a problem for you, aren't I?"

She started to say something diplomatic, tactful, but decided the truth was better. "Actually, you are. Yes."

"Because of what happened the last time you were here?"

"Yes, but that's only part of it. That may even have been only symptomatic. The truth is, I'm at war with myself over you. Part of me wants to be around you, part of me doesn't. And I know that the part that doesn't is right."

"How do you know?"

"Experience."

"Ted versus Royce has become Don versus Royce."

"That's an oversimplification, but probably accurate."

"There's no way I can compete with Ted, but couldn't you be a little more open-minded when it comes to Don?"

"No, I've already made my decision. That's the point. I'm going to marry him."

"Mom? Royce?" It was Christianne.

He went to show the girls where the guest room was and returned a moment later.

"I probably should have used the guest room, too," Anne-Marie said when he was back, "but I changed in your bath. I hope you don't mind."

"No, of course not."

"I guess I just went to the familiar place."

He reached out and touched her cheek affectionately. "I'm grown-up now—I can take it better. But you know what makes this time worse than the last? You seem so close, and yet you're so far away."

She lowered her eyes.

"Do you think we can be friends?" he asked.

"I don't see how. Not friends who actually spend time together. But we don't have a Christmas-card kind of relationship, either, do we? And I don't see how it could become one."

Royce was staring at her mutely. He looked sad. "Well," he said after a while, "I guess I'd better go get into my suit, too. Excuse me."

When he'd gone she wandered out onto the patio, found a chair and sat looking out across the Santa Ynez Valley. After a few minutes the girls came out in their swimsuits. Christianne was still very thin, but womanly curves were beginning to show. Laura was much more developed. They each got a soft drink and came to join Anne-Marie.

"Guess what?" Christianne said. "I invited Royce to my eighth-grade graduation. I hope you don't mind, but he's been real nice, and Laura and I both like him."

Anne-Marie didn't care for the idea at all, but it was Christianne's privilege to invite whom she wished, within reason. And though she didn't like it, she couldn't really object to her daughter's friendship with Royce. "If you want him to come, and he's willing, I guess there's no reason he shouldn't."

"Super!"

Royce came out onto the patio in his trunks, one towel around his neck, several more in his hands.

"Guess what, Royce?" Christianne enthused. "Mom said you can come to my graduation if you want to."

"Great." He glanced at Anne-Marie. "She said I'd need your permission."

"I brought both my kids up to check with me on things."

"It won't be a problem for you if I go?"

Anne-Marie got up. "It's her graduation."

They walked down toward the pool. When they were several yards from the water, Royce handed the towels to Christianne, then ran and dove into the water. She handed the towels to her mother and, with a shriek of glee, dove in after him. Laura followed. The three of them immediately began a water fight. Anne-Marie put down the towels and quietly slipped into the water at the deep end of the pool.

As the fight continued, she swam back and forth, savoring the sensual coolness of the water. Their play amused her, and again she was glad for Christianne's sake that they had come. She wondered, though, how she would handle it if her daughter wished to pursue an active friendship with Royce.

"Mom, Mom!" Christianne shouted amid the splashing. "He's winning. Join our team. Help us dunk him!"

"You picked that fight. I didn't," she called back.

"Come on, Mrs. Osborne," Laura called. "Girls against the man!"

"When you grow up you'll learn a woman can keep her hair dry if she doesn't pick a fight with a man." She laughed to herself at the homespun wisdom.

The splashing abruptly stopped at the other end of the pool, and Christianne and Laura were standing in the water with surprised expressions on their faces. Royce had disappeared.

"Where is he?" Christianne shouted.

All of a sudden Anne-Marie felt something grab her ankles. It was as though a giant octopus had her. Before she knew it she was yanked under the water. She came gasping to the surface a moment later. Royce had his arms locked around her, pinning her so she couldn't move.

"You creep!" she sputtered.

"Lovely mermaids have their vulnerabilities, too," he said into her ear.

"Let go!"

"Hey, Mom," Christianne called to her, laughing, "what happened to your hair?"

Anne-Marie managed to elbow Royce in the stomach, breaking his grip. Seizing the opportunity, she swam to the ladder. She turned and faced the grinning man. "Villain!" she spat, then splashed him angrily.

He laughed as she climbed from the pool. She stood on the edge, her hands defiantly on her hips. "That was a dirty trick."

"Get them while they're unsuspecting. That's my motto."

"Yes, you've proved that. A couple of times."

He roared with laughter.

Seized with an urge for revenge, Anne-Marie leaped in his direction, pulling her knees to her chest to make a large splash. When she came to the surface he was nowhere in sight. Seeing him underwater, beneath her, she screamed and began swimming furiously toward the shallow end.

Royce surfaced and started after her. She could hear Christianne and Laura yelling with excitement as she swam desperately. But he caught her just before she reached the girls.

Grabbing her from behind, he wrapped his arms around her so that she couldn't move. "I've got a prisoner," he said to the girls. "What will you give me for her?"

"You mean, we've got to pay?" Christianne asked.

"You do if you ever want to eat again," Anne-Marie said emphatically.

Christianne put her finger to her cheek as Laura giggled. "This is a tough decision."

"Give him whatever he wants," Anne-Marie said, struggling helplessly to free herself.

"What's your price, Royce?"

"How about ice cream and cake for everyone?" he replied. "It's in the kitchen, if you girls want to go get it."

Their eyes rounded. "Is it okay, Mom?"

"Whatever will placate this sea monster."

"Yippie!" They scrambled from the pool.

"But none for me," Anne-Marie called after them.

Royce edged her toward the deeper water, still holding her firmly as the girls ran up the lawn toward the house. "What's the matter," he said softly into her ear, "afraid you'll lose your girlish figure?"

"You can let go of me now," she said, very aware of his body against her.

He kissed her neck. "I was just beginning to enjoy myself."

"You know how I feel. Let go of me." She made a halfhearted attempt to free herself, and he loosened his arms enough so that she could turn around.

She was facing him, but his hands were still on her waist. She looked at him through water-soaked lashes. "You and your games," she murmured.

He moved still closer. "Games can be a lot of fun."

His face was just inches from hers. She knew he was going to kiss her, and her lower lip dropped just as his mouth covered hers. As they kissed, he crushed her against his chest. She sank her nails into his back, kissing him as much as he kissed her. But then she slipped her hands between them and pushed him away.

"Okay," she said, avoiding his eyes, "we've had our fun. Now it's over." She turned and waded to the ladder at the edge of the pool.

"Anne-Marie!"

She turned.

"Are you sure?"

"I shouldn't have kissed you. It was a mistake." She went over to the stack of towels, took one, and began drying her hair.

On the drive back to Santa Barbara, Anne-Marie hardly said a word. Christianne and Laura were chattering like a couple of parakeets, but she tuned them out, brooding over Royce's kiss. They dropped Laura off and then drove toward home. For a while neither of them spoke.

"It was a fun day," Christianne finally said. "Thanks a lot for taking us."

"You're welcome, honey."

"Royce is really nice, isn't he?"

"Yes."

Christianne looked at her. "Is something wrong?"

"No, I was just thinking about Don, our wedding."

"Oh."

"Do you think you'll ever be as fond of him as you are of Royce?" Anne-Marie asked.

The girl looked at her strangely. "What do you mean?"

"Oh, nothing. I shouldn't have asked. I'm not trying to put pressure on you. Just forget it."

"Mom, what's bugging you?"

"Nothing I care to discuss."

Christianne fell silent, and Anne-Marie wondered if her daughter sensed the turmoil she was feeling. Not that it mattered. It wasn't the sort of thing a woman could easily discuss with her child. Especially considering how pleased Christianne would be. The girl had a crush of sorts on Royce herself.

Anne-Marie went to her room with the intent of regrouping emotionally. All she needed, she told herself, was a little quiet time to sort things out and get on an even keel. In the end her better judgment, her wisdom and experience, would prevail. But first she would have to contend with those girlish, romantic impulses that refused to die.

During recent years, when she felt distraught, Anne-Marie would turn her thoughts to Ted. He had always been a safe harbor for her. But somehow her memories weren't enough just then. Royce seemed to have co-opted even the past. She needed something more tangible, more direct.

In the back of her closet was a trunk of keepsakes she had saved through the years. At first it had served as a repository of things from her childhood and youth. In her early years in America it had been her link with Germany and the past. But as time went on, remembrances from her married life accumulated as well, and now the trunk also served as the archives of her marriage.

She went into the closet, pulled the trunk out and opened it. She sorted through photos and other mementos, touching the past even as she touched them. She looked at pictures of Ted, her eyes growing misty as she remembered the life they'd had together. Then she came to her wedding pictures, studying their faces carefully, trying to recall her emotions and thoughts that day.

She had been very, very happy. She remembered that. But there had also been a vague sadness, too. It had been quite remote, hardly conscious, but it had been there. She knew what it was now more clearly than at any time since that day. It was Royce Buchanan.

Though she had loved Ted—and nothing could take that away from her, nothing—she felt a little resentment toward Royce. He seemed to be robbing her of everything she held dear.

Brushing the thought aside, Anne-Marie delved farther into the trunk. Deep inside she found an old sketch pad from her days at the art institute in Frankfurt. Once Ted had come into her life, she had never done much else with her art, perhaps because, in some perverse way, she had associated it with Royce. She didn't know for sure.

Opening the pad, she flipped through her old drawings, looking at them as if seeing friends from long ago. Then she came to one that made her stop. It was Royce as a young army officer, staring at her from across the chasm of time.

Seeing the sketch, her eyes filled, remembering how desperately she had loved him then. At the time she'd drawn the picture, she wanted nothing more on earth than to be his wife. What irony. What terrible irony. A tear dropped onto the bottom corner of the paper, and she brushed it away.

There was a knock at her door. It was Christianne.

"Mom, do you want me to make dinner tonight?"

Anne-Marie looked at her watch. It was already seven-thirty. She was surprised it was so late. "Are you hungry?" she called to her through the door.

"Sort of. But that's not why I asked. I just thought I'd be helpful."

"That's sweet of you, honey."

"Can I come in?"

"If you want."

The door opened, and Christianne saw her sitting on the floor by her trunk.

"What are you doing?"

"Just looking at some old keepsakes."

The girl walked over and looked down at the sketch pad on Anne-Marie's lap.

"What's that?"

She held it up. "Who does this look like?"

"Sort of like Mr. Buchanan. Or maybe his son."

Anne-Marie laughed. "It's Royce."

"Did you do it?"

"Yes. A long time ago."

"It's pretty good. How come you're sitting here, looking at all this stuff?"

"I got to thinking about your father, so I pulled my trunk out to feel closer to him."

"Oh." Christianne was silent.

"And then I found this old sketch pad."

"It looks like something out of a museum."

"Thanks a lot."

The girl shrugged. "Are you going to show it to Royce?"

She shook her head. "I don't think so."

"He'd probably like to check it out. Has he ever seen it before?"

"I don't believe I showed it to him."

Christianne contemplated the drawing. "You must have been pretty good friends with him."

"I guess we were."

"Was he your boyfriend?"

"Yes. At one time we were quite fond of each other."

"I thought it was something like that."

Anne-Marie looked up at her. "You did?"

"Yeah. I can tell he still likes you."

"We're just friends now. He knows I'm going to marry Don."

"I bet he's not too happy about that."

"Why? What did he say?"

"Nothing."

"Are you sure?"

"Of course, Mom. I'd tell you if he did."

Anne-Marie closed the sketch pad and returned it to the trunk. "Well, that's all in the past."

Christianne sat on the bed while her mother put everything spread out on the floor back into the trunk and shut the lid.

"How come you don't love him now?"

She turned around and faced her daughter. "You know I'm going to marry Don. I have a life planned that doesn't include Royce Buchanan."

Her voice must have been harsher than she'd intended; Christianne became defensive.

"I was just asking." The girl got up and headed for the door. "Shall I try to make that fish casserole of yours, the one with the stuffing?"

"If you like. Go ahead and start it, anyway. I'll be down in a while."

When her daughter had gone, Anne-Marie pushed the trunk back into the closet, then returned to her bed to sit down. She thought. On an impulse she picked up the telephone and called Don. He and Tracy had just finished their supper.

"What's up?" he asked with his usual good-natured tone.

"I've been thinking," she said, "that it would be nice if we got together and had a . . . a romantic evening. Maybe an intimate dinner. Would you like that?"

"Sure. When were you thinking of?"

"How about tomorrow?"

"Yeah, that would be fine. I can make reservations at that French place down on Carrillo . . . what's the name of it? You know the one I mean."

"Chez Alberte."

"That's it. I'll make a reservation there."

"Maybe afterward we can come over here for a nightcap. Normally I don't encourage Christianne to sleep over at a friend's on a school night, but this is the last week before summer vacation. Maybe I can get her to arrange something."

Don chuckled. "Sounds good. What's gotten into you?"

"I guess I just feel the need to be close to you."

"Tracy and I were talking about Carole at dinner tonight, and it got me to thinking about you, Anne-Marie. It's been a while. It would be nice. Shall I pick you up at about seven?"

"Yes," Anne-Marie replied, but she was glad he couldn't see her face.

* * *

They pulled up in front of Anne-Marie's house, and Don turned off the car engine. She took his hand.

"Want to come in?"

"No, thanks. I'll just go on home."

"I'm sorry I didn't manage to get Christianne farmed out for the evening. But when she came home with cramps, I didn't have the heart to push her out of the house."

"I understand. If it'd been Tracy, I'd have done the same."

"We're hampered by our children as much as we're blessed by them, aren't we?"

"That'll all change once we're married."

Anne-Marie sat silently holding his hand, thinking. He could have suggested they go to a motel—or she could have, for that matter—but she knew he'd have felt uncomfortable. It just wasn't Don's style. He'd have worried who might have seen them or recognized his car.

Of course, they could have driven out of town a way, down to Ventura, for example. But she'd have had to come back that night because of Christianne, and it just wasn't worth the hassle. And sex wasn't what had motivated the evening, anyway. She had simply wanted to feel close to Don, to distance herself from Royce.

"The walk along the beach was nice, Don. Thanks for taking me."

"It was fun. I enjoyed myself. You know, it's been ages since I've been there at night. I think Carole and I took Tracy down there one Fourth of July to see the fireworks, but that has to have been ten years ago."

"But this was sort of romantic, don't you think?"

"Yeah. Except for the wind, it was real nice." He chuckled. "We scared those two kids on the blanket, though, didn't we?"

"Maybe we did their parents a favor," she said ironically.

They both were silent.

"We could plan a weekend away," he said, "go someplace where we're not known. Like we did after the first of the year, before the tax season got into full swing."

"I'd like that, Don."

"Let's plan it, then. What the heck." He thought. "Let's see, this coming weekend's out. I've got that golf tournament. The whole firm's playing. I couldn't really duck out at this stage."

"Oh, don't worry about it," she said a bit caustically. "There'll be plenty of other opportunities."

"How about the weekend following?"

She forced a tight smile. "That might be all right. Let's talk about it next week, shall we?"

A frown creased his brow. "You aren't mad, are you?"

"No." Anne-Marie sighed. "A little disappointed, maybe. But we've a whole lifetime ahead of us."

"Or half, anyway."

"Yes, half anyway." She reached for the door handle.

Don stopped her. "I'm sorry, Anne-Marie. And I'm sorry we couldn't be together tonight." He took her jaw in his hand and leaned over and kissed her firmly on the mouth.

She kissed him back, but there just wasn't any feeling. It was her mood. She'd let what began as a pleasant evening get off track. When the kiss ended, she patted his cheek. "Thanks for the lovely evening."

"I'll walk you up."

"No, that's not necessary." She scooted to the door and opened it, slipping out. Closing it, she leaned in the open window and smiled at him. "Give me a call if you have a slow time at the office."

"Oh, by the way. That reminds me. Your friend Royce is coming in tomorrow morning to talk investments. If it goes well, I was thinking of inviting him to lunch. If you're free, would you like to join us?"

"No," she said, stepping back from the car. "I don't care if I never see Royce Buchanan again."

She spun and walked quickly toward the house. She knew that Don must be looking after her with a dumbfounded expression on his face, but she didn't care. She didn't care about him just then, or Royce Buchanan either, for that matter. She was fed up. She'd just about had it with men.

There were only a few dozen people in the auditorium when Royce arrived. He made his way to the front of the hall and sat in the second row, on the aisle. He looked at the others scattered around and saw that Anne-Marie wasn't among them. Perhaps it would be nice to save her a seat, though he wasn't sure she would want to be near him. But figuring that Don Nelson would probably be with her, he decided to save two seats, in hopes that might help.

Gradually the auditorium began filling, and Royce could feel the excitement in the air that special events produced. Girls and boys in their best clothes were scurrying back and forth between family, gathered in the large hall, and their classmates, who were assembling somewhere outside. A teacher began testing the audio system at the edge of the stage, and a middle-aged woman arranged sheet music on a piano sitting off to the side.

Royce watched for Christianne, as well as for Anne-Marie and Don. The seats were being snatched up around him, and he hoped they would see him. He glanced at the program he had been given at the door and found Christianne Osborne's name.

She was a sweet kid, and he was glad he'd had a chance to get to know her. They shared a certain rapport, and that made it more pleasant, though he suspected their friendship was a problem for Anne-Marie. He knew he had to be careful not to let it turn Anne-Marie's feelings into resentment.

The past week had been a difficult one. Royce was sure that Anne-Marie was deceiving herself, and it frustrated him. Even worse, she was fighting her feelings by forcing a commitment to Don. Under normal circumstances time might open her eyes, but she carried a lot of baggage from the past, and she was hurrying the present.

In fact, it might be the past that was the problem. Royce suspected it was Ted Osborne she was struggling with. And he knew he couldn't easily fight her dead husband. He worried that in death, the man was invincible.

She was so sure of what she needed and wanted in a husband. The past, her fears and self-delusions made that man Don. How could he convince her that she was wrong?

As he mulled over his dilemma, Royce spotted Christianne with her friend, Laura. Waving, he caught her eye. She came running over to where he sat.

"You came!"

"Wouldn't miss it for anything." He pointed to the empty chairs beside him. "I saved some seats for your mom. Is she sitting in back?"

"No, I don't think they're here yet. She and Don dropped me off in front because we were a little late. Then they went to park."

"Well, if you see them, tell them I've saved them the best seats in the house."

She beamed appreciatively. "They'll be here any minute. I'll tell them."

Royce watched her run off. About the time she reached the back of the auditorium, he saw Anne-Marie and Don appear at the entrance. Christianne was obviously explaining the situation, making his case for him, as it were, so he turned around and stared ahead, waiting to see if they'd join him.

In a minute or so, they came walking up, Anne-Marie looking beautiful in a white raw silk suit. Don was grinning broadly. She looked a little put upon but not really angry.

"I got here early because of the drive," he explained, shaking Don's hand, "so I thought I'd save you two some seats."

"Hey, really thoughtful of you," Don replied. "Thanks a lot."

"Hello, Royce," Anne-Marie said, extending her hand.

He would have liked to kiss her she looked so pretty, but he stopped at a smile and a handshake. They sat down in the folding chairs, Anne-Marie between him and Don.

The last of the crowd was still arriving, but it was evident from the commotion that the ceremony would be getting under way soon. Don leaned forward, pulling a large envelope from the inside pocket of his suit coat.

"I wasn't sure if we'd be seeing you, Royce, but I brought along some summary sheets of various limited partnerships offered by our clients in the development business. I thought if any of them appealed, I could send along a prospectus or have the principals get in touch with you."

"Thanks, Don," he said, taking the envelope. "These are the ones you were telling me about on Tuesday, I take it."

"Yeah. And some extras I hadn't thought of."

Royce stuck the envelope into his pocket. "Thanks again. I'll look them over." He winked at Anne-Marie, who was watching him out of the corner of her eye. "How are you feeling, Mom? Ready for a daughter in high school?"

"Heavens, I don't know. Kurt wasn't much of a problem, but I understand girls are worse."

"I didn't have a son to make the comparison. There were some sticky times with Sybil, but I didn't see her on a day-to-day basis at the end. Ellen and I were divorced her senior year."

"You haven't talked much about your former wife."

"Not one of my favorite subjects."

Don had turned around and was chatting to a man sitting in the row behind them. Judging by the conversation, they were acquainted professionally.

Royce leaned toward Anne-Marie, speaking in a low tone. "You look beautiful this evening."

"Thank you."

"Really beautiful. Sort of reminds me of the way you looked in your wedding pictures."

"When did you…oh, yes…my father showed them to you."

"One of the most painful experiences of my life."

"You weren't in class this afternoon," she said, quickly changing the subject.

"Did you miss me?"

"I noticed you weren't there."

"I guess I am sort of conspicuous, being the only man."

"Yes."

"Actually, I've decided to drop out."

"Oh? Why?"

"No offense, but I've gotten the feeling you'd prefer to see less of me, rather than more."

"I suppose that's true. But you did pay for six weeks."

"I've gotten my money's worth. My back is a lot better. I'm doing a steady six to eight miles a day on the road now."

She looked at him. "I've thought about what you said…about how you got started running. Was it really true?"

"Yes."

"Then you *were* upset when you returned to Germany and discovered I was married?"

The pianist at the front of the auditorium began playing, bringing the crowd to silence. Royce leaned closer for a final word. "I haven't recovered yet."

Chapter Eleven

Anne-Marie stood by Don in the pleasant sunshine outside the auditorium. Royce was opposite them, his hands casually in his pockets. He seemed at ease, yet under the surface she sensed a latent energy, like that of a cat waiting to pounce. She eased closer to Don, who was enthusiastically describing a business park in Ventura.

Royce was listening politely, but his eyes slid to hers from time to time. When the industrial park discussion had pretty well run its course, Royce adroitly changed the subject from business to pleasure.

"What do you two do for fun? You know, what do you like to do together?" he asked innocently.

Don looked at her. "We've got our kids, of course," he said. "The quiet family stuff."

"Yes, but I mean just the two of you. The interests you share."

Anne-Marie saw that Royce was trying to make a point of some sort, subtly needle her perhaps, and she didn't appreciate it. "Don and I both are into community affairs, charity work, that sort of thing."

"Yeah, that's right," Don added. "There's the United Way dinner dance at the country club next weekend, for example. Of course, we aren't doing much this year but going to it."

"Don was co-chairman of the committee last year," she added.

"What a pain that was," he said with a laugh.

"I admire that," Royce said. "Maybe I can find a way to contribute to some of the local things."

"Hey, there are plenty of service clubs that'd be thrilled to have you aboard," Don said. "Just give me the word if you'd like to visit the Lions. We have a very active chapter."

"I might do that."

Christianne came running up, a big smile on her face. "Well, junior high is history!"

They all laughed.

"You looked really nice," Anne-Marie said, putting her arm around the girl.

Christianne beamed up at Royce.

"I liked the way you took that diploma and shook the principal's hand," he said. "Real snappy."

She blushed.

"You did well," Don added.

Anne-Marie stroked the girl's red cheeks with the backs of her fingers.

"Well," Don said, rubbing his hands together, "who's hungry?" He looked at Royce. "We're all going out for a special graduation lunch. Would you care to join us?"

"Thanks, Don, but I think I'll pass. I've got some things I've got to do out at the ranch."

"Oh, can't you come?" Christianne said with disappointment.

"I'd like to, sweetheart, but I really can't." He glanced at Anne-Marie, who knew he was turning down the invitation because of her.

She felt bad for her daughter, though on balance she was relieved. She didn't feel up to sitting through lunch with the two men. Christianne looked at her.

"Tell him to come, Mom."

"I'm sure he would if he could, honey."

Royce glanced at his watch. "I'm running late as it is." Reaching into his pocket, he pulled out a small box tied with a large pink ribbon. "I got you a little graduation present," he said to Christianne. "Hope you like it."

Her eyes rounded. "Oh, thank you!"

Anne-Marie was touched by the gesture.

"Can I open it now?"

"Sure, if you like."

The girl removed the ribbon and lifted the lid. Inside was a heart locket on a gold chain. "Oh, it's beautiful!" she exclaimed. "I'll wear it on the plane."

"That's right, your big trip to Germany is coming up, isn't it?"

"She leaves Friday," Anne-Marie said.

Christianne was fingering the locket. "Thank you so much."

He reached out and took her by the shoulders. "You were a super graduate, kiddo. The prettiest girl by far."

She blushed again, and he leaned forward to kiss her on the cheek.

"I won't be seeing you before you leave, so have a wonderful trip."

"Thank you."

Royce turned to Don and shook his hand. "Good seeing you. I'll be in touch." Then he looked at Anne-Marie. "Guess you'll be having a mini-vacation yourself with all the chicks out of the nest."

She nodded.

He reached out and squeezed her arm. "Take care." Saluting them all, he turned and walked away.

Anne-Marie watched him go, feeling empty and strangely emotional. When she looked at Christianne, she saw that the girl had been watching her. "Well," Anne-Marie said, "I'm getting hungry. How about that graduation lunch?"

The week was a curious combination of excitement, anxiety and melancholy. Christianne was running around the house, seemingly two feet off the ground, getting more and more agitated as Friday approached. She had packed, unpacked and repacked a dozen times. Whenever Anne-Marie was in the house, Christianne insisted that she speak German, though there wasn't enough time to do much good.

When both her children were little, Anne-Marie had spoken German with them from time to time, but once they were in school, neither of them had cared to pursue it. Still, Christianne had a base to work from, and once she was in Europe the language would come more easily because of her childhood experience.

Anne-Marie herself derived a certain amount of vicarious pleasure from Christianne's excitement. Yet when she was alone, she found herself thinking about Royce more often than not. Her attraction to him as a man—and not just physically—was undeniable. But that didn't trouble her nearly as much as what she was beginning to see as a deficiency in her relationship with Don.

She'd never had any illusions, but in the past she had always regarded Don's shortcomings as inconsequential. Now, alongside Royce, they seemed to stick out more. And the funny thing was, both men seemed equally to blame for the uncertainty she felt about her engagement.

In addition to her annoyance and frustration, Anne-Marie also had an underlying feeling of sadness. Royce hadn't said they would never see each other again, but he had quit her yoga class, and he'd declined Don's invitation to join them for lunch. He hadn't called, and there seemed to be no immediate reason that he would. The uncertainty of it made her want to see him all the more. Doubtless he'd planned it that way. But if that was true, how long would it be before he made some sort of move?

Don, ever the organizer, had raised the question of setting a date for their wedding, and Anne-Marie had put him off for a while longer. The hypocrisy of moving ahead was just too difficult now that she seemed to be struggling to justify marrying at all.

Reason told her that things with Don would fall into place once she'd thoroughly discredited her feelings for Royce or he dropped from the scene. But it seemed as if nothing would progress until she'd dealt with Royce definitively.

On Wednesday she drove Christianne down to Los Angeles for some last-minute shopping and also to look for something to wear to the United Way dinner dance on Saturday. She had several dresses in her closet to choose from, but she had a frivolous urge to find something new and exciting.

One of the more exclusive boutiques in Westwood had a sale on evening wear. Anne-Marie saw a woman's tuxedo, and, on a whim, she tried it on. Christianne stood behind her as she looked at herself in the mirror.

"Hey, rad, Mom. You look super!"

"But it's not very Santa Barbara. Especially not for a charity dinner dance at the country club." Still, the outfit appealed to her sense of whimsy. "Don would just die if I wore this, wouldn't he?"

"Who cares?"

"I do. I wouldn't want to embarrass him."

"I thought you always told me women dress for other women."

"And themselves. That's true."

"Oh, get it, Mom. You'd look really cute."

And so she did, enjoying the freedom of being impetuous.

Kurt called Thursday night from school to tell Christianne goodbye. They talked for quite a while, which pleased Anne-Marie. Then she got on the phone herself.

"Finally going to get a little piece of mind, huh, Mom?"

"It'll be lonely around here. This will be the first time in my whole life I've spent more than a few days alone."

"Builds character." He laughed.

"How are finals coming?"

"I started studying early this year for a change, so I'm in pretty good shape. Another ten days and it will be all over."

"I'm proud of you, Kurt. Keep up the good work." Anne-Marie hung up with a sigh, turning her attention back to the ball of energy at her side.

Christianne clapped her hands excitedly. "Fourteen hours and twenty-three minutes! I can hardly wait!"

Anne-Marie gave her daughter a big hug.

There was a direct flight from Los Angeles to Frankfurt. She drove Christianne down to L.A.X. alone. Don had said he'd go with her if he could reschedule a meeting, but it turned out he was unable to.

In the last minutes before Christianne went through security and out to the gate, Anne-Marie started having misgivings about sending her on such an adventure alone. But it was too late to stop now. Besides, her cousin Kirsten was a very conscientious person and had been looking forward to the girl's visit for nearly a year.

They embraced a final time, and Anne-Marie watched her daughter until she was out of sight. On the drive back to Santa Barbara, she felt a little sad and tried to raise her spirits by thinking about the dance the next evening.

She knew that things were slowing moving toward the moment of truth with Don. Before long she would have to stop procrastinating and make some hard decisions. And something told her the dance would be pivotal.

In a way, she was almost sorry she had bought the tuxedo. Deep down she knew he wouldn't like it, and that wouldn't help matters. She probably owed it to him not to shock him if she could help it. She decided to call him in the morning and tell him what she'd be wearing.

By the time Don was due to pick her up the next evening, Anne-Marie was pretty nervous. He had been a little surprised when she told him about the tuxedo.

"I guess that means I shouldn't get you a corsage," he'd said lamely.

"No," she'd replied, "but maybe a boutonniere."

He hadn't seen the humor in it.

Watching out the window, she saw his Buick pull up in front. She ran to the hall mirror for a final look, hoping that what she saw would give her courage. She really did look great, but that hardly seemed to matter.

For a long time she had debated over wearing her hair up or down. In the end she had decided on a compromise: she'd swept the sides back and secured them with rhinestone barrettes that matched her bow tie, letting the back hang down and curve under.

Her lipstick and nail polish were soft coral, and she'd worn a bit more eye makeup than usual, so there wouldn't be any doubt about her femininity. She straightened her tie as the doorbell rang, then rushed to pull the door open.

Don took her in with a long, curious look. "It's not so bad. You look pretty nice." He managed a smile.

"Not a total bomb, then."

"No, actually, you look real good."

At least he was trying. She was grateful for that. Don extended a small box.

"Your boutonniere."

"You didn't really have to get me one, Don. I was only kidding."

"You don't have to wear it."

Anne-Marie lifted the lid. It was a small red rosebud with a little baby's breath. "It's beautiful."

"I explained to the girl in the florist shop. She said this would probably be best, so I went with it."

She reached up and gave him a kiss. "Thanks."

He beamed, and she felt a little better.

"Ready to go?" he said. "Got your purse?"

"Hey, what do you think I am, a sissy? I've got pockets, buster."

Don gave her an embarrassed smile. "This is certainly going to be a different experience."

Once they arrived, Anne-Marie got lots of attention—some of it amused, some critical, but most of it positive. Don was obviously uncomfortable with the situation, and she was sorry about that.

They spent most of the cocktail hour accepting comments on her outfit. Arnold Bletkoff, this year's dance chairman, a heavyset, gregarious man who was the principal stockholder in Santa Barbara's largest independent bank, pinched Anne-Marie's cheek.

"Let me warn you right now, young fellow," he said, "don't go asking my wife for a dance this evening." He roared with laughter.

Anne-Marie saw Don flush. But it was too late now to be a shrinking violet. "I won't ask Rosemary to dance," she rejoined, "but you can't make me promise not to ask you!"

He roared again. "You've got a deal." He reached inside his pocket and pulled out an envelope. "Shall I put you down on my dance card right now?"

"It looks so empty," she replied with a wink, "I'll take my chances and wait for a rumba."

"And I bet you will, too!"

Soon they went into the dining room. Since Don was on the board as past chairman, they were seated at one of the three head tables. Don sat on one side of her, one of the city council members, a local attorney, on the other.

The guests were filing in to find places at the round tables spread around the room, and Don and the councilman were having a conversation across her. Anne-Marie was staring out at the throng, watching the last few people come in from the bar. Then she was startled to see a familiar face leap into her awareness. It was Royce Buchanan.

She watched him move slowly across the room, looking for a place to sit. He was chatting with a man Anne-Marie didn't recognize, but she decided he was alone when they bid each other goodbye and parted.

As Royce moved generally in her direction, looking for an empty place, she noticed his stylish, double-breasted tuxedo. He looked handsome and sophisticated. She felt her heart pick up at the sight of him.

Finally he settled down at a table about two away from hers. He hadn't noticed her, or at least he hadn't looked her way. Why was he here? she wondered. And how had he gotten in? The tickets had been sold out for more than a month. Perhaps he'd bought one a long time ago. But why hadn't he mentioned it when the subject had come up at Christianne's graduation?

At any rate, she was glad he had come to the dance. Was he here because of her? she wondered.

After a few minutes Arnold Bletkoff got up from his seat at the adjoining table and went to the microphone.

"Could I please have your attention, ladies and gentlemen," he said. "While they're starting to serve the salads, let me just make a few announcements. We're here to have a good time this evening, and I hope that you all do, but we can't forget that the real purpose of this gala event is to raise money for the United Way of Santa Barbara.''

There was applause, and Arnold raised his hands. Anne-Marie glanced at Royce, but he was attentively listening to the speaker.

''So that you can all feel good about yourselves, I thought you ought to know that we expect this dinner dance to net forty-five thousand dollars for the United Way.''

People gasped, and there was more applause.

''That's considerably more than a previous years, and I'd like to say it was because of the skill and hard work of this year's chairman.''

Laughter.

''However, the financial success of this evening is due to the personal generosity of one of our number here this evening. I was approached by a newcomer to our community who wanted to make a special contribution in the amount of ten thousand dollars.''

Whistles and applause. Anne-Marie glanced at Royce, but he still hadn't seen her.

''The donor asked to remain anonymous, so I can't give him public credit for his generosity. The curious among you will have to sleuth it out.'' Arnold thrust his thumbs under his suspenders. ''If nothing else,'' he continued with a laugh, ''it goes to show what a hot ticket the annual United Way dinner dance is!''

There was applause and laughter.

''Well,'' Arnold said, ''you want to eat, not listen to me talk, but I do have to acknowledge all the hard work of our committee members for this year's event. So let me just ask you to show your appreciation to the following people....''

''Ten thousand,'' Don said under his breath, leaning toward Anne-Marie. ''I wonder who it is?''

She looked at Royce, who was listening to the speaker. ''I don't know.''

''Obviously somebody with lots of room on his return for a juicy charitable contribution,'' Don said.

Anne-Marie was still looking at Royce, sure it was he.

At the microphone Arnold had finished acknowledging the committee members. "And one final note of caution to you fellows out there," he said. "When the dancing starts later, if a pretty little fellow with dark hair and orange lipstick gets frisky with you, don't panic. It's not a guy, it's Anne-Marie Osborne!"

Everybody laughed, and Anne-Marie felt herself turning scarlet. People started looking her way.

"Where is she?" somebody in the crowd shouted. "Where is she?" someone else echoed.

"Come on, Anne-Marie," Arnold said. "Take a bow."

She stood up and bowed deeply to the whistles and applause.

"How about a dance?" somebody called out.

"I think there'll be a long line," Arnold said. "Isn't she beautiful?"

Everyone applauded as she bowed again and sat down. Through the crowd her eyes met Royce's. There was a quiet smile of admiration on his face. The people at her table made idle comments, and Anne-Marie glanced at Don, who looked embarrassed.

"Sorry," she said out of the corner of her mouth. "I wouldn't blame you if you took me home after dinner."

"I don't know whether I should take you home or syndicate you." He laughed gamely.

Anne-Marie patted his hand. But off through the crowd she could feel Royce's eyes.

During dinner they exchanged looks a few times, but other than smiling at her, Royce did nothing special. Anne-Marie wondered if he would ask her to dance.

When the crowd finally made its way to the dance floor, she found herself looking for Royce. She began worrying that he might have left. Then, on her way to the powder room later in the evening, she saw him in the bar talking with a couple of men.

On her return several minutes later, he was still there. She paused, wondering whether she should go over and say hello. But then he turned and saw her. She waved, and he excused himself and walked slowly toward her, taking in her outfit as he approached.

"Stunning," he said simply.

"Do you really like it? I hadn't realized what a sensation I'd cause."

"Seeing you in this, I fell in love all over again." He smiled at her wryly. "And just when I was beginning to get over you."

She tilted her head to the side. "Really?"

He chuckled. "Really, what? That I've fallen in love with you, or that I'd gotten over you?"

"Both."

"The first is fact, the second sheer hyperbole."

She smiled with embarrassment. "Why didn't you say you were coming?"

"I didn't know until a few days ago."

"You're the mysterious donor."

"The chairman was right. It's a tough ticket. Bigger than the Super Bowl."

"It was a very generous donation, Royce."

"It's a good cause, and I thought it was important to check this dance out. Next year, I might even want to bring you."

She looked down at her patent leather shoes. "Next year at this time I'll probably be married."

"I like that word, *probably*."

"You know what I mean."

"Don's a lucky man. Does he know how lucky?"

"I think so. We understand each other."

"Is he letting you dance with other men?"

She gave a little laugh. "He was talking about syndicating me after what Arnold said."

"That sounds like something Don would think of."

She gave him a dark look. "He was only kidding."

"So was I. Come on," he said, taking her arm, "let's see if he'd mind if you danced with an old friend of the family for free."

"I think you've already made your contribution, Royce."

They found Don where Anne-Marie had left him. He was talking with some people at an adjoining table. Seeing her approach with Royce, he stood up.

"Royce Buchanan! What a surprise."

They shook hands.

"I understand it's de rigueur to dance with Anne-Marie this evening. Would you mind, Don?"

"Not at all. I'm not much of a dancer, so she might as well have fun."

Royce ushered her onto the floor, slipping his arm around her and pressing her firmly against him. She let herself melt into his arms, surprised how easily and quickly it happened, and how natural it felt. The music was slow, and the gentle swaying of their bodies made her highly aware of him. She inhaled the richness of his cologne, remembering.

"For two cents I'd waltz you right out the door and take you home with me," he whispered into her ear.

"Two cents?"

"Maybe I'd do it for free."

"You'd need my cooperation."

"Wouldn't I have it?"

She laughed. "I've made enough of a spectacle of myself this evening." She glanced around at the other couples. "I think we're dancing too close."

"If they knew what this had cost me, they wouldn't begrudge it."

"That's why you really came? To dance with me?"

"I came because I had to. And once here, I had to see you, dance with you."

"That's very flattering, but I'm not sure it's very a healthy attitude."

When the music ended Anne-Marie started back toward the table, but Royce restrained her.

"One more dance," he said.

She hesitated, then stayed with him. The next tune began, another slow piece, and Royce took her into his arms again. They danced in silence for a while. Images of him kissing her in his swimming pool, making love to her in his bed, kept popping into her mind. And though she felt torn, Anne-Marie knew that there was really nothing in the world she wanted more than to be in his arms.

"You don't really sleep with that guy, do you?" he said after a while.

She pulled back and looked up at him, shocked. "What?"

"I said, you—"

"I heard what you said. What do you mean?"

"I mean you don't really sleep with Don, do you?"

"What kind of a question is that?"

"A serious one."

"Well, it's completely out of line." She stiffened and pulled away from him.

"I don't mean to insult anyone. I just want to know what kind of a relationship you have. That's all."

She looked around, keeping her voice down. "Did it ever occur to you that it's none of your business?"

"I know that. It's just that I don't buy this engagement of yours, Anne-Marie. Don's a nice guy and all that, but you're no more meant for him than the man in the moon."

She looked up at him, her eyes flashing. "Frankly, Royce, I don't give a damn what you think."

"Listen, I'm not trying to pick a fight. I'm trying to open your eyes."

She shook her head. "What gall," she said under her breath.

"All right, so I have no right. But I love you, and I can't stand to see you deluding yourself."

"Deluding myself? I happen to know Don Nelson a whole lot better than I know you. It's no accident I'm engaged to him."

"Can you honestly say that would be true if I'd been on the scene first?"

"What do you think I am?" Her voice had risen, and heads turned their way. She lowered her voice. "This is not first come, first serve."

"That's not what I'm saying. I think you're trying to convince yourself that you should marry Don, when it's really me you love. But you're either too blind or too pigheaded to see it."

She let go of him and moved a step away. "I can't believe you have the nerve to actually say that to me."

"I say it because I believe it. And I think you know I'm right."

"Well, Mr. Buchanan," she snapped, "you've got a real surprise coming. I'm afraid you're not going to get your money's worth tonight!" With that she turned and stomped away toward where her fiancé sat waiting.

When she sat down next to Don, Anne-Marie was still so furious that she hadn't managed to conceal her anger.

Don noticed and turned to her. "What's the matter?"

"Nothing."

"Where's Royce?"

"I don't know, and I don't care."

"Did something happen, Anne-Marie?"

"What does it look like?" she snapped.

Don blinked, taken aback.

"I'm sorry," she said, touching his hand. "I didn't mean to be curt. It's just that Royce Buchanan annoys me sometimes."

"Royce? I don't find him abrasive at all."

"Oh, Don, don't be so damned naive."

"Naive about what?"

"Nothing. Just forget it. I let people get to me sometimes when I shouldn't. I'll be over it in a minute."

"Over what? What did he do?"

"He's just arrogant, and it annoys me."

"Being arrogant's no crime, is it?"

Anne-Marie looked at Don crossly. "Why are you defending him?"

"I'm not, really. He's a prospective client, and I wouldn't want any hard feelings if it could be avoided."

She was so irritated she had all she could do to keep from asking Don what he'd think if she told him she'd gone to bed with Royce a few weeks ago. But her better judgment took control.

Just then somebody walked up beside her. Looking up, she saw Arnold Bletkoff.

"You're such a popular partner this evening," he said effusively, "even the chairman has had to wait in line." He looked at Don. "Could I avail myself, old buddy?"

"Sure, Arnie. Just don't step on her toes."

Both men laughed, and Anne-Marie got up to fox-trot, almost hating Don as much as Royce. As she followed Arnold onto the floor, she had a glimpse through the arched entry of Royce leaving the club. She was glad to see him go, though for some reason she felt as much contempt for herself as she did for him.

Chapter Twelve

During the ride home from the club, Don chatted away until he seemed to sense something was wrong. Then he let the conversation lag. Anne-Marie felt almost sick about the way her feelings for him were deteriorating. It was Royce's fault, but hers, as well. They both were to blame.

But amid her anger, something Royce had said on the dance floor kept coming back to her. He'd admitted that he loved her. He'd almost tossed it off, and at the time she hadn't focused on it. But for the past hour the words had been ringing in her ears. Did he mean it?

Once she'd cooled down a bit, Anne-Marie started mulling over the implications. Royce had angered her practically every time she'd seen him, because he had effectively put her at war with herself. And poor Don was the innocent victim.

But as good-hearted and naive as her fiancé was, Anne-Marie knew that he had to be aware at some level that something was wrong. They'd never discussed it, and she wondered if the time hadn't come. The trouble was, she didn't feel up to it just then. She wanted to be alone.

They arrived at her house, and Don parked the car.

"We didn't get away for a weekend as we'd planned," he said before she could speak, "but maybe now that Christianne's gone it doesn't matter."

He was angling for an invitation to spend the night, and she groaned inwardly. "Don," she said, deciding to face the issue head-on, "I know that you'd like for me to ask you in, but to tell you the honest truth, I'm not in the mood."

He seemed a bit dumbfounded by her directness. "Well . . . I understand."

"No, I don't believe you do."

"People aren't always in the mood."

She almost said, *Don't you see I don't even know whether I want to marry you anymore?* But she lost heart. She couldn't devastate him that way, not out of the blue. She lowered her eyes, uncertain how to handle the situation.

"Don't worry, Anne-Marie. I understand."

"Oh, Don," she said, shaking her head sadly, "why do you have to be so damn sweet? Sometimes it makes me feel just awful."

"That's the first time I've had that complaint."

"I'm not complaining. But I have trouble believing I deserve your patience, your understanding, your goodness."

"That's pretty dumb."

She nodded. "Maybe."

"I hope you had a good time," he said quietly.

"Oh . . ."

He gave a strained laugh. "Your tux turned out to be pretty popular."

"Did I scandalize you too much?"

"No. After a while it was all right."

She took his hand and squeezed it. "Thanks for the evening. Sorry about the way I'm feeling." She started to open the door.

"I'll walk you up."

He got out, and she didn't protest. She waited until he came around the car and helped her out. They walked up to the house and slowly climbed the steps. Anne-Marie felt older than she had in a long time.

At the door he took her hands. "Whatever it is, give it time," he said.

She looked into his eyes. "You know, I don't think I've ever felt the loss of Ted and Carole more than I do right now. I don't mean that as an indictment of either of us. I just feel like we're floundering, maybe kidding ourselves."

Don shook his head. "No, you're forgetting time. Time heals."

"Time heals, but history has a way of repeating itself, too."

He looked at her uncertainly, though he didn't ask what she meant. Anne-Marie rose up on her toes and kissed him lightly. "Thank you," she whispered. She fished her house key out of her pocket and let herself in.

She listened to Don's footsteps as he descended the stairs. Somehow she knew that their engagement was dead, despite his comment about the healing effects of time. And she wondered if, at some level, he didn't understand it, too.

As she dropped into a chair, she heard the Buick start, then pull away. The house was dark and empty. With Christianne gone, she was all alone. Except for a few times when Ted had gone on a business trip before Kurt was born, she had never really been by herself. Now, at least for the summer, with Kurt's over-active schedule, essentially there would be no one around.

As she sat dejected and dispirited, she heard the sound of footsteps coming up the front stairs. For a moment she wondered if Don had come back, but she hadn't heard his car again. She got up just as the shadow of a man passed across the curtains. Her heart began to beat heavily.

The doorbell sounded, bringing a modicum of relief. Surely a burglar wouldn't ring the bell. She went to the door. Still uncertain, she slipped on the safety chain before opening the door a crack. To her surprise, she saw Royce's face in the shadows.

"Hello," he said. "Can we talk?"

She hesitated, then closed the door enough to remove the chain.

"What are you doing here?" she asked.

"I came to talk."

"What makes you think I'm interested?"

"I was just hoping you would be."

She studied his face in the darkness, trying to decide what his motive could be. As she stared, she remembered again him saying he loved her. "How did you know I was home? And that I was alone?"

"I waited for you."

"You were hiding in the bushes?"

A slight smile crossed his face. "Not quite. I was across the street. I parked a few doors up."

She stepped back to admit him, shaking her head as she turned away. "What is it that's reduced us all to behaving like children?"

Royce entered and closed the door. "I could give you the answer to that, but you wouldn't like it."

She turned on a table lamp and dropped into an easy chair, glancing up at his solemn, handsome face. He went to Ted's chair, next to her. She looked at him wearily. "What is it you came to talk about?"

"I'm sorry if I hurt you by what I said this evening. That wasn't my intention. But I meant every word of it. And I want you to know that."

"If you're talking about my feelings for Don, I'm beginning to realize you might be right. Perhaps that's why I got so upset."

Royce looked surprised.

"I'm reconsidering my relationship with him."

"Do you blame me?"

"I thought I did. I blamed us both, actually. Now I'm not so sure."

"He's a nice fellow, but he's not right for you, Anne-Marie."

"So you've said. And I gather that, just because you've had your way with me a couple of times, you think *you* are."

He smiled. "The formulation is a bit cynical but not too far off. The truth is, I do love you, and I believe you love me."

"You really think that's what it is? Love?"

"What would you call it?"

She looked off, thinking. "That's not an easy question. It truly isn't. I know what somebody Christianne's age, or Kurt's age, or your daughter's age might call it. But I'm not sure what it is to people like us."

"Come on, Anne-Marie, what are you trying to say? That you're over the hill? That you're too old to feel the excitement of love? I don't buy it. You're much too full of life to be so jaded or to act so worldly-wise."

"I'm not too old to feel it. But I'm old enough not to be taken in by it. Maybe you're as wide-eyed, Royce, as I am jaded. Maybe it's my tuxedo you love or, more profound still, the body underneath it."

Royce shook his head. "Do you really think I'm that superficial?"

"I don't think you intend to be, Royce. I just don't trust your feelings."

"Hmm." He reflected for a moment. "Perhaps I've farther to go than I'd thought."

"Oh. What did you think? That you were going to come in here and sweep me off to bed?"

"No, but when Don left, I knew I was right about your relationship with him."

She looked at him evenly. "So, the competition's gone, all that's left now is to close in the for the kill."

"I don't believe you're as cynical as you're trying to sound."

She sighed with resignation. "I'm sorry. I'm being bitchy and difficult, I know."

"You're fighting me, and I don't understand why."

"Because I don't trust you, Royce! I've told you that, and you still don't believe me." She got up and paced the room.

"No, it's not me that's the problem. It's your feelings. You don't trust the love you feel." He got up, took her by the arms and looked hard into her eyes. "You're holding me up to Ted, and you're not seeing the same kind of man. That's what's happening. When you look at me you keep seeing that young lieutenant you knew in Germany."

"Maybe that's true. But you are that same person, just a little older."

His expression grew severe. "I made mistakes. But I am not my mistakes. I'm me."

She felt his fingers sinking so deeply into her arms that it hurt. But not as much as the confusing emotion building inside. His eyes were as hard as his hands.

Her face twisted with anguish. "Please don't do this to me."

He pulled her against him then, holding her tightly and protectively in his arms. The emotion in her was beginning to boil over. Royce stroked her hair.

"I love you, Anne-Marie. I really love you. Can't you see that?"

She couldn't help herself. She began to cry, the sobs welling from deep within. He continued stroking her hair, pausing occasionally to kiss her temple or the top of her head.

"Why do people do this to each other?" she sobbed.

"Fear. That's my theory. I went off to Korea out of fear. And I think you're hiding behind Ted for the same reason."

She considered his words as her tears slowly began to abate. She looked up into his eyes, wondering if he could be right.

"If what we feel for each other is as superficial as you think it is," he said, "we'll find out soon enough."

"That doesn't reassure me. Who wants to try to love, only to fail?"

"Ever hear of risk and opportunity?"

"Yes, I know. Nothing ventured, nothing gained."

"I've got a suggestion," he said, taking her face in his hands. "Let's forget the philosophy and just let what happens, happen."

She took a handkerchief from her pocket and wiped her eyes and nose. "That sounds like something a man would say."

He smiled. "Well, I am a man."

"I've noticed."

"And you are a woman."

"I'm aware of that, too."

"History has proven that to be a pretty interesting combination." He kissed her tenderly on the lips.

She felt her insides warm almost instantly. When he pulled back she looked at him through her wet lashes. "How am I ever going to handle you if you keep getting my body to collaborate in your evil schemes?"

He tweaked her nose. "That guy, Arnold, at the dance tonight was right. You are a frisky little fellow."

"Am I the first frisky little fellow you've ever kissed?"

"I've got one advantage Arnold didn't have. I know what's under this tuxedo," he said, tugging on her lapel. He kissed the corner of her mouth.

Anne-Marie put her arms around his neck, letting her body sway against him. She looked into his blue eyes. "I'm not sure if you know what you're talking about or not, Royce. But if this is puppy love, maybe I'm as big a fool now as I was twenty-seven years ago."

"That's an insight worth celebrating. What kind of champagne do you have in stock?"

"I'm afraid I don't keep much of a liquor cabinet. Don likes bourbon. There's a bottle of that in the cupboard...."

"The bourbon has got to go."

"...and there may be a bottle or two of white wine somewhere."

"In the refrigerator, hopefully."

"We can look."

Royce led the way into the kitchen, holding her by the hand. In the back bottom corner of the refrigerator they found a bottle of white zinfandel.

"Fate had this night in mind when it put that bottle there," he said.

"To be honest," she rejoined, repressing a smile, "I think it was Kurt."

Royce laughed. "Where's the corkscrew?"

She got it for him, and he opened the bottle while she took two wineglasses from the cupboard.

"Where's your favorite place in the house?" he asked before he poured. "Your bedroom?"

"I like the bedroom, but my favorite spot is actually my studio, where I do my yoga and meditation."

"Can I see it?"

"If you like."

She led him to her studio, mirrored on two of the opposite walls. The floor was hardwood. There were a few pillows, exercise mats, benches and chairs scattered around for use in her poses. On the walls were a couple of Japanese ink paintings. There was a large arrangement of dried flowers on a table under the window.

"Simple, yet aesthetic." He glanced up at the harsh light of the ceiling lamp. "A bit bright in here, though. You don't meditate with it like this, do you?"

"No, in the evenings I often use candles."

"Ah! Promising indeed."

"I take it you would prefer candlelight."

He smiled in reply.

She lit a candlestick on the table while Royce extinguished the ceiling light. He pulled one of the thin foam mats into the center of the room, plus a small bench, on which he placed the bottle of wine and the glasses. Sitting at one end of the mat, he gestured for her to sit on the other.

She placed the candle between them, kicked off her shoes and sat cross-legged, facing him. He poured the wine and handed her a glass.

"Will there be a toast?" she asked.

"Yes." He thought for a moment. "To our mutual enlightenment."

She smiled, and they clinked glasses over the flickering candle before sipping their wine.

Anne-Marie watched the shadows shimmering on his face. His expression was seductive, producing the effect in her that he undoubtedly intended.

"You know, it isn't like this after a year or two," she said. "It becomes much more important whether you can work out a compromise system of changing the baby's diapers in the middle of the night."

"Are we going to have children?"

She flushed. "Definitely not!"

"All right. That's okay with me, too."

"You're acting as though an offer was made and accepted."

"Am I getting ahead of myself?"

"Ahead of me, anyway. I was trying to point out that this . . . this candlelight conversation is just . . . theater. Something to be recognized for what it is."

"Okay. We'll agree that it's meaningless."

She pouted. "You're making fun of me."

"I thought we were going to leave the philosophy downstairs."

"Better I get drunk and let you seduce me?"

"That could be fun. But I'd prefer to love your mind before I love your body."

She stared at him, lifting her wineglass to mask her expression, though she continued looking at him over the rim. "That's a very nice sentiment, actually."

"And heartfelt."

"All right. Suppose we make love and it's just wonderful. Suppose we do it two, three, ten nights, *twenty* nights in a row, even. You really aren't so naive to believe it would go on like that forever?"

"No, nice as that sounds, I admit there would be days when your skepticism would get to me, and I'd snap at you, and you'd be offended, and we'd yell at each other a little. And there'd be other days when my assertiveness would bug you and you'd tell me to back off, and I'd get miffed and tell you to mind your mouth, and you'd take a swing at me."

She chuckled. "Maybe you're more of a realist than I give you credit for."

"I have no delusions, believe me. Though twenty nights sounds like an interesting challenge."

She gave him a look, then her expression turned thoughtful. "Some people would rather be in an unhappy relationship than lonely. I don't happen to be one of them."

"Ah! I'm beginning to understand." He sipped his wine. "You think to yourself, poor old Royce is divorced, living alone. His daughter is married and gone...he's rattling around in that big empty house like a marble in a shoe box. His life is empty, so he latches on to the first dame who comes along and catches his fancy.

"But Anne-Marie, on the other hand, has her life together. She's got her career, her kids, her place in the community. She has known married love, and it was different than this. She's not desperate, but obviously old Royce is. That about sum things up?"

She was smiling.

"Did I say something funny?"

"No. You were doing it again—commenting on my train of thought."

He rubbed his chin. "So I was. I've been trying to avoid that."

"Don't worry, it doesn't bother me like it did your wife."

"Good. That's one less strike against us."

She cleared her throat. "We're getting off the subject."

"That's right, you wouldn't enter an unhappy relationship just because you were lonely. That's where we were, wasn't it?"

"Yes."

"Look, Anne-Marie, I said we'd shout a little. I'm enough of a realist not to believe in fairy tales. But I didn't say we'd declare all-out war. I think on balance we'd be very happy."

"How can you be so sure? You don't really know me. Not deep down."

"Not as well as I will, that's true. But the more I see you, the better I feel about us."

"If I seem so wonderful, then you have to be deluding yourself, Royce. Everyone has flaws. If you looked at me realistically, you'd recognize mine and you'd have a dispassionate talk with yourself before you decided you could or couldn't deal with them."

"I already know that you're stubborn. That will take some getting used to. And you're not very flexible in some ways. That I think I can help. I know we're going to butt heads a lot. That's almost a given. The question is if we can learn to do it gently, and with grace."

She took a long drink of wine. "You've really got this all figured out, don't you? It's as if I'm a business you're planning on acquiring. You've studied the balance sheet, the profit-and-loss statement, the management, the plant and equipment, and you're ready to make your offer."

"We're definitely going to have to wean you from all that accountant jargon."

Anne-Marie couldn't help laughing. "But I am serious."

"Listen to you. A minute ago you were chastising me for not looking at our relationship dispassionately, now you're criticizing me for being too calculating in my analysis. The fact of the matter is you're trying to shoot me down, whether you have cause or not, and all I'm trying to do is love you."

"Love's not enough."

"Have you ever had a conversation like this with Don?"

"No, of course not."

"Have you ever *really* communicated with him?"

"No. That's one reason I probably won't marry him."

"'Probably won't'?"

"All right. Why I won't marry him."

"Well, I submit that the fact that we can talk like this is proof we've got an awful lot going for us. Being able to communicate is half the ball game."

"What's the rest?"

A quirky smile touched his lips. "Some of it we'll get to later. The rest is common values and common interests."

"Do we have common values and interests?"

"We're both into yoga, athletics and taking care of ourselves and our children. And we both seem to be on the same wavelength, even if there's been some static. I'm sure as time goes on, we'll discover a lot more that we share."

He took the bottle from the bench and poured them each more wine. Then he looked at her for a long time, his eyes continuing to say what his mouth no longer uttered.

There was an intangible something about Royce Buchanan that did things to her. And it wasn't just glandular. It really had nothing to do with sex.

"What are you thinking about?" he asked.

"Sex."

He raised his eyebrows.

"I mean . . . I was thinking how this really has nothing to do with sex."

"No, but that can be part of it. You know what I was thinking?"

"What?"

"That I only got one and a half dances with you this evening, and I should have gotten two."

She smiled, remembering. "Yes, that last one ended abruptly, didn't it?"

"Do you have any music around here?"

"There's a tape deck under the table. But I'm afraid most of the music I've got here is more suitable for meditation than dancing."

"Mind if I try?"

"No."

Royce went over and fooled around with her sound system for a while, finally locating some soft background music. "It's not exactly Johnny Mathis," he said, returning, "but we can try." Extending his arms, he took her hands and lifted her to her feet with one motion. She stood before him, inches from his chest, looking up into his eyes. "I do love you, Anne-Marie."

Then he kissed her, holding her gently, as though she were fragile. His lips were soft, his touch affectionate, loving. When the kiss finally ended, she took an urgent breath and saw the candlelight flickering in his eyes. She didn't have to tell herself that this was something different than anything she'd ever experienced before. She knew.

Royce held her close, and they began moving to the music. Looking over his shoulder, she saw their reflections in the mirrors. Their bodies and the flame of the burning candle trailed off in an infinity of duplication. It was as though the future and the past were conjoined.

And the couple she saw was surprisingly harmonic. There was no incongruity between the woman in the tuxedo and the man who held her. The figures looked as though they belonged together, and the physical imperative was, if anything, reinforced by the words of love he'd expressed.

A powerful feeling passed through her. Sensation collided with insight. It was almost as if he had looked beneath the surface and into her heart. She looked again in the mirror as they turned around and around. Was it the wine, or was this real?

"Are you looking at us?" he whispered into her ear.

"Yes."

"Do you like what you see?"

"Uh-huh."

"It can be even more beautiful, you know."

They both stopped moving, and she lifted her eyes to him, her mouth dropping slightly open. And as the ethereal Eastern rhythms played in the background, Royce took her jacket by the lapels and eased it back off her shoulders and down her arms, tossing it to the floor a few feet away. Then he unfastened her bow tie, tossed it aside, too, and began unbuttoning the studs on the front of her shirt.

"I've never taken a tuxedo off anyone else," he said.

"I've never had one taken off me."

"Then this is new for both of us."

When the shirt had been cast aside, he unsnapped her bra where it fastened between her breasts. She wondered if he could feel the thumping of her heart beneath his fingers.

Anne-Marie looked up into the eyes that wouldn't quit her, and she felt something almost tangible between them, something more certain than his words, his own unbowed confidence. And then he looked down at her breasts, cupping his hands lovingly under them. She glanced into the mirror, seeing the glow of candlelight on her naked skin, seeing the man ten feet from her touching the woman and, beyond them in the distance, the other couples, each identical but more remote.

Then he leaned over and took her nipple into his mouth, coaxing it into erection with his lips and tongue. She held his face against her breast as he gently sucked on her, exciting her and drawing her eyes to the erotic couples in the mirror.

Pausing to kiss her lips, Royce unbuttoned her trousers and let them fall to the floor. When she stepped out of them, he kicked them aside and quickly peeled down her panty hose so that she stood completely naked before him. Then he took her in his arms once more and they began dancing to the quiet strains of the music.

The couple she saw now was very different from the one she'd seen before. The white of her skin against his dark tuxedo made her seem fragile. Their inequality was strangely arousing, powerfully arousing.

"Do you like what you see now?"

"Yes," she whispered. "I like it."

They danced until her desire became so acute that she begged him to take off his clothes. Royce kissed her long and deeply before he stepped back and slipped off his coat. Then, as he began to undress, she dropped down on the mat to watch him, setting the candle on the little bench, next to the wine bottle.

She lay back, observing him as he slowly unbuttoned his shirt. He seemed to be in no hurry, teasing her a little, almost as a woman might play with a man. When he slipped off his shirt, revealing his broad chest and the soft mat of fur covering it, she saw that he had had a lot of sun. His skin was a deep coppery brown in the candlelight, making his teeth and his blue eyes stand out even more.

He removed his shoes and socks, unfastened his trousers and let them drop to the floor, stepping out of them and kicking them aside. He had been looking at her steadily all the while, taking pleasure in her pleasure.

Anne-Marie rolled to her side and rested her head on her hand. She liked to look at his body. Despite his age, it was lean and hard from all the running. He paused, standing in nothing but his briefs, his arms hanging casually at his sides. His eyes were on hers. She looked him over, taking in the sight unabashedly.

"Do you like what you see?" he asked.

"Yes, very much. But you aren't going to stop there, are you?"

The question was brave, and she felt herself blush as the smile on his face widened. But she made herself stare into his eyes. He slipped his thumbs under the waistband of his shorts, then paused, teasing her, challenging her, before slowly slipping them down and off his legs.

He got down beside her, pressing his warm flesh against her. He kissed her tenderly, ever so softly on the lips. The tips of her breasts just touched his chest until she lowered herself on the mat and looked up at him, waiting.

There was love in his eyes, and admiration. He ran his fingers along her jawline as he gazed down at her. "You're so beautiful, so very beautiful."

She heard a slight tremor of emotion in his voice and sensed the depth of his feelings. And she felt love for him, as well, though it was harder for her to be as free with it as he was. Something made her hold back a little.

"Why am I afraid?" she whispered.

"Because in a way you're as much a virgin as you were that first time . . . in the woods. Do you remember that day? It was warm and sunny."

"I remember."

"I worshiped you."

"You were young and in love with the idea of love."

"But it was very special with you, Anne-Marie."

"I was terribly frightened, but I had no doubt about wanting you."

"Do you doubt now?"

"I'm not afraid of you. I want you to make love with me, but the meaning of all this is still hazy. I don't see the future clearly."

He leaned over and softly kissed her chest, just above the breastbone. "Don't think about anything except what you feel when I touch you."

Then he ran his tongue lightly over her skin, leaving a moist trail behind. She trembled.

As she watched him, he ran his fingers over her, lightly caressing her, tracing each curve and hollow. She didn't move; she merely accepted the sensation.

"Close your eyes," he whispered.

She did. Then she felt his lips and his warm breath on her belly. His tongue scored her flesh. And when his finger lightly touched her, she was moist, alive with sensation and receptive.

"Do you want me?" he whispered into her ear.

"Oh, yes, I want you very much."

He stroked her thighs with his palms, gently easing her legs apart. And when she was open to him, he moved between her knees and gently lowered his body onto hers.

His skin felt almost hot. Her breasts arched against his chest, taking his weight. As she put her arms around his neck, pulling him down upon her, she could feel the bulge of his loins against her. He was turgid, ready to take her.

Fire rose from within, and she clutched him to her. His mouth took hers forcefully as his teeth sank into the soft flesh of her lips.

"Oh, take me," she gasped. "Take me, Royce. Please take me."

Reaching down, he guided himself into her gently, but with one long, sure stroke. She felt him at the very depths of her, and she gasped.

He froze then, exquisitely pinioning her to the mat. She felt so full of him, and he was so large. Slowly she pulled her knees up until she was able to wrap her thighs around his waist.

He lifted his head to see her more clearly in the flickering candlelight. Their faces were inches apart, their eyes locked.

"I love you," she murmured.

Royce lowered his mouth to the side of her neck and kissed her. Then, with his face buried there, his pelvis rocked slightly, causing him to withdraw partially. But he thrust again, filling her as before. She drew a breath at the sensation, but as he continued she began to relax, opening herself to him, submitting completely.

In moments the storm in her started to build. She began moaning to the heightened rhythm, losing herself in the sensation. As her control began slipping, Anne-Marie's head rolled to the side. And through her hooded eyes she saw them, him on top, his golden body thrusting, the taut muscles of his buttocks driving into her. She supine, receptive, submissive.

The sight of the couple beside them sent her soaring. She cried out as her climax took her, and he exploded, filling her with the warm flow of his love.

As the shattering sensation slowly trailed away, she felt their mutual love. She sensed a bond between them, and she felt closer to him than she had to any other man.

Chapter Thirteen

When Anne-Marie awoke, Royce was on his side, looking at her, his head on the pillow. "Good morning," he said cheerfully as she yawned and stretched. He brushed her cheek affectionately with his fingers.

"How long have you been awake?"

"I don't know. Not long. Maybe twenty minutes."

"Have you been lying there all this time, watching me?"

"Uh-huh."

"I hope I didn't do anything dreadful."

"Well, you didn't snore, if that's what you mean. But you did keep babbling my name."

She poked him. "I did not."

He grinned.

"You were really watching me sleep?"

"Yep."

"And what were you thinking?"

"I kept telling myself that if I can hang on for just nineteen more nights, it might last forever."

"You did not," she scoffed.

"Well, I think twenty will be a cinch."

"What I said last night isn't a laughing matter."

"You're afraid I'll wither up and blow away."

"Figuratively speaking, you might."

"Nope. But I refuse to debate the point now. I guess I haven't told you, but I never get into an argument before breakfast."

"What about after breakfast?"

"I turn into a tyrant."

"Now you tell me."

"It's before breakfast, isn't it?"

"But it's after last night."

He laughed and tweaked her nose. "Would I be overdressed if I went down in my tuxedo?"

"Poor baby! You don't have a lot of options, do you? Tell you what, I'll get one of Kurt's bathrobes. He wouldn't mind."

"Want to bet?"

She nodded. "On second thought, you may be right. Maybe I should have said, what he doesn't know won't hurt him."

Royce threw back the covers and sat up on the edge of the bed. "What's for breakfast?"

"I don't eat eggs myself."

"Me either."

"Or bacon."

"I agree. Too much cholesterol." He grinned at her. "You see? We're made for each other."

Anne-Marie got up and sat beside him. He put his arm around her waist. She leaned against him, and they looked down at their nude bodies.

"Not bad for a couple of senior citizens," he said.

"Speak for yourself. I've already made up my mind to defer old age indefinitely."

He chuckled. "I'm going to defer it at least nineteen more days."

She slapped his leg. "You'll have me sorry I ever said that."

"I should have insisted on a continuing option for twenty more. That was my only mistake."

"At that rate," she said, getting up, "you'd soon need a depletion allowance."

"Brave lady."

Anne-Marie got a silk dressing gown from her closet and put it on while he watched. "Let me see what I can find for you," she said, and left the room.

After she had gone Royce sat for a moment, thinking. Normally his feet would no sooner hit the floor than the urge to get out and run would strike him. But this morning, for some reason, he didn't feel it. He wasn't sure why—Anne-Marie, perhaps, or the contentment she brought—but the thought of a quiet morning doing nothing but being with her made him happy.

Their lovemaking had been different than the time at his house—different for him as well as for her. Feelings on both sides were deeper, and there wasn't the same urgency as there had been the first time. Now he was more confident of shared feelings. Before, she had been a lovely phantom coming back into his life as in a dream, and he had grasped at her.

But the past wasn't dead yet. He sensed they still had a way to go. Yet, somehow, it seemed they had turned a corner. She was beginning to trust her feelings, beginning to feel all right about him, and, most important, she had stopped deluding herself about Don.

Anne-Marie returned a minute later with a terry bathrobe over her arm. "I found this in Kurt's closet. It should get you through breakfast, anyway."

He kissed her, and they went downstairs, arm in arm. It was nearly ten o'clock, and the sun was shining brightly. There was a power mower humming somewhere in the neighborhood, and Royce almost had that domestic feeling a Sunday morning can give a man. It was something he had rarely had, even during his marriage.

"What will my job be?" he asked.

"Oh, you don't have one. A man should be pampered one day a week. I'll fix it. You just sit there and keep me company." She went to the cupboard.

"Hey, you're sounding better and better."

"Don't get used to it."

"Will I have the opportunity?" he asked, pulling out a chair. She turned and looked at him thoughtfully. "I don't know."

It was a hopeful sign, but he knew not to make anything of it. Anne-Marie turned back to what she was doing. He watched her, liking the thought of her naked body under the light silk gown.

"Decaf okay?" she asked.

"Fine."

"You're a juice person, I know, but my selection is a bit more pedestrian than yours." She opened the refrigerator. "It's either orange or apple."

"What are you having?"

"Apple, I think."

"Exactly what I was thinking. You see, our common tastes are legion."

She gave him a look. "I think I'll put a sedative in your coffee."

Royce sat back happily and watched as she brought him his juice, coffee, wheat toast and a bowl of natural whole grain cereal with skim milk. He took a banana from the fruit bowl in the middle of the table and sliced it onto his cereal.

"Just like home," he said with a broad smile.

Anne-Marie put a plate with several slices of toast on the table for herself, then sat down with him. Their eyes met, and he imagined that the same sort of recollections from the night before were going through her mind as were going through his.

"What shall we do today?" he asked cheerily.

"I don't know about you, but I'm going to clean house."

"Is that some kind of psychological thing?"

"No. The house is a mess. That's all."

He frowned. "I would have preferred a more momentous response."

"What is it about men that their egos won't rest unless the ground continues to tremble for at least twelve hours after sex?"

Royce laughed uproariously.

Just as his laughter was dying, they heard the front door creak open, then slam shut. Anne-Marie's eyes rounded as heavy footsteps crossed the living room floor. She started to get to her feet when a voice in the other room broke the brief silence.

"Mom! You home?"

She gasped. "My God, it's Kurt!"

She looked down at his robe, and Royce knew what was going through her mind. She was visibly upset, biting her lip and looking around as though she were trying to find some place for him to hide. Then he remembered. It wasn't just the embarrassment of being found in a morning-after situation. Kurt was going with Don Nelson's daughter.

Anne-Marie seemed to panic, turning abruptly so that she inadvertently bumped her chair, causing it to scoot back noisily. The footsteps could be heard again, this time coming in their direction. Royce heard an anguished cry from Anne-Marie just before the door swung open.

Kurt Osborne, wearing a T-shirt and jeans, came walking in, the expectant expression on his face freezing, then fading as he saw them.

"K-Kurt," Anne-Marie stammered, "what are you doing home?"

He blinked incredulously, his eyes going back and forth between his mother and Royce. He started to say something but obviously couldn't find the words. His neck slowly turned red.

Anne-Marie glanced at Royce, then lowered her eyes. Kurt's face twisted, his anger replacing the incredulity.

"What the hell's going on, Mom?"

"Kurt," she said in a low but firm voice, "this has nothing to do with you."

"Nothing to do with me?" He shook his head, glaring at Royce. "You're my mother, aren't you? And this guy spent the night in our house."

"I'm an adult. I can—"

"What about Don?"

Royce could see Anne-Marie begin to tremble. He wanted to do or say something to help, but he knew it wasn't his place. This was between her and her son.

"Mom, this isn't like you...." There was pain in his voice.

"There's no reason for you to jump to any conclusions."

He shook his head. "Jump to conclusions? Supposedly you're going to be marrying my girl's father in a couple of months, and here you are with...with somebody else." He looked Royce square in the eye. "Dammit, if that's not bad enough, he's wearing my robe!"

Anne-Marie sighed anxiously. "I'm sorry, Kurt, we had no idea you'd be walking in on us."

"Obviously."

"What people do in privacy is nobody else's business."

He was glaring at her now. "I can't believe this. My own mother. And all these years I respected you. I idolized you."

"Your mother's done nothing for you to be ashamed of," Royce said, unable to hold his tongue any longer.

"How would you know what I'd be ashamed of and what I wouldn't?" Kurt shot back.

Anne-Marie looked at Royce. "Please," she implored quietly.

"What are you saying?" Kurt went on. "That it's your fault, not hers?"

"Please," she interjected, "don't take this personally."

He threw up his hands in disbelief. "What am I going to say to Tracy? How can I face her and Don?"

"I told you, it's not your problem."

"No, *you're* my problem, Mother."

"Kurt!"

Anne-Marie and her son stood facing each other, he with real anger on his face. Royce reached out and touched Anne-Marie's arm. "Would it be easier for you if I left?"

"No," Kurt said with disgust. "Don't bother. I'm leaving. I'd rather not be in this kind of house." He turned and stomped through the doorway.

"Oh, Lord," Anne-Marie said hopelessly. Then she went after him.

Royce got up when she had gone, feeling her agony. The problem was, he didn't quite know what was best to do. What did she need? Would she want him to stay, or would she want space? All he could do was make it as easy for her as possible. He'd have to take his cue from her.

He could hear their voices in the living room but not their words. Then the front door slammed. Several moments later she returned to the kitchen, her eyes glistening.

"Dammit!" she said through her teeth. "Why did he have to come home this morning, of all mornings?"

Royce put his arms around her, but she was oblivious, totally preoccupied with what had happened.

"Now I've got Kurt to worry about . . . on top of everything else."

"Whatever he's feeling, it isn't permanent. He'll get it in perspective. Moms are always all right in the end."

"I know. But I've created a big problem for him. He, more than anyone, was in favor of my marrying Don. I think I even let his enthusiasm for the idea infect me a little."

"What happens now?"

"I've got to talk to Don."

"I'll come with you."

"No, Royce. Thanks, but no. This is something I have to do myself."

"Are you sure? I want to be there for you, Anne-Marie, in case you need me."

She laid her head on his shoulder. "I appreciate your saying that. I really do. But your presence would only complicate things."

"Then I'll wait for you here."

"No. Go on home."

"All right. But come out after you've talked to Don."

She kissed his chin. "I'll call you when I get home."

"Promise?"

"Yes."

He studied her, trying to detect any unexpressed feelings, any subtle signs of danger. "Are you sorry I stayed?"

"To be honest, I think it was a mistake not to resolve things with Don first. I owed him that much."

"You can tell him now. Surely Kurt won't say anything."

"No, I asked him not to. I told him I'm going over there as soon as I've cleaned up and gotten dressed."

"Then everything will be all right."

She shook her head sadly. "Kurt may not stop loving me because of this, but he'll never respect me the way he did before."

"Nonsense." He wanted to be reassuring, but nothing he could say would convince her.

She pulled up in front of the Nelsons' house and turned off the engine. Kurt's Mustang was in the driveway. Knowing he was inside with Tracy and Don, and knowing what he must be thinking of her, Anne-Marie felt dreadful. And yet she knew this was something that had to be done.

She got out of the car and walked slowly toward the front door, absently fiddling with her engagement ring. She glanced down at Carole Nelson's rosebushes along the brick walkway. Her friend had loved roses. They were cared for by the gardener now that Carole was gone, and were neglected by comparison. Seeing them, and thinking of her friend, Anne-Marie felt unworthy. She wondered if Don would hate her.

Standing at the door, she took a deep breath and rang the bell. Don answered, brightening at the sight of her.

"Well, good morning!" He was in his golf clothes. "Kurt said you were coming over, but not why." He gestured for her to enter. "What's up?" He gave her a peck on the forehead.

"Are you playing golf this morning?" she asked, looking at his clothes.

"Played already. Teed off at six. It was probably just as well I didn't stay over last night."

She glanced into the front room. "Where are Kurt and Tracy?"

"Out in back."

"Good. I want to talk to you." She looked into his eyes for the first time, knowing this was one of the hardest things she'd ever have to do.

"Let's go back into the kitchen. I was just making coffee. Care for some?"

"No, thanks."

"That's right, you drink decaf," he said, leading the way back. "I've got to remember to get some of that."

They entered the kitchen, and Anne-Marie went right to the table, feeling the need to sit down. Don was getting a mug out of the cupboard.

"You know," he said, "I've been thinking about your health food fetish and wondering if I'll really be able to hack it. I know I need it," he said, putting both hands on his stomach, "but I was wondering if two or three nights a week we couldn't eat normal."

"That's what I've come to talk to you about."

"Diet?" he said, pouring coffee from the percolator on the counter.

"No, about us. Our engagement."

He saw she was in a serious mood, and he walked slowly to the table, carrying the overfilled mug carefully. "What about it? What's the matter?"

As he sat down, she reached out and took his hands. "Don, I don't have to tell you how I feel about you—you already know. But I can't marry you."

He looked shocked. "Why not?"

Anne-Marie closed her eyes. "Because we've only been engaged a short time, and I've already been unfaithful to you. There's someone else, and I can't in good conscience keep your ring." She slipped the diamond off her finger and put it in his hand.

He was visibly stunned. "I don't understand. What do you mean, unfaithful?"

"I've been with someone else."

"Who?"

She took a deep breath. "Royce Buchanan."

His eyebrows rose slightly, but his expression grew composed. There was surprisingly little emotion on his face.

"I know it's a terrible thing, but all that's left is to be honest with you. I suppose I should have told you before that Royce and I weren't just friends when we knew each other in Germany. We were lovers. And . . . well, I guess we've become lovers again."

Don didn't say anything. He simply looked at her with a blank, unaccusing expression.

"I've been resisting him," she went on, "thinking our engagement might insulate me. But it didn't work. I was afraid to admit it, but the truth is, I still care for him."

Don fingered his mug. "Maybe it's a passing thing."

"No, I don't think so. I don't know what will come of it at this point, but my feelings are very strong. I suppose I love him."

"It's probably an infatuation."

"Well, maybe. But the point is, I can't feel that way about him and be engaged to you."

"Why not?"

"Don! Last night I slept with the man. He came over after you dropped me off, and I slept with him!"

"I'm not pleased about that, of course. I wish you hadn't. But I don't see why we should throw the baby out with the bath water."

"Don, didn't you hear me? I slept with Royce Buchanan."

"Yes, I heard. But I also know that we share something special. These things happen. It doesn't necessarily mean anything."

She shook her head incredulously.

"After Carole died," he went on, "I had a sort of mid-life crisis myself. There was a secretary in Walter Benton's office I developed a crush on. I took her to lunch a couple of times and almost convinced myself I cared for her. I suppose it could have led to sex if I hadn't woken up and said to myself, 'Don, this girl's twenty years younger than you. Who do you think you're kidding?'

"I pulled back then, and pretty soon I started seeing it for what it was. I was lonely and wanted to feel young again. I was using this girl for that purpose."

"This isn't like that, Don. Besides, you weren't engaged to anyone at the time."

"If you think being engaged makes this incident a horrible sin, don't worry about it. Better it happen now, rather than after we're married. Although I'm sure we'd be able to weather it then just as well."

She was stunned. "I can't believe you're saying this."

"Anne-Marie, I don't believe in taking a shortsighted view of things. Why should a moment of weakness spoil what we have? It's what we share over the long run that matters . . . the reasons we got engaged in the first place. Physical attraction is a passing thing. Home, family, companionship are the things that carry a couple together into their golden years."

"I admire you for your open-mindedness, Don. But what I feel for Royce is not mere physical attraction. And what happened last night is not only an incident."

"How can you be sure? It just happened. What do you really know about this fellow? What do you know about his life? I mean the way he lives it every day. What was his marriage like? Why didn't it work? What are his priorities, his values? Does he share the same devotion to home and family that Ted did? And wasn't that important to you?"

"Please, Don. I didn't say I'd agreed to marry Royce."

"I'm sorry if I seem to be badgering. I don't mean to. But I care what happens to you, and I value what we share."

"And I've valued it, too. But I'm not sure it's enough. Maybe *we've* been kidding ourselves. Our children are close. They might even marry one day. But isn't it possible our relationship is more a product of habit and duty than love?"

"That depends on what you mean by *love*. You aren't saying that you feel nothing for me, are you?"

"No, of course not. I never would have agreed to marry you in the first place if I didn't feel respect and affection for you, if there weren't things we shared."

"Well?"

"That's not enough."

Don thought for a moment. "It's probably silly for us to debate this, Anne-Marie. A person can't be talked into or out of a relationship. When I had my mid-life crisis, I had to discover it for myself. So I'll take the ring back if you don't want to wear it anymore.

"But I'll tell you right now, I don't consider our engagement to be off, just tabled. I think the best thing you can do is continue your relationship with Royce. You'll find out soon enough if it's infatuation or something mature and meaningful. But the main thing is, I'll be waiting. I'll understand. And I'll be here for you."

She shook her head. "I don't know if you're a fool or a saint, Don."

"It doesn't matter which."

"No, perhaps it doesn't." She looked at him, feeling very sad. He was a dear man, but she knew she could never marry him, no matter what. If she was sure of nothing else, she was sure of that.

How things would turn out with Royce, she didn't know. Only time would tell. But Royce had taught her one thing—marriage couldn't be approached as nothing but a master plan for one's golden years, the way Don regarded it. She couldn't say that was wrong, only that it wasn't right for her.

She glanced out the window and saw Kurt and Tracy walking hand in hand. Though Don had a surprisingly mature attitude about what had happened, she knew she couldn't expect the same from her son. Working things out with him might be the most difficult challenge of all.

Don glanced out the window to see what she was looking at. "Which of us should tell the kids?"

"Kurt already knows. He walked in on us this morning. I had no idea he was coming home this weekend."

"I was wondering what was wrong with him. He seemed depressed."

"I'm afraid his mother really let him down. He's devastated."

"He's young. He'll learn that these things happen."

"I don't think he'll ever forgive me."

"Sure he will. I'll talk to him. If he sees I can take it, he should, too. After all, it's not the end of the world."

She looked into his eyes. "You really are a wonderful person."

"No, just a very practical man."

She squeezed his hands. "If it's all right with you, I'd like us to tell them together. Tracy is going to think little enough of me. I don't want to skulk off."

"Whatever you wish."

"And I'll ask Kurt to come home before he goes back to school, so we can talk."

As they got up, Don quietly slipped the ring into his pocket. It was a sad moment, but Anne-Marie knew it marked a new turn in her life—like the day Royce Buchanan had kissed her goodbye and gone off to Korea.

Chapter Fourteen

She drove home with a great sense of relief. Kurt had agreed
to meet with her before going back to San Luis Obispo. He was
taking Tracy to a beach party that afternoon but had promised
to come by for dinner. He had cooled off some, but Anne-
Marie could see that he was still deeply hurt.

Don had handled it well when they told the kids they were
breaking off their engagement, and that had made it easier for
her. He'd been right about Kurt reacting positively once he'd
seen how well Don was taking it. Part of Kurt's problem was
embarrassment and hurt pride, and the way Don treated the
matter took away the sting.

But now the question was what to do about Royce. Her feelings were very strong—she loved him—but her conversation
with Don had raised some serious questions. What did love
mean?

Don had said many of the things she had been telling herself: that what she felt for Royce might be infatuation, that it
might not last, that it might not be anything more than a mid-
life crisis. And now she was free to meet the issue head-on.

With her engagement behind her, she could really look at her relationship with Royce, free of guilt and fear.

Of course, she wasn't about to jump into anything permanent. Royce hadn't even proposed, though his intentions were undoubtedly serious. He seemed completely convinced they should be together. And maybe the blind single-mindedness of that bothered her, too.

Perhaps, deep down, that's what troubled her—his undying belief in his love. But Royce wouldn't be marrying his feelings, he'd be marrying her—her tastes, desires, prejudices, needs and passions. With Ted she had been compatible enough to be happy, and their devotion to each other had defined their love. With Royce there were still so many unknowns.

When Anne-Marie arrived home, she knew she'd have to call him right away. He'd be worried, and he'd want to see her. But she'd already decided she needed a little time to think things through and center herself.

She went to the phone in her bedroom. He answered on the first ring.

"Well, it's done," she said.

"You okay?"

"Not really. I feel pretty lousy about myself."

"Did Don give you a bad time?"

"No. To the contrary, he was quite understanding. And very helpful with Kurt."

"What, exactly, did you tell him?"

"Everything. The truth."

"And he didn't mind?"

"I wouldn't put it that way. But he encouraged me to go ahead and have my fling with you. He's convinced nothing will come of it . . . that it's an infatuation . . . that I'll get over it."

He scoffed. "He's treating you like a child. How would he know about our feelings for each other?"

"That's not fair, Royce. Don was really incredible . . . especially considering the circumstances. And it wasn't his ego talking, either. I think he was completely sincere."

"You aren't implying that it's ego in my case, are you?"

"I wasn't implying anything at all. Please don't be defensive if I feel a little compassion for him. After all, I did have feelings for the man. We go back a long, long way."

"I'm sorry. I didn't mean to upset you. But I've been worried, thinking I shouldn't have let you go over there by yourself."

"I know. We're both on edge. It's been a rough day. Let's just forget about it."

"I don't like to see you sad and upset. Come on out here and we'll have dinner. I'll do a barbecue. I've got some great salmon in the freezer."

"No, I can't. Kurt's coming over for dinner. I've got to make peace with him, try and salvage my respectability."

She could tell Royce was disappointed.

He hesitated, apparently weighing his words. "Is there anything I can do?"

"No. Thanks, but I think Kurt and I will have to have a heart-to-heart talk."

"Is he going to spend the night?"

"No, he's got to be back at school first thing in the morning."

Royce didn't say anything, and Anne-Marie could tell he was hoping she would suggest he come over later, or volunteer to drive out to his place. But she couldn't think about that yet— not until she and Kurt had talked.

"Maybe you and I should talk, too," she said.

"That sounds ominous."

"No, but I think we should both understand where we're coming from."

"I know where I'm coming from," he joked, "so we'll just have to figure out where you're coming from."

She didn't laugh.

"I know, it wasn't very funny," he added dryly.

"Bear with me, Royce. I've got an awful lot on my mind."

"Sure. I'm in your corner, though—remember that."

He sounded sincere, which made her feel slightly better. "What are you doing tomorrow for lunch?"

"Not a thing. Shall we meet?"

"That's what I was thinking. But I won't have long—only an hour and a half between classes, and they're five miles apart."

"Then to save time why don't I pack us something," he said. "We can go to the beach and have a picnic."

"I'd like that."

"Then it's done."

He sounded so good to her, and simply talking to him put her at ease. But she had to guard against falling into his arms. Now that she was free to be with him, it was even more important to keep a clear head and evaluate her feelings logically. Still, she was reluctant to let the conversation end. "What are you going to do this evening?"

"The air's wonderful." There was a long pause, then he added, "I was thinking I might go for a run."

When he'd hung up, Royce walked out onto his patio. Anne-Marie was having a rough time, and he felt bad for her. It was a damn shame, he thought, that nothing in life was ever easy. If it wasn't one thing, it was another. Get rid of the fiancé, then the son gets in the way.

Oh, well, it was probably best for her to get that resolved while she had the chance, he thought. If the boy went off with things up in the air, she'd agonize until she saw him again. Hopefully he wouldn't give her too rough a time.

But Royce knew that however it came out, it would take a while before Kurt accepted him. From what Anne-Marie had said, the kid had everybody's life pretty well figured out. Their relationship had to be a blow, and over the long haul Kurt would undoubtedly blame him, not his mother.

He picked up a stone in the flower bed and threw it in a long, high arc over the yard and the pool and into the paddock beyond. Then he gazed down at the sun shining on the aqua water, remembering his horseplay with Anne-Marie, remembering the way she had kissed him.

He wanted her so badly, hating the fact that she wasn't with him now. But, as before, he'd have to be patient. He'd had months, years, to get to the point where he was. And only a month or so ago, Anne-Marie's life had been headed in a completely different direction.

Royce had just gone inside to change into his running clothes when the telephone rang. He expected it to be Anne-Marie again. Perhaps she'd changed her mind about coming out after Kurt left. He picked up the receiver, but the voice was different and seemed to come from very far away.

"Daddy, it's Sybil."

"Sweetheart! What a surprise. How are you?"

There was a silence. Then he thought he heard a sob.

"Sybil?"

She sniffled.

"Sybil, what's wrong?"

"It's Mike . . . we had a terrible fight. I think we're going to get a divorce." Then she started crying.

Royce felt his gut wrench. Her tears had always done that to him. No matter what the reason, whenever his little girl cried, he turned to jelly. "What happened?"

"I don't even know," she sobbed. "We were arguing over something stupid, and then before long we were yelling at each other. I said some things, and he said some things, and then he left. He's never coming back. I know it."

"Of course he is. People don't get divorced because they've had a fight. Look how long your mother and I lasted."

"That doesn't make me feel a whole lot better," she moaned.

"Well . . . what I meant was, it takes a lot more than just one argument."

"It wasn't the first."

"I'm sure it won't be the last, either."

"He doesn't love me anymore."

"Of course he does. People aren't themselves when they're angry. When did this happen?"

"Last night. He didn't come home. It's the first time he didn't come home. We never fought like this before."

"I'm sure you'll be hearing from him soon."

She sniffed. "I don't think so, Daddy."

"What does your mother say? She knows him better than I do."

"She isn't home. I tried calling a couple of times, but there was no answer. She's probably on a cruise or something. She may have mentioned it to me. I don't remember."

"Well, don't worry. I'm sure it'll work out, sweetheart."

"I can't stand sitting here waiting, not knowing where he is, what's happening."

"I understand. It's rough."

He wanted to help, but he wasn't sure what was best. There was a delicate line between being supportive and meddling. Offering to fly back smacked too much of interference, particularly when Mike returned to the scene. On the other hand, if Sybil chose to fly out to California, his assistance would be simply supportive, even in his son-in-law's eyes.

"If you feel the need to get away, you can come out here, honey. You haven't seen my place yet."

"Actually, that sounds good. It would serve Mike right if he came home and I was gone. Would you mind?"

"I don't think revenge is the best motive, honey," he cautioned, "but if you feel the need to get away for a while, I'd love to have you."

"All right. I'll call for reservations. Hopefully I'll be there by tomorrow afternoon. I'll let you know as soon as I book a flight."

"Okay. But leave a note for Mike, telling him where you are."

"Why should I?"

"Somebody's got to make the first move. That was one of the problems your mother and I had. Neither of us was committed enough to make the first move."

"Thanks, Daddy, for being so understanding. I love you."

Royce put down the phone, full of mixed feelings. There were no shortcuts. Everybody had to learn by their own mistakes, and maybe, if they were lucky, by the mistakes of others.

Kurt arrived at about seven-fifteen. He greeted Anne-Marie briefly, then went upstairs for a quick shower. She was just putting dinner on the table when he came down. He took his usual chair. Their eyes had hardly met.

"How was the beach party?"

"Fine."

She handed him the potatoes, which he scooped out in several large dollops onto his plate.

"Tracy have fun?"

"Yeah."

"Then what happened this morning didn't spoil her day?"

"She survived." He served himself a broiled chicken breast and some vegetables.

"How about you?" she asked.

He looked up at her, engaging her eyes for the first time. "I'll survive, too."

"This morning wasn't so horrible," she said, wanting to get right to the heart of the issue, "though I admit the way it happened made it look bad."

"What you do is your business."

She looked at him, but he lowered his gaze. "You say that, but you don't sound like you mean it."

"What am I supposed to say...that I'm thrilled you and Don broke up?"

"No, but you could understand that my first obligation is to be true to my feelings."

"Is that what was going on here last night? Feelings?"

"You don't have to be snide."

"It's not every guy that gets to see his mother that way."

"Kurt, the only bad thing was that I hadn't yet talked to Don. I should have done that, and I intended to right away, whether you'd walked in on us or not."

"Sure. If you say so."

"Don't you believe me?"

"Does it matter?"

"Yes, it matters. I care what you think."

"Kind of late for that now, isn't it?"

"What are you saying? That I don't have a right to be with whom I wish? I'm a grown woman, Kurt. And I'm free to have the relationships I choose."

"Who said you didn't?"

"I wish you really believed that. Look, I know you've been protective of me ever since your father died. We've been pretty close, and that's natural. And it's obvious enough why Don was acceptable to you. But I can't live my life based on your preferences, any more than I would expect you to."

"Have I asked you to do that?"

"Not in so many words. But to reject me because I…I don't choose the man you'd prefer is…unfair. I certainly wouldn't have put pressure on you to marry Tracy just because Don and I were getting married. And if the two of you broke up, it wouldn't have affected my relationship with Don."

"Look, Mom. I know you've got to be true to yourself, but so do I. I don't like that guy, Buchanan, and nothing you can say will change my mind."

"How can you say that? You don't even know him."

"I don't like him. That's all I know."

Anne-Marie fell silent. There was no point in arguing. She couldn't change his feelings. They ate for a while without speaking.

"It's one thing if you don't like Royce," she finally said, "but I wish you'd accept the fact that I care for him, the same way I'll accept your choice of a wife whether I like her personally or not."

"So, it's marriage already?"

"No, I was speaking hypothetically. To illustrate a point."

"Do you want to marry him?"

"I don't know, Kurt. I love him. Or at least my feelings for him are very, very strong."

"That's what you said about Don, too."

"I cared for Don…I still do…but my feelings aren't the same as they are for Royce. It's different. But I'm not sure at this point whether it's the sort of thing that will lead to marriage. It's certainly possible."

"Why are you telling me all this?"

"After this morning, I want to be honest with you so you'll understand my position and hopefully accept it. It would behoove both of us to try to work it out. It's conceivable Royce could end up as your stepfather."

Kurt took a big bite of potatoes, chewed and swallowed hard. "Sounds like you've already made up your mind."

"No, not at all. I simply don't want any more surprises for you. Or any false hopes. Don doesn't believe our relationship is over, but it is. That much I'm sure of."

"Why can't you keep an open mind about that?"

"Because I know."

"Sounds like you've already got a case for Buchanan."

"Perhaps I do."

Kurt stared at her for a long time.

"What are you thinking?" she asked, increasingly uncomfortable under his gaze.

"I was wondering what would have happened if he'd come back when Dad was still alive."

There was a terrible indictment implicit in the remark, and it wasn't at all frivolous. Perhaps, subconsciously, she'd been wondering the same thing. Maybe that was another reason she was uncomfortable with her feelings for Royce. In a way, he had brought into question all that she had believed in and considered important in life. Was loving Royce now belying, in some fashion, all that had gone before?

"Well?" Kurt said.

"I loved your father, and we were very happy. But that has absolutely nothing to do with what's happening in my life now."

She looked down at her plate, wanting to believe what she had just said, knowing that she herself wasn't convinced.

The next afternoon at twelve Anne-Marie came out of the club, wearing a gray-and-purple jogging suit. Her hair was up in a ponytail, and she had on a headband that matched her suit. She felt pretty good despite the rough night she'd had and the cloud that still hung over her relationship with her son. The anticipation of seeing Royce had sustained her, and once Kurt had left, her thoughts turned more fully to Royce.

When she saw him sitting on the fender of his car, she waved. He smiled and stood up as she approached.

"Hi," she said.

He took her by the shoulders and kissed her. "Hello, beautiful," he replied, looking into her soft gray eyes. He took her hand, rubbing her bare ring finger between his thumb and forefinger.

She looked down at their hands, sensing immediately that the rules of the game had changed. Then their eyes met. There were so many questions, so much uncertainty, yet his magic, his effect on her, was always the same. It was almost as if she was one person in his presence, another when they were apart.

"I've packed us a lunch," he said. "You hungry?"

"Yes." But the hunger she felt was to be with him.

"Shall we take my car?"

"I'd only have to come back to get mine. Maybe we'd better take both. Shall I follow you?"

"You know the beaches. Why don't you lead the way?"

They didn't waste any time. Anne-Marie hurried to her car and got in. She drove out of the parking lot with Royce following. She led the way to Goleta Beach, which wasn't too far. Being a weekday, it wasn't crowded.

They walked a hundred yards from the parking area, then Royce spread out the blanket on a flat place in the sand, well away from the water. They plopped down, and he opened the picnic basket he'd carried.

Anne-Marie was sitting with her arms wrapped around her legs, looking out at the surf. The sea breeze was blowing tendrils of hair at the side of her face. He watched her until she became aware of his gaze. Then she turned a little self-consciously and smiled.

"How did it go with Kurt?"

"Okay, I guess. We're speaking. He came around partway. But he made it pretty clear he wasn't pleased."

"Not pleased with me, would be my guess."

"Well, you're not one of his favorite people right now."

"I'm sorry about that. Especially for you."

She looked at him. "I made it clear that I live my own life."

"And that if you wish to associate with the likes of me, you will?"

"I didn't quite put it that way."

He took a sandwich out of the basket and handed it to her. She began unwrapping it aimlessly.

"How about you?" he asked. "How are you feeling?"

"About us?"

"Yes."

She touched his hand. "Nothing has changed, except perhaps I've realized that we should let our relationship develop more slowly."

"Do you feel rushed?"

She stroked his arm. "Whenever I'm with you, I never seem to have a choice. Whatever happens, I do willingly. It's like I was a kid again, more irresponsible than ever."

"And when I'm not around you're much more level-headed?"

"It sounds silly, I know."

"Does it worry you?"

Anne-Marie was still holding the sandwich, but she hadn't taken a bite. "I don't know if *worry* is the term I'd use. But I wonder what keeps holding me back."

"You must have a theory."

"Obviously my emotions and my reason are counseling two different things."

He took a sandwich from the basket and absently tossed it up and down in his hand, thinking. He didn't know whether it was best to pursue the discussion or get right to the bottom line. His instincts told him the latter.

"So, what do you want to do?"

"I want to take things slowly. If that's possible with you."

"You're asking for my cooperation, in other words."

She smiled. "I know what I'm like when I'm around you."

"Kissing you good night at the door will be torture, if that's what you have in mind."

"I just want to get to know the man I have this terrible and wonderful passion for."

"Hoping he won't turn out to be a chimera."

"Hoping the quiet moments are as wonderful as the others."

He took her hand and pulled it to his lips, kissing it softly. "I'll do my best, Anne-Marie."

She stroked his head, looking into his eyes. Then she seemed to grab control of herself, looked out to sea and took a bite of her sandwich. He removed the plastic wrap from his and began to eat, as well.

"I had a kiddy problem of my own last night," he said.

"Oh?"

He told her about Sybil's call and the fact that she was arriving that afternoon.

"The poor thing. She has to be terribly upset. How long has she been married? A year?"

"Only six months. I'm sure they'll straighten it out. They're both young and headstrong. And, I think, kids have it rougher these days in some ways. With the roles not dictated so much like they were when we were young, there's a lot more for a couple to work out in a relationship."

"Maybe that's what you and I are going through ourselves, Royce. In a way, we're like kids again. It's a different world with different rules."

He thought about what she'd said, liking the mixture of sincerity and innocence in her eyes, her girlish spirit and mature beauty. "You know what, Mrs. Osborne?"

"What, Mr. Buchanan?"

"I love you." And with that he pulled her down on the blanket, held her face in his hands and kissed her. "Let's just forget who we are for five minutes," he whispered. "Then we'll play the game your way."

Chapter Fifteen

The next morning Anne-Marie lay in her studio in *Savasana*, her body completely relaxed, stretched out on the mat she and Royce had made love on. During her workout she had thought of him, the memories a sweet dream she could return to at will.

Though he had kissed her on the beach, managing to arouse her in just a few brief minutes, he had behaved himself after that. They had finished their picnic and walked back to the cars hand in hand.

"I'd like for you to meet Sybil," he had said before she drove off to her class. "I'm sure she'll be out of sorts this evening, but why don't you tentatively plan on coming out for dinner tomorrow night? She's young, but she's a hell of a chaperon," he added with a laugh.

And so she'd agreed, glad for the opportunity to have a glimpse of another aspect of Royce Buchanan.

At ten that morning she had a consultation with an orthopedic surgeon and a patient who required therapy, and she had a yoga class that afternoon. Afterward she planned to come back to the house to clean up before going to Royce's.

Though her mind was more active than it should have been to do *Savasana* properly, Anne-Marie did manage to slip into a deeper meditation. Several minutes later she came out of it refreshed.

After a quick shower she dressed, had a light breakfast of fruit and toast, then went out onto the porch to check her mail. There was a special-delivery letter from Christianne. Anne-Marie eagerly tore open the envelope.

Dear Mom,

It's only been a few days, but I LOVE Germany. Everything is so rad, I don't know how you could have left. Kirsten is really, really nice. She's been super and has taken me lots of places already. We speak German all the time, and I'm really getting good. Maybe I can skip right to German II or III next year. Wouldn't that be rad?

The best of all is a boy I met. He lives near Kirsten, and his name is Erik. He's just WONDERFUL! He's tall and really, REALLY cute. Much better than any of the boys in Santa Barbara. Yuk.

Erik speaks English better than I speak German, but he promised to help me speak German like a native. *Ich liebe Dich!* By the way, he has brown hair and blue eyes. He's fifteen, but he looks much, MUCH older! Can you believe it?

Well, I've got to go. Erik is coming over, and we're going to go for a bicycle ride. Kirsten is letting me use her bike. Did you know they ride their bikes in the woods here? It's so pretty in Germany. I love everything about it. Thanks for letting me come.

Love,
Christianne

Anne-Marie stared at her daughter's familiar hand. It had only been a few days, but what a change. Boys had hardly meant a thing to her, except as a topic of conversation with her girlfriends. And suddenly she sounded obsessed. This Erik was the first boy she'd ever shown a serious interest in.

It was puppy love, doubtlessly, and she smiled at the thought. The whole thing was probably innocent enough, and Kirsten would be keeping an eye on Christianne.

Still there was something vaguely disconcerting about the letter. Anne-Marie knew it was because her daughter was so far away. Within a week or two Erik would probably have passed from the scene, but there was the romance of being far away and in love for the first time. Surely Christianne wouldn't let things get out of perspective, though.

She folded the letter and put it on the kitchen counter. She decided to answer it right away and get in a little maternal caution. Christianne knew that all the rules from home applied, but those involving boys hadn't been put to much use—until now there hadn't been a need.

Anne-Marie shook her head. For a while it looked as though Kurt would be her only worry over the summer. Now she could see that her daughter would be troubling her from afar. She hoped the crush would fade quickly; she had no desire for sleepless nights.

She sighed, knowing that the next few years would get worse before they got better. Why did she have to be alone? Why did Ted have to die so young?

Then Anne-Marie thought of Royce, and Christianne's friendship with him. What would he be like as a stepfather? she wondered. Would he be someone who could offer stability and mature guidance to a girl's life, or was he only the type who brought the excitement of a horseback ride or a wild water fight in the pool?

It occurred to her that the question she'd been asking about her own relationship with Royce was not a lot different. Their romance had begun at a dance in Frankfurt. Even now, years later on a California beach, he could still take her breath away. Was that all there was to Royce Buchanan, or was there more?

The sun was just setting behind the hills to the west when Anne-Marie arrived at Royce's place in the Santa Ynez Valley. She had been eager to meet his daughter and see him in the role of father.

Having reflected on the subject, she had decided that Royce was really a pretty shadowy figure to her. He was the young officer, and he was the wealthy businessman living alone on a ranch in semiretirement. But what had he been in between? She didn't know.

Royce greeted her at the door, looking tanned, relaxed and very happy to see her. He was wearing a powder-blue polo shirt and beige slacks. He kissed her briefly, then, with his arm around her, he took her into the living room where the dark-haired young woman she had seen in the picture in his bedroom sat waiting.

Sybil was young but poised and even prettier than her picture. She shook Anne-Marie's hand warmly. "I almost feel as though I know you," she said, smiling with the same perfect white teeth as her father. "Daddy's talked about you so much."

"Hey," he protested, "I thought we were going to pretend I'd hardly mentioned her."

Sybil rolled her eyes with mock dismay. "Do you have any idea what it's like having a father who's almost fifty acting like a teenager in love?"

"He's a big tease," Anne-Marie replied, glancing at him.

"Women just can't keep their mouths shut when they think they've got a guy where they want him," Royce objected lamely.

"Oh, Daddy, every woman's flattered by attention, and you know it."

Anne-Marie stuck her tongue in her cheek. "Sounds like you've got the old man figured out."

Sybil looked at him and smiled affectionately. Then she put her arm around his waist and leaned her head against his. "We're pals, aren't we, Pops?"

He kissed her forehead and winked at Anne-Marie. "Like in the old days . . . especially when you wanted a new dress or had gotten your third speeding ticket in a month."

She looked at him. "You always said that's what fathers were for. I was simply taking your word for it."

He laughed. "I've always been a sucker for a pretty face. And you two are the best proof I know." He gestured toward the couch. "Sit down, ladies. Anne-Marie, how about a drink?

Sybil and I are having a glass of white wine. May I pour you one, or would you prefer something else?"

"Wine would be nice."

He nodded and left the room as the women sat side by side on the couch.

"So," Anne-Marie said when he was gone, "is this your first visit to your dad's ranch?"

"Yes, Mike and I were supposed to come out a couple of months ago, when he had a business trip scheduled to L.A. But it was canceled." She looked down rather sadly, her expression changing. "Unfortunately, I ended up coming under very different circumstances."

"Royce mentioned that. Have you heard from your husband?"

Sybil shook her head. "No, not a word. I'm beginning to think I won't, either."

Anne-Marie felt compassion for the girl and wanted to do or say something comforting, but she didn't feel she knew her well enough to be too personal. "It's nice that you've got your father at a time like this."

Sybil glanced toward the door where he had exited. "Dad's super. He's always been there for me."

Anne-Marie saw the emotion in her eyes. "I gathered you were close, but I had no idea what kind of a relationship you had."

"He was always my friend as well as my father. I lived with my mother most of the time after they divorced, mainly because it was easier. But she and I were never as close as I was with him. Daddy and I always understood each other." She smiled a bit wistfully. "No matter what, we always had a lot of fun."

Royce returned carrying both a glass of wine for Anne-Marie and the open bottle, which he put on the coffee table. "Who had a lot of fun?"

"You and I did, when I was growing up. I was telling Anne-Marie about our relationship."

"Did you tell her about the time when you were three and you pulled down your pants with the neighbor boy, and I had to tan your little behind?"

Sybil blushed. "No. And you didn't tan my behind. You started giving me a lecture about birds and bees. Don't you remember?"

Royce rubbed his chin. "Maybe I'm confusing it with the time you were thirteen and I caught you with that kid with the long legs and the big ears."

She reached over and gave his knee a playful slap. "You didn't paddle me then, either."

"No, but maybe I should have." Royce took her hand and held it affectionately, smiling at her. Then he looked at Anne-Marie. "I think I was too softhearted to be a good father."

"You were a wonderful father," Sybil insisted. "And you still are."

"What do you think Anne-Marie? Knowing me as you do, what kind of a father do you think I would have been?"

"Judging by what I see, you must have been first-class."

"You see?" Sybil said. "It's obvious."

Anne-Marie and Royce exchanged looks. "Frankly," she said, "I've never seen this side of you before. It's . . . a change from what I'm used to."

"I've always been alone when we've known each other," he replied. "It was either before I had a family or after they were gone."

So, he'd been aware of it, too, she thought. And she realized they'd really had unequal opportunities to see the kind of people each of them were. "Yes," she said, nodding, "that's right."

"You look sort of shocked, Anne-Marie," he said with a grin.

She caught herself. "I guess I just have certain associations with you in my mind, and I'm not prepared for what I'm seeing."

"I've often thought," Sybil said, "that Daddy must come off as a rake to women who don't know him well. But he's really a pussycat."

He shushed her. "You're going to give away my secrets."

Anne-Marie laughed. "You haven't managed to hide all your good points, Royce, but it is refreshing to hear about you from someone who should know."

"Then you didn't see me as a 'rake,' as my darling daughter so artfully put it?"

She repressed a smile. "Let's just say other women see a side of you that a daughter doesn't."

"All right," he said abruptly, rubbing his hands together, "I think it's time to change the subject. Who's getting hungry?"

Anne-Marie and Sybil both laughed.

Royce poured more wine into his daughter's and his glasses, then lifted his. "Here's to discretion."

They laughed again. He took a long swallow of wine, then rose. "I'll go and check on dinner if you two promise to talk about something sensible... like fall fashions, or the condition of the stock market."

"I'm beginning to think your daughter and I could teach each other a lot about you," Anne-Marie teased.

"That's what I'm afraid of."

Royce went to the kitchen, and Sybil suggested that they go out onto the patio to enjoy the evening air. Outside they looked down at the pool, and Anne-Marie thought again of the afternoon she and the girls had spent there. It was strange, but after their conversation, she saw that day in a slightly different light.

"You know," she said, "I never pictured your father as a family man. Would you describe him that way?"

"Well, not really. He and I are close. And I think we have a good relationship—we always have. But Dad was not your typical family man. He and my mother didn't have a very good marriage, needless to say."

Anne-Marie wondered about his relationship with his wife. It had been something she had been curious about for a long time, but she didn't feel she could ask Sybil about it, not without the girl first volunteering to discuss it.

They looked out over the valley and the oranges, yellows and violets of the western sky. Sybil took a deep breath, and Anne-Marie could tell she was dismissing some nostalgic thought about her husband. She felt sorry for her and wished she could help.

Sybil sipped her wine. "California's nice, isn't it?"

"Yes, it's home to me now. It has been for a long time." She turned to her. "I'm from Germany, originally."

"I know. Daddy's told me all about you."

"All about me?"

"All that he dare."

She chuckled. "That's a relief."

"He told me that you knew each other in Frankfurt, and how he ran into you by accident here in Santa Barbara."

"Talk about surprises!"

"I think it was one of the most fortunate things that's ever happened to him, Anne-Marie. He loves you very much."

She turned to the girl. "Did he tell you that?"

"Yes, in his way. I can tell how much you mean to him."

"It's an awesome responsibility...to be loved."

Sybil mused. "He's not desperate, but he feels he missed an opportunity with you the first time."

"I know. But it was different with me. I was happily married, and that makes what's happening now different for me than for him."

"You feel disloyal to your husband?"

"I don't know if I'd put it that way, though there may be a grain of truth to it. Perhaps it's more a matter of having experienced two different loves and trying to understand them in the context of each other."

"When I met Mike, I was sure there would never be another man I'd even look at."

"But you found that not to be true?"

"Oh, it's not that. There isn't anyone else, for either of us. It's just us. Sometimes we really clash. I guess we're both strong willed." She smiled. "Daddy says it's his fault for bringing me up with the independence of a boy."

"It's not easy being a woman these days. Or a man either, I suppose. But I don't think the fundamental issues are all that different than they used to be. If two people care for each other, and they're willing to commit themselves to the other person's happiness—treating them as they want to be treated—then there's a good chance the relationship can succeed."

"That's a good philosophy, Anne-Marie. Maybe that's where Mike and I have gone wrong. Maybe we're both too selfish and self-centered."

She turned to the girl, and as she did she saw a figure behind them. Royce was leaning against the doorjamb.

"A beautiful philosophy, Anne-Marie," he said softly, his eyes on her.

Sybil looked back, too.

"Dinner's about to be served," he said, looking back and forth between them. "Anybody hungry?"

Royce had blackened some fish, Cajun style, steamed some broccoli and carrots, made some whole grain rice and fixed a fruit salad for dessert. During dinner they talked about when they were young, Anne-Marie and Royce recounting anecdotes for Sybil's benefit. The girl was particularly struck by the way it had been for Anne-Marie growing up in her father's house.

They were just finishing dessert when the telephone rang. Royce got it in the kitchen. He returned a moment later, grinning. "Sybil, it's Mike."

Her face lit up, and she almost jumped from her chair.

"You can take it in my bedroom if you want, sweetheart. I'll hang up here when you get on the line."

She ran off without a word. Anne-Marie and Royce exchanged happy smiles. He stepped back into the kitchen to hang up the receiver, then came back and sat down.

"I hope that works out," he said with a grin. "For two days I've had visions of being 'with child' again."

"There isn't anything fundamentally wrong with their relationship, is there?"

"No, they're just young. They're learning."

"I'm not so sure age has anything to do with it," she said.

"Maybe not. Ellen and I tried for nearly twenty years and never managed to get on track."

She looked at him, but he was gazing off into the distance. "You've never told me about your wife, Royce, or your marriage."

He sighed. "It's a difficult subject for me. Even now."

"We don't have to talk about it."

"No, it's something we should discuss. It was as much a part of me as your marriage was a part of you. You're entitled to know about it." He paused.

"I guess our fundamental problem was that neither of us was really committed to the other's happiness...what you were talking about out on the patio. And we were both at fault, not just one of us. I don't know if we ever really cared for each other enough to make it work. We thought we loved each other at one time. But maybe our heads weren't in the right place. I know mine wasn't."

"How so?"

"I was wrapped up in my career, making a success of my company. It wasn't that I didn't care about Ellen. But our relationship didn't count foremost for me. And she had other priorities, as well.

"After our marriage broke up, there was a period when I was a little cynical about women, about life generally. Sybil was always a bright spot for me, but obviously she wasn't enough. I knew she had her own life to lead. So once I sold my company, I started looking inside myself, knowing that if I was ever to find happiness, it would be there. But I was still floundering when something happened to change everything. I found you again."

She lowered her eyes.

"Does that bother you?"

"It flatters me that you should feel that way. But being loved like that can be a heavy burden. I can't be responsible for your happiness, Royce. Nobody can do that for another person. I said that to Sybil earlier."

"I understand what you're saying. And to be honest, I may have been thinking in those terms in the beginning. I was lonely and looking for something or someone when you came back into my life. There was an emptiness to it—I was deeply aware of that. And maybe I did grasp at you, at first. But gradually I came to know that even that was more an indication of the love I felt than any desperation. After all, finding female companionship has never been a problem for me."

"I'm sure it hasn't. But at a certain point in life, that in itself isn't as important as it once was. Mature people chase rainbows as much as younger people. But they're different rainbows."

He was grinning. "There are a lot less challenging rainbows to chase out there than you, Anne-Marie."

"Maybe the challenge is what appeals to you."

"No. I love you. I'm certain of it. And I feel your love, too."

She nodded. "Yes, and you're not the only one who's had to adjust. I've been trying to accept the fact I could have loved Ted, been happily married to him and still be able to love you."

"Is that what you've been fighting?"

"Partly."

He reached over and took her hand, slowly rubbing the back of it with his thumb. "You know, if we ever get our kids straightened out, maybe we can actually end up enjoying this summer."

She smiled, seeing a slightly different person than she had the day before. Maybe this new glimpse of him had rounded him out in her mind. Royce *was* a good deal more than the brash young officer or the confident older businessman she'd seen during the past few weeks. She was beginning to feel comfortable with him as a person.

Just then Sybil came running back into the room. "Daddy, Mike's flying out tonight. He wants me to meet him in Los Angeles, and then he wants us to go on to Hawaii."

"Hey, that's great, sweetheart."

"Do you mind?"

"You don't need my permission."

"No, but I need to get to L.A."

Royce laughed. "The old keys-to-the-car routine."

"I can get a connector flight if you'll drive me to the airport."

"No, don't be silly. I'll take you to L.A.X. It's only a couple of hours. And I feel like a drive."

"Are you sure?"

"Yeah. Find out when Mike's flight arrives, and we'll have you there with bells on your toes."

"Oh, thank you, Daddy!" She ran off again.

Anne-Marie turned to Royce, seeing that beneath his grin he was a little misty-eyed. She patted his hand. "Isn't it wonderful? She's thrilled."

"Yeah. Now I can go back to walking around here with nothing on if I feel like it."

"Oh, it was good for you to have her out. And it was probably good for her and Mike, too."

"Sure. There's always a reason for everything. Like that backache I came down with. Where would we be without that?" He gestured broadly. "You'd be doing your thing, content as a clam, blithely marrying the wrong guy."

"How *is* your back, by the way?"

"When I do the yoga, it's fine."

"Haven't you been keeping it up?"

"Sometimes."

"The results depend on the effort you put into it."

He was contemplating her, obviously thinking about something else. And judging by the seductive look in his eye, she decided it wasn't something she should ask about.

Sybil returned, euphoric. There were happy tears in her eyes. "He's in Houston, on business. His flight is arriving at eleven-thirty."

Royce looked at his watch. "We'd better get going. How long will it take you to pack, sweetheart?"

"Just a few minutes."

He turned to Anne-Marie. "Feel like a drive to L.A.?"

"No, you two haven't had much time together," she replied. "I wouldn't want to interfere."

"Oh, you wouldn't be interfering," Sybil insisted. "Besides, that way Daddy would have company on the ride home. Please come, Anne-Marie."

She looked at Royce, who had an easy smile on his face. "I brought her up to look after her old man."

"You do make a wonderful team."

"Oh, great!" Sybil said. "I'll get to packing." She headed off.

He sighed and looked at Anne-Marie. "Do you have anything scheduled for the morning?"

"No, nothing till the afternoon."

"Great. That way if we're too tired for the drive back, we can stay over and come back in the morning. Why don't I give the Bel-Air Hotel a call and see if they'll hold a room for us?"

"The Bel-Air?"

"Yeah. I believe they have a massage room. Maybe I can get that sports massage Dr. Gilchrist suggested."

"Royce, you're incorrigible."

He smiled. "Everything happens for a reason."

Chapter Sixteen

It was well past midnight by the time they exited the San Diego Freeway in Los Angeles. They drove east on Sunset toward Stone Canyon Road. Royce turned left at the traffic light and proceeded along the twisting road.

"I take it you've been here before," Anne-Marie said gamely.

"Whenever I came out to the coast, I tried to get a room here. It's not your typical businessman's hotel, but I like the way they pamper you." He reached over and ran the backs of his fingers across her cheek.

They soon drove through the hotel's arched entry, over the bridge that was all lit up, and pulled to a stop at the main entrance. A parking attendant appeared immediately. They had no sooner gotten out of the car than a bellhop came down the steps and took the overnight bag Anne-Marie had insisted Royce bring.

After Royce had checked in, they were taken to their suite. He gave the bellhop a tip, and the man saluted them and left. Anne-Marie stretched out on the bed and watched as Royce stood at the desk, going through the hotel directory.

"What is it about you that makes me feel so wicked?" she asked.

"Wicked?"

"Deliciously wicked."

He smiled at her. "That's better." He turned back to the directory.

"What are you doing?"

"Checking out the massage business."

"You're really serious about having a massage?"

"Of course," he said wryly. "What do you think I've been after all these weeks? I want that therapeutic massage of yours."

He picked up the phone and called the desk.

"May I help you?"

"Yes, the last time I stayed here, I had a massage, and I don't recall who I talked to about it. How can I arrange to get the use of the massage room?"

"For what time, sir?"

"Now."

"But Mr. Buchanan, it's nearly one in the morning. The masseur won't be in until seven o'clock."

"That's all right. I brought my own masseuse."

"Sir?"

"Can you arrange for someone to get us into the facility? I'd like the use of the table, the steam room and so forth."

"Give me a few minutes to make arrangements, Mr. Buchanan. I'll ring you back and have someone come up."

"Thanks." He hung up the phone and turned to Anne-Marie.

"When you get your mind made up, you plunge right ahead, don't you?" she observed.

"It did strike me as the perfect opportunity."

"How am I going to give you a massage, dressed like this?"

"I'll arrange for some robes. Since we know each other, it's okay if you're dressed a little informally."

"Royce, you're planning a seduction, not a massage."

"I'm planning a massage. Of course, one never knows what might happen when two volatile chemicals are brought together. But then, that's up to nature, not me."

He walked over, extending his hand to her. She took it, and he pulled her to her feet. Then he embraced her, kissing her softly on the lips. "Sorry if I lack willpower, Anne-Marie, but there's something about you that foils my best intentions."

She kissed him on the chin. "Yes, I know the feeling."

Royce lay nude on his stomach on the table, his body limp and in ecstasy. She had been working his back, shoulders, arms and legs for more than half an hour. Zen Shiatsu was not an ordinary massage, he saw. It was like having yoga applied to your body. The sensation was wonderful.

When Royce opened his eyes, he saw the perspiration on her brow. She was working very hard. And her hands were strong, incredibly strong.

"It's a cliché, I know," he said, "but I feel like putty in your hands."

"How's your back?"

"Terrific." He moaned with pleasure as she dug her elbow into the meaty place just below his shoulder blade. "It can't be much fun for you, though."

"It's a workout, believe it or not."

"I believe it." He luxuriated in the sensation. She was wearing a light terry robe, and, knowing that she was naked underneath, his mind kept turning to erotic thoughts. "Are you warm?"

"Yes, very," she said, working his lat muscles.

"Take off the robe. The door's locked."

"That's not very professional, Royce. I'll keep it on."

"A woman with high principles," he groaned.

"Around you, that's all I've got to cling to. Even then, it's not enough."

"Sounds promising."

"Why don't you meditate?" she rejoined.

"Whenever I do, I think about what's under that robe of yours."

"I think you're about ready for the cold shower."

"Is that part of the treatment?"

"No, but in your case, I'm prescribing it."

He reached back blindly and managed to catch the flap of her robe.

"Royce, let go."

But he held on, turning over and grasping the other flap firmly in his hands. He pulled her down close to him.

"This is not part of the massage. I'm not finished."

"Let's take a love break."

"There's no such thing."

"It's a Western concept. We ought to try it. Things are always best when East meets West." He pulled her an inch closer and kissed her lower lip.

"Royce . . ."

Then he kissed her again, and she kissed him back, her mouth opening to receive his tongue. She was leaning over his prone body. The tie of her robe had come loose.

"Come up here with me," he whispered.

It was a narrow table, but she managed to get astride him. She looked down, her face suddenly sensuous. He saw the desire in her eyes.

The robe was hanging open, and her breasts were exposed. He reached up and massaged them gently, all the while his eyes locked with hers. Then Anne-Marie let the robe slide off her shoulders and fall to the floor.

Slipping his hands around her sides, he pulled her down on him and kissed her again. Both their bodies were moist, and the friction of their skin was exquisite.

Anne-Marie sat up again. She was astride his loins, and he felt himself hardening against her. He reached up and touched her face with his fingertips.

"You're so lovely. So very lovely."

She kissed his hand.

"There could never be anything else as wonderful as this," he said. "I love you."

"Every man falls in love with his masseuse. Just like every man falls in love with his nurse."

"I don't want anyone else. I want you." He arched himself against her, feeling that she was moist. She closed her eyes, letting her head drop back, exposing her throat to him.

She was so beautiful, sitting erect upon him, her shoulders and back straight, her stomach taut, her thighs squeezing his sides.

"I have to be in you," he murmured.

She rose enough to permit him to enter her, but from that point she was in control, affecting the depth of his penetration, the rhythm of their movements. For a time she rocked on him, the motion of her pelvis inciting him.

Despite the fact that the steam bath and massage had sapped his strength, the storm of his climax came quickly. She gasped at the depth of his penetration, crying out as he came. And when she collapsed on him, her breathing erratic, he knew that he had fulfilled her, too. He kissed her wet temple as she lay against him.

"My darling, my darling," he said, holding her tightly.

She cuddled against him, stretching her legs out so that her full weight was on him. He stared up at the ceiling, caressing the back of her neck, feeling her breathing as she lay on him, very still.

"This isn't the time to say this, probably. It really calls for candlelight and champagne, not a massage room," he said. "But I can't help myself, Anne-Marie. I want you to be my wife."

She blinked her damp lashes against the side of his neck. Her body was still pulsing from their lovemaking.

She didn't answer him for a moment. She simply clung to his body, enjoying the sensation of his fingers on the back of her neck. "Oh, Royce, how can I even think, much less make decisions, when I'm with you like this?"

"Just do and say what you feel."

"I'd be in bed with you all the time."

"Is that so bad?"

"It's not very practical, is it?"

"Well, I want to marry you. And I've got you where I want you now, so give me your answer."

"I love you, Royce." She kissed his chin. "I really do. But I don't want to make a commitment in the heat of passion."

"Let's take a cold shower. Then you can make a commitment."

"I'm serious."

He looked at her. "But you must have thought about it."

"I thought that it could come to this eventually, yes."

"Then you're not pleased?"

"I am pleased, because I love you. And I'm flattered. But I didn't want us to rush. I want to get to know you better. I want us both to feel comfortable with each other's values and way of life." She paused for a moment. "I want to make sure there's a solid foundation. Love and a wonderful sex life aren't enough."

He lay back with a sigh. "Why are women so damned cold-blooded about this sort of thing?"

"You're content to go with the emotion?"

"Yes. I mishandled the situation years ago, in Germany, and five minutes after I saw you this time, I knew we should be together."

"Royce, you could marry half the women in the world on that basis."

"Perhaps feel attraction, but not marry. Believe me, I know about these things."

"You're a hopeless romantic. And anyway, your track record isn't very good."

"One learns more from one's mistakes than one's successes."

"Your certainty scares me, too, to be honest." She pressed her cheek against his and lay holding him for a while. "Have I hurt your feelings?"

"No."

"What are you thinking?"

"I'm wondering, exactly, what it is that you want."

"Time. Just time."

"I think we need to be together more. Since Christianne's gone, I think you should live with me at the ranch."

"No, I'd only get addicted to you. That won't solve anything. Besides, Kurt's coming back from school next weekend. He'll be home for the summer."

"He's a big boy. You don't have to take care of him."

"That's true. And if it was best that I live with you, I wouldn't let Kurt stop me. But I don't think that it is best. Not now."

"What do you want, Anne-Marie? To go out to dinner and a movie every Saturday night?"

"For a while."

He groaned.

"Does that upset you?"

Royce kissed her temple. "If you want me to walk on hot coals, I will."

"I just want you to give me time."

She lifted her head and looked into his eyes, hoping to find understanding. He was smiling faintly.

"I do love you, Royce. Believe me."

"When will you know?"

"It's hard to say. But I'll tell you. And if you still want me—"

He put his fingers to her lips. "It's okay. However many movies it takes."

For the first few days after their trip to Los Angeles, Anne-Marie felt happier than she had in months. It was as though whatever had been hanging over her head had suddenly disappeared. Perhaps it was that everything was finally out in the open, that she and Royce had an understanding of sorts.

When he had dropped her off at home, they did make a date for Friday night. "Dinner and a movie," he said.

And that's what they did. Royce picked her up, and they went off happily.

At dinner he told her that he had a trip planned for the following week. "I've got some business back East to attend to, and I want to check out some investment opportunities up in San Francisco. I've been putting it off, so I decided I might as well get it out of the way."

"How long will you be gone?"

"All next week and most of the week after."

"Oh." She was disappointed at the thought of not seeing him for such an extended period.

"It's going to be a long trip, I know, so I thought maybe you could spend the weekend with me at the ranch."

"I'd like to, but I can't. This is Kurt's first weekend home. I think I'd better stay around the house."

Royce didn't reply, though he looked disappointed. "I also thought you might join me in San Francisco next weekend—sort of combining business with pleasure."

"It sounds like fun. Maybe. But I'd better wait and see how things go with Kurt first."

She could see that troubling thoughts were going through his mind, but he was censoring them. Instead of commenting, he looked at his watch and said, "We'd better hurry if we want to make that movie."

Later, after they left the theater, Royce drove her home. He'd been strangely quiet, and Anne-Marie was afraid that in declining his invitation, she'd hurt him.

Kurt's car was out front, and the lights were on in the house as they pulled up. Royce parked behind the Mustang.

"Is it all right if we sit out here for a while? Your son won't be too annoyed?"

"Please don't be sarcastic. I know you're upset . . ."

He glanced up at the house, then pushed a button to lower their windows. "I don't know if I like this role reversal," he said sardonically. "I'm almost afraid to kiss you."

Anne-Marie sighed but didn't say anything for a while. She could tell Royce wasn't pleased. "You're upset because I wouldn't go out to your place."

"I'd prefer it if you had, of course."

"Well, it didn't make a lot of sense to go all the way out there and then have you drive me back."

"I still don't see why you couldn't have spent the night."

"Because I said I preferred not to," she replied. "Not until things get on an even keel with Kurt."

"Anne-Marie, you talk a good game about being in control of your life, but when it comes down to it, you're tiptoeing around your son."

Her eyes flashed. "I happen to care what he thinks."

"You're sending him the wrong messages if you let him think you'll live your life around his sensibilities."

"I'm not living my life around his sensibilities."

"Would you come home with me tonight if he weren't here?"

"I might. Of course, if you badgered me like this, I might not want to."

"Badgered you? I want to be with you because you happen to be important to me." Now his eyes flashed. "Maybe I'm not the problem, Anne-Marie. The problem may be your priorities. Maybe it's *your* attitude that needs adjusting, not mine."

With each exchange her anger had been rising, and so had his. It made her wonder just how understanding he was. If he wasn't so selfish, he'd realize that she couldn't simply run off with him without giving due consideration to her children. "Well," she said after a few moments, "we obviously don't see eye-to-eye on this issue."

"No, I suppose we don't."

She glanced at him. He was looking straight ahead, his jaw muscles working. "You said once we'd butt heads."

"I told you I had no illusions. I knew you could be stubborn."

"And I knew you could be incredibly self-indulgent."

He turned his head slowly to look at her. He was very angry, and she suspected she'd gone too far. But she was pretty worked up herself and didn't care at the moment if she had offended him.

"Is that the way you see my love, my feelings for you? You consider it selfish?"

"I think your lack of understanding about Kurt is selfish, yes."

"Well, dammit, maybe I don't know you as well as I thought I did."

His voice had risen, and the invective in it stung her. She felt for the door handle. "This conversation has pointed out deficiencies in us both, hasn't it? Maybe it's a good thing it happened now, before our relationship got too far along." She managed to get the door open.

"Anne-Marie, wait. You can't leave with things like this."

She was already halfway out the door, but she stopped. "Why not? Am I wrong? Is there any point in bickering?"

"I don't like the bickering any more than you do, but you're wrong. Wrong to leave."

"Well, I am leaving." She got out and slammed the door. Then she leaned over and looked in the open window at him. "I can't imagine we've got anything more to say to each other." She started up the walk toward the house.

"Anne-Marie," he called after her.

She ignored him. She heard his door opening, but she was almost to the stairs.

"Anne-Marie!"

She climbed the steps, then turned around when she reached the porch. He was standing at the door of his car, looking over the roof at her.

"Please come back."

"I have no desire to talk to you, Royce." With that she turned and marched into the house.

Royce stared at the house for several minutes after the door had closed. The blood was still pumping through his veins, but he was already beginning to feel remorseful. He shouldn't have let himself get angry.

True, she'd said a few things to provoke him, but he shouldn't have lost his cool. Anne-Marie had no way of knowing he'd gone to a lot of trouble to have a very special weekend—a catered dinner for the two of them, a harpist from the university school of music. Of course, he could have told her, but that only would have made her feel worse.

And it wasn't her fault that he was going away. Obviously the weekend in San Francisco was shot to hell, too. He cursed silently. The only reasonable thing was to apologize. He didn't see any point in putting it off. If he acted promptly, he might be able to salvage something.

Reaching in and taking his keys from the ignition, he walked up to the house, his gut churning as he pushed the doorbell. He waited a long time, then rang it again.

Finally he heard footsteps inside, but when the door opened it wasn't Anne-Marie. It was Kurt, standing there in jeans, a muscle shirt and stocking feet.

"Hi, Kurt. I'd like to speak with your mom."

The young man's expression fell just short of gloating. "She doesn't want to come to the door."

"Would you explain that . . . I'm . . . here to apologize?"

"She asked me to tell you she doesn't want to talk to you."

"I know she's upset, but please relate that I want to speak with her."

Kurt looked more bored than pleased. "All right. Hang on. I'll tell her." He closed the door.

Royce waited impatiently, cursing his stupidity in having let things get out of hand. The situation reminded him of Sybil and Mike's spat, and his embarrassment over it was nearly as great as his remorse. A minute later, Kurt returned.

"She's already undressed and getting in the tub. She said it would probably be better to talk later, anyway."

Royce started to send the boy back with another message but thought better of it. Instead he settled for a question. "Did you tell her I wanted to apologize?"

"Yeah."

He wasn't sure if Kurt had but knew he had little choice but to trust him. "Thanks," he mumbled. "Please tell her that I'll talk to her later."

He turned and went back down the stairs and headed for his car, the empty feeling inside reminding him of another time long ago—when he'd left Herbert Keller's house on a snowy winter day without the girl he loved.

When Anne-Marie came downstairs thirty minutes later, Kurt was at the kitchen table, eating a bowl of ice cream. She was in her bathrobe and hadn't bothered to dry her hair. It was combed back, and her skin was still tingling from her hot bath. Her face felt flushed, and she wondered if it was noticeable that she'd been crying. She got a container from the refrigerator poured herself a glass of juice, then sat down at the table.

"What happened?" he said, taking a bite of the ice cream.

"Oh, nothing."

"Did he get out of line?"

"Nothing improper. We had an argument."

"Mr. Wonderful's not so wonderful, huh?"

She gave him a look. "I don't need your sarcasm, too."

"You were pissed off because he was sarcastic?"

"No."

"Then what?"

"It doesn't matter. Never mind."

Kurt took another bite of Rocky Road, watching her.

Anne-Marie looked over at the counter and saw the ice cream carton. "I'm glad you're finishing that off."

"I was wondering how it ever survived Christianne."

"She was rather distracted her last few days." She watched him scrape the bottom of the dish. "What, exactly, did Royce say?"

Kurt gave her an amused smile. "You're pissed off but not that pissed off, huh?"

"Never mind the editorial comments. What did he say?"

"He wanted me to tell you he apologized."

"He should have."

"If you guys are arguing already, it's not a very good omen."

"No, it's not."

Kurt pushed the bowl back, and Anne-Marie immediately got up, carried it to the sink and rinsed it out. She dried her hands on a tea towel. Then she turned to her son. "Did he seem upset?"

"Yeah, I think you could say that."

"So, when I wouldn't come down . . . he just left?"

"Uh-huh."

"I suppose I was being rather immature. Probably as bad as he was."

Kurt looked at her. "What's with you and this guy, Mom? Do you love him?"

"I don't know what I feel at the moment."

"You don't sound pleased."

"No, I guess I don't. I'm rather unhappy, as a matter of fact."

"Is he serious?"

She looked at him, then drew a long breath. "He wants to marry me. Or at least he did."

"Is that why you're upset?"

"No." She sighed with resignation. "He's upset because I wouldn't go to his place for the weekend."

"The horny bastard."

"Kurt! Royce loves me. That's no way to talk about him."

"So, why didn't you go?"

"Because...I didn't think it was fair to you, your first weekend home."

He shrugged. "I don't care."

"That's not the point. I resented the fact that he didn't appreciate my sensitivities."

"He's got other priorities, obviously."

"Yes, I think we both came to that conclusion."

"So, what are you going to do."

She put her head in her hands. "I don't know."

Kurt scooted back his chair and crossed his legs, watching her until she looked up.

"I imagine you'd be glad if I didn't see him again."

He rolled his eyes. "You know how I feel."

"I guess this doesn't help your opinion of him, either."

"It's your life. Whatever you want is okay with me."

She reached over and stroked his arm. "I suppose that's progress."

Kurt gave her a weak smile. "I guess all the women in this family are having romance problems."

"What do you mean?"

"This boyfriend of Christianne's, Erik."

"You know about them?"

"I got a long letter extolling the virtues of German guys in general, Erik in particular."

"Good heavens. She must really be smitten. I had a letter about him, too."

"She's roaring out of puberty like a runaway train."

"Kurt! That's no way to talk about your sister."

"Well, it's true. One minute boys are the stinky things she has to sit next to in class. The next minute they're the gods of the earth—or at least this guy, Erik, is."

"That's what hormones do to a person. You weren't so different yourself."

"Were you that way?"

"I don't remember it being so abrupt. And I was a little older than Christianne when the first big love of my life came along."

"Buchanan?"

"Yes. Royce."

"It's kind of strange when you think about it, isn't it?"

"Yes. And I'm not sure whether it says more about me then or now."

He contemplated her for a moment. "I'm glad this didn't happen when I was younger, still living here at home."

"You're home now."

"Yeah, but only for the summer. And if he's going to be around, I plan to make myself scarce. Of course, I'll be working days and spending most of my evenings with Tracy, anyway."

"Do you really dislike him that much?"

"I guess I'm just not used to the idea."

"Maybe if you try to keep an open mind, Kurt, you will get used to it."

"It sounds like you've forgiven him."

"I certainly regret what happened, maybe as much as he does."

The telephone rang, and Anne-Marie got up to answer it.

"That's probably your chance to tell him so," Kurt said, rising. "I'm going over to see Tracy. She had to baby-sit tonight, if you can imagine. See you later."

Anne-Marie waved to him as she reached for the phone. "Say hello to her for me," she called after him.

"Yeah. All right, I will."

Kurt went out the door as Anne-Marie picked up the receiver. "Hello."

"I'm sorry."

"Oh, it's you." Though she had already forgiven him, she wasn't going to let him off the hook too easily. Besides, she wasn't so sure what had happened wasn't a bad sign. Reason told her to be cautious.

"You were right. I was being selfish."

"I could have been a little more tolerant. I'm not without fault."

"No, you were within your rights. I can't blame you."

"It takes two to make an argument."

"But only one fool to start it. I have a bad habit of expecting to have things my way. Years of being the boss, I guess. I don't suppose a rotten marriage helped, either."

"At least you have the maturity to recognize it."

"I'm not without my flaws. I'll slip again, I'm sure."

"That's hardly encouraging, Royce."

"Don't tell me there were never any problems in your marriage."

"Ted and I never had an argument like that. Not where we shouted at each other."

"Never?"

"No, I don't believe so. We expressed our displeasure from time to time, but—"

"I find that hard to believe."

"It's true."

"Forgive me, Anne-Marie, but your marriage sounds...I don't know...boring."

"It wasn't."

"I didn't mean to be critical. But there is truth to the old saw that there's a silver lining behind every cloud. Making up can be fun. Sometimes it's even worth the fight."

"I don't believe it would be worth it to me."

"That's because we haven't made up yet."

"Haven't we?"

"Not completely. With all the trimmings."

She smiled to herself. "I won't ask what that entails."

"Come out here tomorrow and find out."

Royce was making an effort, and she was tempted to let it end the way he wanted it to. But something kept telling her there was a serious problem here that shouldn't be overlooked. "I don't mean to be difficult, but I think it would be better if I didn't."

"Then you're still upset with me?"

"I want to think about what happened. Not that it's the end of the world. I know it isn't. But during my bath I did some thinking. Maybe your business trip is a good thing. Maybe we should be apart for a while and get a little perspective."

Royce didn't say anything for a moment. She was sorry the conversation was taking place on the telephone; she would have liked to see his face.

"Okay," he said after a while. "That's fair enough. I can appreciate your feeling that way. But you do accept the fact that my apology is sincere?"

"Yes. And you have my apology for my contribution to the problem, as well."

"Good. Sounds like we've cleared the air, anyway."

"I suppose we have."

"Is it okay if I give you a call when I get back?"

He was being polite, not sarcastic, but she heard an edge to his voice. She wondered if she hadn't been a bit too severe. "Yes, of course. I want to talk to you."

"Then I'll call."

"Please do."

"Good night, Anne-Marie."

She felt her heart sink. "Good night."

Chapter Seventeen

Kurt was scheduled to start work Monday at the lumberyard where Don had gotten him a job, so Sunday was his last day of leisure. He and Tracy were driving down to Los Angeles, and Anne-Marie was left alone.

It was a pleasant, sunny day. She decided to go out into the backyard to get some sun. She slathered herself with oil, put on her bikini and her hat, then went out to the lounge chair on the small patio Ted had built one summer.

Lying in the sun, she thought of the irony of the situation. She had turned down a weekend with Royce—had even fought with him over it—because she hadn't wanted to offend her son. And the first thing Kurt did was go off and leave her alone. Of course, she didn't begrudge him his freedom, but she couldn't help resenting the fact that her sacrifice was for naught.

What was worse, her relationship with Royce seemed to be up in the air. Their spat wasn't the problem so much as what it said about their relationship. She wasn't used to fighting, and she wondered what it portended.

But the more she thought about him, the more she realized her misgivings seemed to be games of reason. She found herself rationalizing what had happened, making excuses for him, and wanting to find the silver lining he had spoken about.

It was especially hard knowing Royce would be leaving for a couple of weeks. She wanted to call him, make amends and perhaps even arrange to see him if he still wanted to. But her pride and her uncertainty about his feelings kept her from calling. He had agreed that they should be apart for a while. Perhaps it was best to leave well enough alone.

That evening, after she had showered, and poached herself some fish, steamed some vegetables and made a fruit salad, she had a solitary dinner. As she ate she found herself listening to the traffic sounds in the street outside, hoping somehow that Royce might have taken it upon himself to drive in to see her before he left town.

But he didn't come by. After dinner she sat on the front porch for a while as it grew dark. Finally she got restless and decided to go for a walk around the neighborhood. It was a rare night, when the sea breeze didn't come in bringing the usual cooling marine air. People were out on their lawns, and she exchanged a few words with those she knew.

It was the sort of evening you wanted to be with someone you loved. In the past, she would have thought nostalgically of Ted. But it was different this time. Royce Buchanan, despite what had happened, was foremost in her mind.

Half an hour later she was home again. As she mounted the front steps, she could hear the phone ringing. She hurried to unlock the door, then ran to the kitchen and grabbed the receiver, hoping it was Royce. Instead it was Don Nelson.

"How are you doing?" he asked.

Anne-Marie had trouble disguising her disappointment. "Fine, Don. How are you?"

"Can't complain. Same as always, I guess."

"What's up?" she asked.

"I called to let you know that Kurt and Tracy won't be making it home tonight. They had some car trouble in L.A. and are going to stay with Carole's sister, Molly. Kurt said it's nothing serious, but he won't be able to get the car fixed until morning. He tried to reach you but said he didn't get an answer. They asked me to let you know."

"Thanks, I appreciate the call."

"No problem." He hesitated. "So, how's everything going?"

"Fine."

"Really?"

Anne-Marie suspected he had gotten word of her tiff with Royce. He was probing to see if her interest in him might have been rekindled. But she felt surprisingly resentful on Royce's behalf—almost protective of him and of his place in her heart. "If you're inquiring about Royce and me, Don, we're in a testing phase."

"I see."

"It seems the kindest thing for me is to be direct with you."

"Uh . . . yeah. I guess so."

"Thanks for letting me know about the kids. I would have worried."

"You're welcome."

She hung up, feeling bad. She missed Royce more than ever. Anne-Marie looked at her watch. It was much too late to see him, and a call would only be torture. Better that she wait until he returned. The separation would tell her much more about her feelings for him.

On Monday morning she met with Dr. Gilchrist and one of his patients—a woman with a shoulder injury from an automobile accident—to plan out a yoga and massage therapy program. When she got home, there was a letter in the mail from Christianne, devoted primarily to Erik.

The girl definitely had a crush on the boy, and Anne-Marie was beginning to worry about the timing of it—on her first extended trip away from home. Things had a way of getting blown out of proportion under such circumstances, though she knew Christianne was a good girl and basically levelheaded.

She discussed the situation with Kurt that evening at dinner. He didn't seem too concerned, though the suddenness of it struck him.

Anne-Marie wasn't quite sure what, if anything, to do. She had already written to her daughter, giving some rather low-key maternal advice. There was only a passing reference—a gesture of reassurance—in Christianne's most recent letter. Perhaps it was time to write to her cousin to ask if there was anything to be concerned about.

At the beginning of the following week she received a special-delivery reply to her letter from Kirsten. Anne-Marie had to struggle through the German, and, though her cousin's intent was to reassure, she was alarmed by what she read.

Kirsten recounted how well they were getting along, how much fun Christianne was having, and how readily she had made friends. There was a reference to Erik, but her thrust was to play down the seriousness of it—the usual teenage thing, Kirsten seemed to be saying.

But most distressing of all was the suggestion that Anne-Marie ought to consider letting Christianne spend the school year in Germany. Being an exchange student was a common thing, and having the opportunity to stay with a relative was a double bonus, Kirsten argued.

Under other circumstances, particularly if Christianne was more mature, Anne-Marie would have considered it. But in light of the sudden and dramatic ascendancy of this boy, Erik, an extended stay was out of the question. It worried her so much that she decided to phone Germany.

It was already pretty late in Frankfurt, but she made the call anyway. Kirsten answered the phone, and they chatted for a while, Anne-Marie trying not to sound panicky. She started out by questioning her cousin further on the suggestion of the extended stay. Then she expressed her reservations.

Kirsten was understanding, though notably disappointed. Anne-Marie asked to talk to her daughter, who greeted her in German. They bantered a bit in the language at Christianne's insistence; she was obviously proud of her new linguistic skill.

"What's this about you wanting to stay for the school year?" Anne-Marie asked in English.

"Don't you think it would be great, Mom? I'm really excited. Kirsten said we can talk to the people at the school here when you give your permission."

"That's the trouble, honey. I'm not so sure it's a good idea. This is your first year of high school. Kids usually do a year abroad when they're juniors. I think it might be rushing things a bit."

"Mom, you aren't saying no?"

"I don't want to be arbitrary. I'm sure there are some good points to the suggestion. But it seems to me the disadvantages outweigh them."

"But I have to stay. I can't go back now. I can't."

"I didn't say you have to come back now, Christianne. You still have a few weeks . . . the rest of July."

"But that's not enough."

"You've had a very nice trip, and it's not over yet."

"Can I at least stay till school starts? Can I stay through August? I have to, Mom."

"What's so important about staying in Germany? You have your friends here, and you'll be starting high school in September."

"I don't care about anyone there. I don't care about anyone but—" She cut herself off.

"But who? Erik? Is that what all this is about?"

"You wouldn't understand."

"Of course I would. But you're very young, Christianne. There's plenty of time for boys."

"I don't care about other boys. I love Erik."

"I'm sure you're very fond of him, but—"

"I *love* him!"

"Christianne—"

"I don't care what you say, I'm not leaving! I'll renounce my citizenship!"

"Christianne, this is getting completely out of hand."

"I told you, I love him. Don't you understand that? You, of all people?"

"Of course I understand. But I can't let you do something irresponsible."

"Oh, Mother, how can you do this to me?" she cried. "I hate you! I won't leave Erik, I won't!"

Anne-Marie heard the phone slam down, and then it went dead. She stood for a moment, listening to the dial tone. She felt so helpless that she had to deliberately try to calm herself.

She took a deep breath, then dialed Kirsten's number again. Her cousin answered.

"*Es tut mir leid*. I'm sorry, Anne-Marie. I don't know what's happened to her. She's been just fine until now. The boy means more to her than I thought."

"*Es ist in Ordnung*. That's all right. These things happen. Could you put her on the line, please?"

"She ran to her bedroom, crying. Wait a moment."

Anne-Marie waited, her heart pounding, feeling the distance as she never had before. Finally Kirsten came back on the line. "I'm sorry, but she won't come to the phone. She's upset, but I'm sure she will be all right soon. I will have her call you when she calms down."

"Okay. Please do, Kirsten. I'll wait."

For the next hour or two Anne-Marie paced, anxiously waiting for the phone to ring. Finally she realized it was too late in Europe for a call to come now. Perhaps she would hear from them that night, when it was morning in Frankfurt.

She went upstairs to her studio and did some stretches, trying to relax her taut muscles. But it was useless. Christianne's outburst had upset her. It was so unlike the girl. She'd always been spirited but never hostile or disrespectful. Clearly, her relationship with Erik was even more momentous than Anne-Marie had thought. And that worried her.

Thinking about it, she wondered whether she ought to fly over and take charge of the situation. If she hadn't heard from Christianne by morning, she decided, she would.

When Kurt came home from work, Anne-Marie told him about what had happened.

"Spare the rod and spoil the child," he said ironically.

"That's no help. Even if it were true, it wouldn't do any good now." She sighed woefully. "What do you think I ought to do, Kurt? If she won't talk to me, I almost have to go over there."

"It's probably just a bid for attention."

"No, your sister's not that way. Besides, she doesn't want attention from me, she wants permission . . . a green light. But she's much too young to be intimate with a boy."

"How do you know that's what she wants permission for?"

"It's enough that that's what it could be. It scares me to death."

"Well, does she know about birth control?"

"We've discussed it in the past. But the entire subject of sex disgusted her at the time."

"How quickly they learn."

"Kurt, you're not being at all reassuring."

"Tell Kirsten to get her some birth control and then forget about it."

"I might as well encourage her to have sex!"

"What else can you do from here?"

"That's the point. Nothing. I've got to go. That's all there is to it."

"You'll probably get there and find out all that's happened is that she let the guy kiss her."

"I hope that's exactly what happens. Will you be all right here alone?"

"Sure. I love TV dinners."

"It wouldn't hurt for you to learn to cook."

"Mom, don't worry about me. Go take care of the brat. What the heck, make a vacation of it. If you go that far, you might as well."

"I can't. I've got classes. I'll lose students if I let them down. A few days for a family emergency, they'll understand. Besides, what fun would it be to roam around Europe alone? And I'm sure your sister would be miserable company."

"Whatever turns you on."

She thought for a moment. "I would like to ask a favor of you, though. If Royce calls when he gets back to town, would you tell him what happened?"

"Yeah, sure."

"I'll try to drop him a note before I go."

"Don't worry. I'll take care of your boyfriend, too."

She gave him a long look. "That's another thing that's been bothering me."

Royce arrived home midmorning on Wednesday, a day earlier than he'd told Anne-Marie. He called her first thing. There was no answer, so he left a message on her machine and decided to go for a run.

It was a hot day, and he soon worked up a sweat, moving at a steady but leisurely pace. He had managed to get in a little jogging on his trip but not the kind of distances he liked. The one exception was in San Francisco where he had driven to Golden Gate Park one morning, managing to get in better than eight miles.

But he faithfully did the yoga poses Anne-Marie had prescribed, and his back was feeling fine. During the trip he had thought about her incessantly, and about the incident that had shaken their relationship. It pained him whenever he remembered her anger, and he felt bad about the way he had behaved.

But what troubled him most was the way she had reacted. He hadn't lived up to the standard of her husband, and Royce knew that it meant she hadn't yet fully accepted him for himself. At some level, in some way, she continued to evaluate him in terms of Ted.

It had been torture being away from her, but it had been good, too. Before, when she was never more than several miles from him, the pain was more acute, the urge to see her overwhelming. But knowing she was hundreds of miles away, the longing had been quieter, more dispassionate.

Wherever he went, she was never far from his mind. Her face came to him out of nowhere, whether he was riding an elevator, standing in line at an airport, or listening to a real estate broker pitch a property. Though he was tortured with uncertainty about the way she would react when he saw her, his absence had made him crave her all the more, and his return to Santa Barbara was that much sweeter.

When he completed his run, he had a shower and dressed. There was still no answer at Anne-Marie's, so he left another message. He decided she probably had a full teaching schedule. As he recalled, she didn't have an evening class on Wednesday, so he expected her to return his call soon.

By dinnertime she still hadn't phoned, and he began to worry. What could be wrong? Was she still upset with him? She'd wanted space, and he'd made an effort to give her that.

He didn't feel much like cooking, so he got himself a beer and went out onto the patio to watch the sunset. At about dusk he saw a car turn off the highway and head along the drive toward the house, its headlights shining in the falling darkness.

He got to his feet, watching it, deciding it had to be Anne-Marie. It was difficult to see the car, and when it drew close he realized it wasn't hers. It was an older, American-made vehicle. As it circled the house below him, he recognized Kurt's Mustang.

Royce walked around the house wondering why Kurt, of all people, would be coming to his place. By the time he reached the front, the young man was hurrying up the walk. He stopped when he saw him. They stared at each other for a moment, Kurt breathing heavily, his face flushed.

"I need to talk to you, Mr. Buchanan."

"What is it?"

"It's Mom."

Royce felt his stomach drop. "What about her? What's happened?"

"She called from Germany. Christianne's run away with her boyfriend."

"Anne-Marie's in Germany?"

"Yes, she left a couple of days ago. Christianne was getting weird, and now she's run off. Mom's about to come unglued. I'm not sure what to do."

Royce looked at the boy's distraught expression. "I'm glad you came to me. We'll do something to help her. If necessary, I'll fly over. Do you have a number where your mother can be reached?"

"Yeah, she's at her cousin's, near Frankfurt." He pulled a slip of paper from his pocket and handed it to Royce. "Mom called right when I was getting home from work. She didn't know you were back from your trip. But before she left, she asked me to tell you where she was if you called. When I got your message off her tape machine, I decided I'd better drive out here. I figured she'd want you to know about Christianne, and, well . . . to tell you the truth, I thought it might be a little easier to explain everything in person."

"I'm glad you came, Kurt. It sounds like we've got a lot to talk about. Come on in, and I'll check on flight schedules. Then we'll call your mother."

Anne-Marie waited for him outside customs, pacing back and forth. In the hours since Royce called there had been no word on Christianne, and she was convinced something terrible had happened. The police had been notified, but she could tell that runaway teenagers were not a very high priority in the absence of foul play.

As she paced, she kept watching the door leading from customs, hoping to see Royce's familiar face. During their brief phone conversation they hadn't discussed their relationship— the topic of concern was Christianne. But his readiness to be with her when she needed him was evident. For that she was grateful, though she didn't know what he would be able to do that hadn't been done already. Still, having him there would be a comfort.

Anne-Marie didn't know whether her desire to have him at her side was a healthy sign or not. Wanting him out of weakness wasn't good, but her longing for him had begun before the crisis had erupted. Besides, looking to him in her time of need might be an indication of how profound her true feelings were. All she knew was that she was too needy just then to care.

Finally she saw him walk briskly through the door, looking around for her. Anne-Marie almost ran to him, eager for his reassuring embrace. He dropped his small carry-on bag and took her into his arms.

"Darling," he murmured. As she began crying, he kissed her eyelids. "No word yet?"

She shook her head, fighting back the sobs. "I'm so glad you've come. I've been hating the fact that we fought, that I let things get blown out of proportion."

"Let's not worry about that now. What matters at the moment is Christianne."

"I don't know what's happened to her, Royce. I'm so upset."

He stroked her head. "Don't worry, she'll turn up. We'll find her."

They picked up his bag and began walking toward the terminal building, his arm around her shoulders. "The last week or so has been the worst of my life, apart from when Ted died. First us, then Christianne. It's even worse than when you went off to Korea and left me behind."

He squeezed her. "That was the low point until now?"

"It was pretty close to the bottom."

"Lord, I hate to think I've been in the middle of your worst experiences."

"I've thought about what you said...about the silver lining, and how good could somehow come of our fighting. All I came up with is that our love must run pretty deep."

"The question is whether we bounce back, whether we care enough about each other to make things right."

"Do you think it would always be that way?"

"We'll have disagreements—we couldn't be very interesting or stimulating people if that weren't true. The trick is what I told you once before—learning to disagree gracefully. This last go-around I failed miserably on that score."

"So did I."

He leaned over and kissed her temple as they walked. "We're on the right track, Anne-Marie. We'll just have to learn to help each other."

She sighed, feeling much better. "I think you were right about how much fun making up can be. I like it already."

Royce gave a full-throated laugh. She liked hearing it. She felt safe, and hopeful again.

"Were you able to get me a room at the Schlosshotel?" he asked.

"I tried, but they were booked. So I reserved a room in the village. It's a modest little place with a few rooms over a restaurant, but it was all I could find. If it's no good, I'm sure we can find you something closer to Frankfurt."

"It'll be fine."

"There's not enough room at my cousin's, otherwise you could stay there."

"Once we get Christianne back, and we can sneak out for a coffee or ice cream together in the village, I'll be the happiest man alive," he said with a twinkle in his eye.

"It almost seems we've come full circle, doesn't it?"

They made their way to the parking lot, where they got into Kirsten's car. Anne-Marie reached over and put her hand on his. "I'm so glad you're here, Royce."

He leaned over and tenderly kissed her on the lips.

Forty minutes later, after a drive through the countryside in the hazy sunshine, they entered the town of Kronberg. Royce looked around, remembering the familiar old buildings, the church steeple and rooftops profiled on the hill above the main shopping street.

Many of the facades were different, and there was a new energy and prosperity, but it was the town where Anne-Marie Keller had lived, and where he had experienced some of the most beautiful and painful moments of his life.

Just off the main square she drove into a small parking lot wedged between two old stone buildings, one the small hotel where she had reserved him a room. Royce got his bag, and they went inside.

The proprietor, a thin, middle-aged man with a broad smile, came out from behind the bar when they entered, greeting Anne-Marie. He shook hands with Royce, introducing himself in English as Uve Felsing, while Anne-Marie went into the adjoining room to call Kirsten.

"You've come all the way from California today?" Felsing said. "You must be tired."

"Today and last night. I managed to get a little sleep on the plane, though."

"They say because of jet lag it's best to stay awake and get on the new schedule." He went around behind the bar again. "What can I offer you to drink?"

"When the plane was coming in, I was thinking about some of that good beer you've got here."

"Pale beer?"

"Please." Royce sat on a bar stool and watched as the man tilted a slender glass against the tap, letting the amber liquid trickle down the side of it. "Why is German beer so frothy?"

"That's the way the customers like it. If the beer doesn't have a big head they won't drink it." Felsing waited until the foam dissipated, then added a bit more. He finally put the glass on the bar in front of Royce. Just then, Anne-Marie returned.

"Still nothing," she said, climbing onto the stool next to Royce.

He squeezed her shoulder, then leaned over and kissed her temple. "It may take a while, but she'll turn up." He pushed her dark hair off her face with his fingers. "Want a beer?"

"No, thanks. But I'll sit with you while you drink."

Royce filled out the registration slip the proprietor brought him. When he had finished his beer, Felsing summoned a plump, rosy-cheeked girl from the kitchen to carry his bag up and show him to his room. Royce and Anne-Marie followed the girl up the twisting staircase to a second floor.

The room had a high ceiling, a wash basin in the corner, a big double bed with a bolster and fat pillows and an armoire against the wall. The girl left before Royce could tip her. Anne-Marie went to the open window, where sheer curtains were billowing in the gentle summer breeze.

He put his arms around her, locking his hands over her stomach. She leaned back against him, and they stared out toward the square.

"Remember when we walked along there together, hand in hand, years ago?" he asked.

She sighed. "I wish I could enjoy the memories, Royce. But I keep seeing Christianne running from me, desperate to get away...to be with Erik."

"Maybe you're remembering the feeling. There was a certain desperation in our relationship. Remember?"

"That's the trouble. I'm even feeling guilty about my father and what I put him through. I'm stuck between my duty as a parent and my sympathy for Christianne." She turned to face Royce. "I'm so afraid."

He led her over to the bed, where they kicked off their shoes and lay down, holding each other. She looked up at him, and he wiped the tears from her eyes with his finger.

"Who would have thought twenty-seven years later we'd be here together again, under these circumstances?" he said.

"I'd give anything if she's all right."

"Do you think the police are making a serious effort?"

"Who knows? It's obviously not terribly important to them."

"Maybe we should hire a private investigator, offer a reward for information. Has there been any publicity? Has it been in the papers?"

"No, I don't believe so. I don't think anybody cares so much as I do."

"What about Erik's parents?"

"Kirsten and I went to see them. They're nice people, and they're concerned, but not like I am. They're not frantic. I guess because he's a boy. Better a son than a daughter."

"What sort of kid is he?"

"He seems nice enough. When I met him, he was respectful. Nice looking. But he seemed too mature for Christianne. Of course, she seemed to have aged a couple of years herself since leaving home."

"You were just a schoolgirl when we met, remember? A few months later you were ready to run off to Korea with me."

"Please, Royce, don't even mention it. If she feels even half as strongly as I did then . . . I . . . I don't know what." She dug her nails into his arm. "I keep telling myself she's much younger. And she is. Nearly three years."

"And that'll make a difference in the end. She can't be thinking of marriage. They simply couldn't stand the thought of being separated." He paused for a moment, thinking. "What happened, anyway? Did you argue?"

"Yes. I told her she couldn't stay in Germany, that she had to come home with me." Anne-Marie shook her head. "I'm sure I mishandled it entirely. But there was no way I could let her stay."

"She probably understands that, too. It's just a matter of putting it to her in a palatable form."

"I wish you had been here."

"I'm here now, darling."

She snuggled against him, and Royce closed his eyes, terribly fatigued but content to have Anne-Marie in his arms. It was different somehow, knowing that she not only desired him, but that she needed him.

So long as they got Christianne back unharmed, the girl's escapade might turn out to be a blessing. For once Anne-Marie might be able to relate to him as something other than a lover. Wonderful as it had been between them, he, too, had felt that something was missing. What he had wanted more than anything was for her to see him as a husband, and as a stepfather to her children. Perhaps the dream that had begun in Kronberg twenty-seven years ago was coming to fruition. God, it seemed, was giving him a second chance.

Chapter Eighteen

That afternoon they had just sat down to tea at Kirsten's when the telephone rang. Anne-Marie tensed as her cousin, a sturdy woman in her mid-thirties, rose and moved quickly from the table. Anne-Marie looked at Royce, feeling in her bones that the call concerned Christianne. She listened to Kirsten's voice in the other room but couldn't clearly hear what she was saying. Then the woman called to her.

"Anne-Marie! *Kommen Sie her!* They found them. Hurry!"

She got up and ran to the other room. Kirsten was clutching the phone, looking at her with round, intense eyes.

"It's Erik's father. He's had a call from the police. They found them at a youth hostel in Frankfurt."

"How's Christianne?"

"He says they are both fine. They are all right."

Anne-Marie sagged with relief and felt Royce come up behind her. She put her arms around him and continued listening to her cousin.

"Erik's father is going to Frankfurt," Kirsten said. "He asks if you wish to get Christianne or if he should bring her to you."

"We'll go. Tell him we'll drive. But we need the address."

Kirsten got all the information and hung up.

"Thank God," Anne-Marie said, dropping her head against Royce's chest. He rubbed her back, and she felt tears of relief welling.

"Shall I drive you to Frankfurt?" Kirsten asked.

"No, I think it's better if Royce and I go. I'm sure it's going to be difficult for Christianne." She touched her cousin's arm. "Thanks, but we've already disrupted your life enough."

"You know I feel responsible, Anne-Marie."

She kissed Kirsten on the cheek. "Don't. It's nobody's fault. These things happen in life."

They hurried to Frankfurt, Royce following the directions Anne-Marie related from Kirsten. When they arrived at police headquarters, Erik's father and mother were already there. They were sitting with the kids in a small reception room, waiting. Christianne stood up when Anne-Marie and Royce entered.

"Oh, Mom!" the girl said, hurrying over and throwing her arms around Anne-Marie. "I'm sorry. I'm sorry."

They embraced for a long time, both of them crying. Royce glanced over at Erik, a nice-looking, fair-haired boy with a worried, sheepish look on his face. His mother was next to him, his father standing. Anne-Marie and Christianne were still hugging and talking softly to each other, so Royce introduced himself to Erik's father, who began apologizing earnestly.

Finally Anne-Marie turned to them, wiping away her tears. She shook hands with Erik's parents. Her arm was still around Christianne, and they chatted for several moments in German.

Royce watched, not understanding much of what was said, though the gist of the conversation was clear enough. After a moment or two, Christianne slipped away and joined Erik on the couch. There was a bit more conversation, then Anne-Marie signaled to her daughter that it was time to go.

Christianne got up tentatively, glancing back at Erik. "Will you let me see him again, Mom?"

"We'll discuss it."

"I've got to know. It's important to me."

Anne-Marie sighed. "Before we can worry about the future, we've got to deal with what's happened."

For the first time Erik spoke. "It's not Christianne's fault, Mrs. Osborne. It's my fault. Please don't be harsh with her."

"I appreciate your attitude, Erik, but the issue isn't fault. Right now, Christianne and I have a lot to discuss."

"Please understand," the boy said, "that I didn't hurt her. She is okay."

"I understand." She looked at her daughter again. "Come on, Christianne."

The girl hesitantly turned to Erik, then kissed him on the cheek before walking to where her mother stood. They said goodbye to Erik and his family, Royce shaking hands with the father again before they headed out the door.

"Gee, Royce," Christianne said as they walked along the corridor, "I didn't expect to see you."

"Your mom was pretty worried, kiddo. I came over here because she was so upset."

"I didn't know it was that big a deal."

"We all love you," he said, patting her shoulder affectionately. "And we were concerned." The girl hung her head. "But we're glad you're back safe and sound."

She looked up at him, managing a tiny smile. "I hope it wasn't too much trouble for you to come with Mom. But I'm glad you did. Thanks."

They exited the building, walking in the late afternoon sun to Kirsten's car. After they had gotten in and Royce started out of the parking lot, Anne-Marie turned to her daughter in the back seat.

"Did Erik tell the truth? He didn't hurt you?"

"No, of course not. He loves me."

"As a . . . a lover?"

"Mom!"

"I need to know, Christianne. It might be embarrassing, but I have to know."

"We didn't have sex, if that's what you're worried about. He wouldn't do anything like that. We love each other."

Anne-Marie glanced at Royce, who was repressing a smile. "Sex isn't so awful, Christianne. It can be a very beautiful and wonderful part of people's lives. But one does have to be ready for it . . . understand it . . . and be able to deal with it."

"Please, Mom. I don't ask you about your sex life."

"And you aren't my mother."

"Could we just forget it?"

"All right. If you assure me that nothing happened, we'll let the matter drop for now. But we still need to talk about your running away. That we won't drop."

"I told you I was sorry."

"Christianne, saying you're sorry doesn't resolve the issue. What you did was wrong. It says something about you. And it says something about our relationship. Until we get to the bottom of it, we've got a serious problem."

"What do you want me to say?"

Anne-Marie glanced at Royce, who was driving and keeping his mouth shut. "Perhaps we should discuss it later, when we're alone."

"If you're saying that because of Royce, don't bother. I'm glad you had him come instead of Don."

"Don and I are no longer engaged. I broke it off after you left. With all the commotion, I guess I neglected to mention it."

"You aren't going to marry Don? That's great!"

Anne-Marie gave her a surprised look. "You don't have to act so pleased, do you?"

"I am pleased. I was hoping it would be Royce, instead. Are you two engaged?"

"No, we aren't. We're . . . friends."

The girl slunk back in the seat, putting her hand over her mouth.

"That's all right, Christianne," Royce said, glancing back at her in the mirror. "I love your mother. We just haven't figured out what kind of a relationship we're going to have. It's sort of like you and Erik."

"Well," Anne-Marie said, "let's not go mixing things up." She looked back at her daughter. "You and I still have to discuss this running away business. It upset me that you felt you had to resort to that sort of thing, Christianne."

"Didn't you say that you almost ran away with Royce when you were a teenager?"

"I was a few years older than you. Anyway, we didn't do it in the end." She looked at Royce, feeling uncomfortable all of a sudden.

"But you didn't talk to your father about it. You wanted to run away and get married, didn't you? You told me Grandpa Keller was very stubborn and unreasonable, and that it made it very hard for you."

"Is that what gave you this idea of running away? My telling you that story?"

"No."

"Then why did you?"

"Because you said I couldn't stay in Germany."

"What did you expect to accomplish? You didn't think you were going to get married, did you?"

"No, I'm not old enough."

"I'm glad you recognize that. And the fact of the matter is, young lady, you aren't old enough to be away from home for a year."

"Then why not for the rest of the summer?"

"Your behavior hardly inspires trust, Christianne!"

"Oh, Mom, you don't understand!"

Their voices had risen, and Royce could tell matters were about to get out of hand again. He suspected it was the same sort of conversation that had preceded the girl's flight. "I don't mean to interfere, but could I suggest that we have a nice dinner somewhere and discuss this more calmly?" he said.

Anne-Marie sighed wearily. "All right, if you think that will help. I'm at my wits' end."

"Have you eaten yet, Christianne?"

"No, and I'm starved."

"Why don't we go to the Schlosshotel in Kronberg? Have you ever been there?" he asked, glancing in the mirror.

"No."

"Your mother and I used to go there, years ago. In fact, I made one of the biggest mistakes of my life there."

"Then how come you want to go back?"

"Because one of the marks of a successful person is the ability to learn from your mistakes. And sometimes," he said with a glance at Anne-Marie, "Providence is kind enough to give a man a second chance."

The sun had set behind the hills to the west, and the three of them walked from the dining room to the lounge where Anne-Marie had waited for him that time years before. It looked much the same as she remembered it, and she wondered if Royce was recalling that day. She sneaked a look at him, but he betrayed no sign.

"It's a nice evening," he said. "Shall we go out on the terrace?"

They went out into the warm air, pungent with the smell of grass from the fields. There was also a vague hint of smoke and something sweet, like a flowering vine.

It was a pleasant evening, though things with Christianne were still unsettled. There were problems, but her daughter was safely back. And Anne-Marie was once more in the home of her youth. Best of all, Royce was with her. It was all so bizarre, yet in another way, it seemed so natural.

During dinner, Royce had steered the conversation, telling Christianne about Anne-Marie wearing the tuxedo to the dance, and how beautiful she'd been. And he told her what her mother had been like as a girl in Kronberg—the way he would pass each anxious week waiting until he could get a day of leave so that he could see her.

"I loved your mother as much as a young man could love a girl," he had said at dinner.

"So why didn't you marry her?"

"Because, as a wise person once said, love's not always enough."

Christianne had scratched her head. "What is enough?"

"That's not easily explained. Sometimes a person can go all through life without finding out exactly. As I said before, you can learn from your mistakes. The trick is not hurting yourself and others too badly in the process."

Christianne hadn't understood what he meant, but Anne-Marie had. And it made her wonder just where the truth lay. She knew she was right about taking Christianne back to the

ates with her. But Royce was helping her to see that the way
was done was nearly as important as the decision itself.

"Would you ladies care for an after-dinner drink?" he asked,
sturing toward the tables on the terrace.

"I'm full," Christianne said, shaking her head.

"How about you, Anne-Marie?"

"If you're having one, I'll join you."

Royce seated her, then signaled to the waiter, who was
nding nearby. He ordered two cognacs. "I don't know about
u, Christianne, but when I'm full, a walk makes me feel
tter. Would you like to go for a stroll out there with me?"

The girl looked at her mother. "Sure."

"You wouldn't mind if we talked a bit, would you, Anne-
arie?"

"No, not at all."

They went down the steps of the terrace and out along the
th that she and Royce had walked along years before. She
tched them go, he with his arm around her daughter's
oulders.

They walked very slowly, and Anne-Marie could see that they
re deep in conversation. It was a father-daughter chat they
re having, something Christianne had never really had the
nefit of. She was glad for his gift, glad that he was there now,
en it was probably more important than it had ever been.

She wasn't sure what Royce was saying, but somehow she
sted that it would be beneficial. She herself was at a loss,
owing that she couldn't give in, yet feeling that she had fallen
o the trap her own father had—having to take a categorical
sition.

So Royce's help was particularly welcome. And it might not
n matter a great deal what he said. It was enough that he was
re, that Christianne liked him and that he could act as a
ffer.

Watching them moving slowly down the path, she realized
at she was seeing a different Royce Buchanan, or at least a
ferent side of him. And the more she thought about it, the
re she realized the warmth she felt toward him was very
ilar to the serenity and contentment she had felt in her

marriage. Was it Royce who had changed? Was it she? Or w
it the situation itself?

Perhaps it was all of those things. Anne-Marie wasn't su
But she knew in her heart that something important had ha
pened. Maybe it was as simple as her own fear fading, but it w
very real.

The waiter brought the cognacs Royce had ordered, a
Anne-Marie picked up her snifter, watching the man she lov
talking earnestly with her child. Though he was no longer t
impetuous, cocky young officer she'd walked with in that ve
field, Royce was the same man, self-possessed, confide
mellowed now with age and wiser with experience.

Nor was she the love-struck young girl she'd once be
though at heart she was the same person. The love they felt
each other—then and now—perhaps rose from the same sou
deep within each of them. But it was better now, if only
cause they were wiser.

Anne-Marie sipped her cognac as her eyes followed the f
ures in the distance. She realized that to love again was not o
possible, it was right, when once it had been wrong.

Her eyes were still glistening with emotion when, seve
minutes later, Royce and Christianne came walking back to t
hotel. There was a big smile on her daughter's face.

"Mom," Royce said with a wink at the girl, "we've go
proposal for your consideration."

"What sort of proposal?"

"Christianne and I have been talking, and she sees why y
might have a little trouble with the idea of her staying on
Germany. On the other hand, I think I've convinced her t
appreciate the importance of her relationship with Er
So... we've come up with this idea.

"If you're in agreement, I'll talk to Erik's parents and se
they'd let him come to California for the rest of the summ
and stay at the ranch, with me. That way Christianne, a
maybe some of her friends, could come out regularly, and th
could ride horses, swim and generally see each other so
more."

"That's a very generous offer."

"Well, it's certainly no problem for me, and the kids can
end a little more time together that way—under our super-
sion."

Christianne nearly bounced in her chair. "Is it all right,
om?"

"If Royce is willing, I guess it's up to Erik and his parents."

"Oh, Mom, thanks!"

"Well, don't count on it yet."

Royce patted the girl's hand. "We've discussed how even if
doesn't work out for this summer, there may be opportuni-
s in the future. If things are meant to be, they have a way of
ppening."

Anne-Marie felt her eyes fill at his words. He reached over
d touched her cheek as a tear slid down against his fingers.

"Mom," Christianne said, "I've got to know if Erik's parts will let him come. Can I go ask him?"

Anne-Marie looked down at her cognac. "Well, honey, we've
st gotten our drinks."

"Oh, you don't have to take me. His house isn't all that far.
I ran, I'd be there in ten or fifteen minutes."

"Wouldn't it be easier to wait and we'll drive over later?"

"No. Please."

"All right. But don't stay more than half an hour. I'll expect
u back at Kirsten's no later than nine-thirty."

"Oh, thanks!" She jumped up and kissed her mother on the
eek. Then she went around the table and kissed Royce, too.
really hope you get to be my stepfather someday," she said.
think life would be a lot easier at home."

She scampered like a rabbit back along the path and across
e field, toward the town. Anne-Marie watched her for a mo-
nt, then waited until Royce turned to her.

"What, exactly, did you two talk about there?"

"We discussed our romantic interests."

"Evidently."

"It was for Christianne's good."

She couldn't help smiling. Royce took her hand.

"I don't have to tell you how much I love you, do I?" he
d.

She slowly shook her head.

He sighed, looking out at the gently falling dusk. "Just bei here makes it all so poignant."

"I was thinking the same thing. And I was also thinking h I'm beginning to see you in a different light. Perhaps appre ate you more as a person than I did before."

His blue eyes sparkled, and that characteristic grin of crossed his face. "Are you trying to tell me there's hope us?"

A smile touched her lips as she nodded. "There's hope."

"How long will it take you to get ready for a wedding?"

"Probably I could be ready by the time your housegu leaves."

Without a word, he rose and pulled her to her feet. "Co on, let's walk for a bit."

They went out along the path, as they had those long ye ago, their arms around each other. When they had gone a c tance from the *Schloss*, Royce stopped and turned to face h They looked into each other's eyes.

"Last time we were here, I asked you to wait two years me," he said. "It's been nearly thirty, but I finally succeed What do you suppose that means?"

"I guess it means that there was a lot more to that love th we realized." She paused. "And that when something is s posed to happen, it has a way of happening." She smiled.

He gently pulled her close, then kissed her on the lips. "I a lucky man, Anne-Marie."

She buried her face in his neck. And though it wasn't w ter, as it had been the last time, she shivered in his arms.

"You aren't cold?" he whispered.

"No, I'm just remembering."

"I loved you then, and I love you now. But I'm much wis if that makes a difference."

She looked up into his eyes, seeing his love. "We both a Royce. We both are."

* * * * *

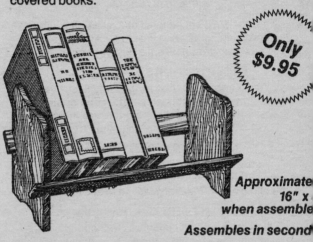

COMING NEXT MONTH

#493 PROOF POSITIVE—Tracy Sinclair
Tough divorce lawyer Kylie O'Connor privately yearned for a happy
marriage and bouncing babies. But cynical Adam Ridgeway wasn't
offering either, and Kylie's secret couldn't keep for long....

#494 NAVY WIFE—Debbie Macomber
Navy officer Rush Callaghan placed duty above all else. His ship was
his home, the sea his true love. Could vulnerable Lindy Kyle prove
herself the perfect first mate?

#495 IN HONOR'S SHADOW—Lisa Jackson
Years had passed since young Brenna coveted her sister's boyfriend.
But despite recently widowed Warren's advances, Brenna feared some
things never changed, and she'd forever be in Honor's shadow.

#496 HEALING SYMPATHY—Gina Ferris
Ex-cop Quinn Gallagher didn't need anyone. Yet sympathetic Laura
Sutherland saw suffering in his eyes—and her heart ached. She'd risk
rejection if her love could heal his pain.

#497 DIAMOND MOODS—Maggi Charles
Marta thought she was over Josh Smith. But now the twinkling of
another man's diamond on her finger seemed mocking... when the
fire in her soul burned for Josh alone.

#498 A CHARMED LIFE—Anne Lacey
Sunburned and snakebitten, reckless Ross Stanton needed a
physician's care. Cautious Dr. Tessa Fitzgerald was appalled by the
death-defying rogue, but while reprimanding Ross, she began feeling
lovesick herself!

AVAILABLE THIS MONTH:

JOIN BESTSELLING AUTHOR
EMILIE RICHARDS
AND SET YOUR COURSE
FOR NEW ZEALAND

This month Silhouette Intimate Moments brings you what no other romance line has—Book Two of Emilie Richards's exciting mini-series Tales of the Pacific. In SMOKE SCREEN Paige Duvall leaves Hawaii behind and journeys to New Zealand, where she unravels the secret of her past and meets Adam Tomoana, the man who holds the key to her future.

In future months look for the other volumes in this exciting series: RAINBOW FIRE (February 1989) and OUT OF THE ASHES (May 1989). They'll be coming your way only from Silhouette Intimate Moments.
